RAVES FOR
THE NOVELS OF
MADELINE HUNTER

"In this fascinating, danger-tinged novel...
Hunter seamlessly marries seductive wit
with smoldering sensuality."
—*Booklist*

"Passions blaze in this complex story that
pairs another marvelously singular couple...
to the delight of all concerned."
—*Library Journal*

"Delightful...excellent...Entertaining."
—*Publishers Weekly* (starred review)

"Intelligent and memorable...Readers may
be reminded of Jane Austen."
—*RT Book Reviews*

"There are some writers who are born to
write...It is Madeline Hunter's writing that
lifts it above...[A] sublime end...Stellar."
—Examiner.com

TALL, DARK, AND WICKED

MADELINE HUNTER

JOVE BOOKS, NEW YORK

JOVE

An imprint of Penguin Random House LLC
375 Hudson Street, New York, New York 10014

TALL, DARK, AND WICKED

A Jove Book / published by arrangement with the author

ISBN: 978-0-515-15517-4

PUBLISHING HISTORY
Jove mass-market edition / October 2015

PRINTED IN THE UNITED STATES OF AMERICA

10 9 8 7 6 5 4 3 2 1

Cover photography by Claudio Marinesco.
Cover design by Rita Frangie.
Text design by Kelly Lipovich.

Penguin
Random
House

TALL, DARK
AND WICKED

CHAPTER 1

Loyal
Good-humored
Intelligent
Uninhibited
Passionate
Accommodating

Lord Ywain Hemingford—Ives, to his family and clos-est friends—read the list of the qualities he required in a mistress. He had jotted them down, in no particular order, during an idle moment the day before. Only the first one deserved its ranking without question. In fact, it should be underlined. There were other qualities that attracted him, too, but these six, he had learned through experience, were paramount.

He tucked the paper behind some pages, to be returned later to its current duty as a marker in his book. He settled into his favorite chair, propped his legs on a footstool with his feet aimed toward the low fire, and again turned his attention to a novel he had been meaning to read for four months now.

Vickers, his manservant, set a glass and two decanters, one of port and the other of water, on a table next to the chair, then stepped back out of view.

"If your brother the duke should come by this evening, sir, should—"

"Deny him entrance. Bar the door. I am not home to him. If God had any mercy he would have inspired Lance to remain at Merrywood Manor, not allowed him to venture back up to town where he will be a nuisance to all whom he encounters. I am done with being his playmate, or his nursemaid." At least for a while, he added to himself. After a recent, renewed week of barking, the hounds had again retreated, but they had not given up the hunt.

Ives did not mind being his brother's keeper. He resented very much playing the role for a brother who treated his advice like it came from an old aunt. One would think that a man under suspicion of murder would be more circumspect in his speech and actions, and want to create favorable impressions, not stick out his tongue at society whenever he could.

"Very good, sir."

Padding steps. A door closing. Peace. Ives closed his eyes and savored for a moment that rarity in his life—freedom to do whatever he damned well pleased, whenever he chose, with nary a claim on his time or attention.

Several developments allowed this respite besides the dwindling interest in Lance by magistrates out for blood. No cases awaited his eloquence in court for at least a fortnight. By coincidence his mistress had a week ago been most disloyal, giving him the excuse he had sought for some time to part with her.

That left him free of her too. Of attending on her. Of purchasing gifts. Of feeding her vanity. Of joining in little parties that she liked to hold that bored him more than he ever let her know.

It did, of course, also leave him free of a sexual companion. That was not a situation that he by nature welcomed, but he did not mind too much. Contemplating with whom to end his abstinence would give his forays out on the town an enlivening distraction.

He anticipated a glorious stretch of pointless activity. Several long rides in the country beckoned, following whim more than roads or maps. A stack of books like this one waited, too long unread. He could indulge in regular practice with sword and fists, to improve his prowess at fighting with both. And he looked forward to at least one good long debauch of drunkenness with old friends too long neglected.

"Sir."

Vickers's voice, right at his shoulder, surprised him. He had not heard Vickers return.

"Sir, there is a visitor."

"Throw him out, I told you."

"It is not your brother. It is a woman. She says she has come on business. She says you were recommended to her."

Exhaling a sigh, Ives held out his palm.

"She gave me no card, sir. I would have sent her on her way, but she would not indicate just who had recommended you, and the last time such an unnamed recommendation came your way it was from—"

"Yes, quite right." Damnation. If someone, or even Someone, thought to interfere with the next fortnight by having him running around England on some mission or investigation, Someone was very much mistaken. Still, he should at least meet this woman and hear her out, so he could construct a good reason why he could not help her.

He stood, and looked down at himself. He wore a long banyan over his shirt and trousers. The notion of dressing again raised the devil in him. Hell, it was long past time to call at a lawyer's office, even if Someone recommended him. He would be too informal for a stranger, or for business, but he was hardly in a nightshirt. This woman would just have to forgive him his dishabille. With luck she would realize she had interfered with his evening, which she rudely had, and make quick work of whatever she wanted.

He walked to the office. She was probably a petitioner for some reform cause, or the relative of a friend looking for his advice on which solicitor to hire. Her mission this evening no doubt could have been completed more humanely by writing a letter.

He opened the door to his office, and immediately knew that his visitor had not been recommended by anyone significant, let alone *Someone* really important. Her plain gray dress marked her as a servant. He could not see one bit of adornment on either it or the dull green spencer buttoned high on her chest. The simplest bonnet he had seen in months covered her black hair and framed her face.

Eyes lowered, lost in her thoughts, she had not heard him. He considered stepping out just as silently, and telling Vickers to send her away. He placed one foot back to do so.

Just then she lifted a handkerchief to her eyes— glittering eyes, he could not help but notice, with thick, black lashes that contrasted starkly with her pale skin. Radiant skin, as it happened, giving her face a notable presence, if he did say so, even if she was not a beautiful woman. Handsome, however, even if somewhat sharp featured.

She dabbed at tears. Her reserved expression crumbled under emotion.

He hated seeing women cry. Hated it. His easy sympathy had caused him nothing but trouble in the past too. Still . . .

Hell.

He waited until she composed herself, then walked forward.

*   *   *

Padua sniffed, and not only to hold back the tears that the day tried to force on her. She also checked for the tenth time to discover if her garments smelled.

Newgate Prison reeked. The stench that London gave off seemed to concentrate in the old city, but Newgate smelled like the source of it all. She had never experienced anything like it. It remained in her nose, and she worried that it had permeated her clothing.

She sat rigidly on the chair the servant had pointed out. Her surroundings caused some trepidation. She had perhaps been rash in following the advice to seek out this lawyer. Probably so, considering the person who had given the advice had been a bawd incarcerated in the prison.

Normally, she would not take advice from a prostitute or a criminal. Yet when that woman called her over as she found her way out of the prison, and showed sympathy, she had not been herself. Just talking to someone eased her distress. After hearing her tale of woe, that woman advised she get a lawyer, and even provided the name of one who had aided a relative who was wrongly accused. Suddenly the prostitute appeared as an angel sent by Providence to offer guidance out of the Valley of Despair.

Now she awaited that lawyer's attendance. Not only a lawyer, but also a lord. She thought it odd that a lord was a lawyer. She would assume the bawd erred on that, except the servant here did not blink when she used the title in requesting an audience.

Now that she was here, she could believe the lord part. Although she sat in his chambers, this was no apartment, nor merely a set of offices. Rather she sat on the entry level of what appeared to be a new house facing Lincoln's Inn Fields. There had been nothing to indicate that others lived or worked above. This lawyer had a good deal of money if this whole building was his home.

The mahogany furniture and expensive bookbindings said as much. Her feet rested half-submerged in the dense pile of the carpet on the floor. Her rump perched on a chair that must have cost many pounds. Real paintings decorated the walls, not engravings done after famous works of art.

His fees were probably very high. She doubted she could afford them. The bawd had guessed as much. *If you've not the coin to pay him, he'll probably take other payment, dear. Them that works our side of the Old Bailey almost all do.*

Could she agree to that? She recoiled from the idea. Then again, it would be no worse than the bargains most women struck in their lives. Had her mother not taught her that the loveless marriages to which most women were subjected were merely economic arrangements prettied up by legalities? Experience of the world had shown that view to be harsh, perhaps, but essentially accurate.

She closed her eyes, and immediately was back in

the prison, peering into a cell full of men. The stench, the dirt, the ugly sounds all assaulted her senses again. Hopelessness and death reigned in Newgate Prison. No one would leave a loved one inside it, if she had the means to get him out.

Tears pooled in her eyes. She dabbed them away with her handkerchief, and fought for composure. She never cried, but this was not a normal day in so many ways.

"You asked to see me."

The voice jolted her out of her reverie and drew her attention to the man suddenly standing ten feet in front of her.

Oh, dear. Goodness. He was not what she expected. Not at all.

She had pictured a man of middle years with gray hair and spectacles and a face wizened with experience. He would wear dark coats and a crisp cravat and be accompanied by a clerk or two.

Instead the man assessing her—there was no other word for the way his gaze took her in—could be no older than thirty or so. He possessed classical features and fashionable locks of dark brown hair of an enviable hue. He wore a long banyan that could pass for a greatcoat if not made of midnight brocade instead of wool.

An impressive man. His green eyes captivated one's attention. Very attractive eyes. Intelligent. Expressive. This lawyer was not merely handsome, but handsome in a way that made fools out of women when they saw him.

She found her wits, lest she appear just such a woman.

"Are you Lord Ywain Hemingford?" She had no idea how to pronounce Ywain. Surely not *JA-wane*, as the bawd had. She tried *EE-wane* instead. His subtle wince said she got it wrong.

"I am he. It is pronounced *eh-WANE*, by the way, at least by my family. There are half a dozen options. Almost everyone chooses the wrong one, so I long ago retreated into the name Ives. Think of me by that name, if it is easier." His perfect mouth offered a half smile. "By either name, you have me at a disadvantage."

"My apologies. My name is Padua Belvoir." She took in his informal dress. "I have intruded at the wrong time. I am sorry about that too. I have been so distraught I have not paid proper mind to the hour, and I could not rest until I sought the help I need anyway."

"You told my man you were recommended to find me. May I ask by whom?"

By a prostitute in Newgate Prison. "I do not think she wants me to tell you her name."

He strolled across the chamber. "I assume you are here regarding criminal matters."

"How did you know?"

"Because that is the only reason she would not want her name used, and because I believe you visited the prison today." Ever so calmly, he opened one of the windows. A crisp breeze poured in.

She felt her face burning.

"Please, do not be embarrassed. The prison is a fetid place," he said. "I had a coat that had to be burned after I wore it there one summer day."

"It is not only fetid, but horrible in every way. The conditions are disgraceful. The inmates are wretched."

He settled his tall body into a chair near hers. He sat in it like a king might sit on a throne. His arms rested along the tops of its sides, and his hands hung in front of its carving. "Have you come to request a donation, perhaps to further a campaign to improve those conditions? I will contribute, but I must warn you that yours is a noble yet futile quest. People tend not to worry overmuch if criminals are not comfortable."

"I am not here to ask for a charitable donation, although someday I hope to have the time to devote to such good causes."

"A budding reformer, are you?"

"There is much in our society that could use some reform."

"As there has been in every society down through time."

Oh, dear, he was one of those. The kind who saw no point in trying to better the present because such efforts in the past had failed. "I know history, sir. I have received a liberal education. With our superior knowledge, I think we can be more enlightened than our forefathers."

He resettled himself in that chair, and angled his head. "I would ask which reforms you want to see first, but let me guess instead." His gaze scanned her from head to toe. "Workers' rights. Educational reform." He scanned again. "Universal suffrage, including the vote for women. If you are educated, you would not like being denied a right enjoyed by others who have no more training of their mental faculties than you have."

"Your conclusion is accurate. However, my reasons are less elevated. I simply believe that since there are many men who now vote who are stupid and ignorant, there can be no logic in denying the right to any others, stupid or ignorant though they might be as well."

He laughed lightly. An appealing laugh. Quiet. Warming. His eyes showed new depths. "I do not think I have ever heard it said that baldly before. Like a wily math tutor, you have insisted that a different equation be solved, one that puts me at a disadvantage should I want to disagree."

His insight with that math tutor comment unnerved her. How had they veered onto this topic? "My opinions do not signify, of course. My original point was that not everyone in that prison is a criminal, so the suffering there cannot be excused."

He offered that half smile again, no more. "Since you do not want money, and you do not want to discuss reforms, perhaps you will explain what you do want."

"I want your eloquence and skill to help my father, who has been so affected by prison that he is too weak to help himself. He has been wrongly accused of a crime."

He did not actually sigh at hearing this most predictable topic, but his expression retreated into one of bland patience. "How long has he been there?"

"At least two weeks, but perhaps a month. I only learned about it yesterday. I received a letter, from whom I do not know, telling me. Normally I receive news from him at least once a month. It has been some six weeks since I last received one of his letters, so I had become concerned."

"Why did you not visit him, and see what was wrong, if the letter did not come?"

"We are somewhat estranged. There was no argument between us. He is just much engaged in his own pursuits. I could not visit, because I do not know where he lives in London."

"Did you see him when you went to the prison today?"

"I was allowed to visit him. He is in a large cell with many rough fellows. He is unwashed and unshaven and frightened. I fear he will get ill there. So many others are sick."

"Why was he put there?"

"He would not tell me. He only said to leave and not come back." Her voice almost caught on the last sentence. The visit had been horrible. If an iron door had not separated her from Papa, she thought he would have physically driven her away.

The green of his eyes darkened while he thought. She did not take the pause as a good sign. Not at all.

"Miss Belvoir, I am sure you were dismayed to find your father in a cell with men unsuitable for polite society. However, if you do not know the crime of which he is accused, how can you know that he is wrongly accused? His refusal to speak of it even with you suggests the opposite."

"My father is no criminal, sir. He is a scholar. He has taught at universities throughout the Continent and had a position as a teacher at Oxford until he married my mother. He spends all his time on his research and his books. There can be no justifiable reason for him to be imprisoned, unless being an intellectual has now become a crime. A serious miscarriage of justice is about to occur."

It poured out nonstop, the way her excitement sometimes betrayed her. Lord Ywain—Ives—just sat there, listening, exerting a presence that crowded her despite his sitting six feet away. He did not appear especially interested.

"You are sure of this?" he said.

"I am positive."

"And yet you do not even know where he lives in London." His words did not dismiss her outright, but his expression almost did. His eyes had narrowed with skepticism.

She felt her best chance to help her father slipping away.

"I told him that his silence was foolhardy. That is why I am here. I was told that some people have lawyers at their trials now. I was told that you at times speak for those accused." *Slow down. Stop gushing words.* "My father is incapable of defending himself, and may even be unwilling to do so. The accusations are insulting, and he is the sort to refuse to engage in the insult by refuting it."

He had not moved during her impassioned plea.

Those hands still rested at the end of the chair's arms. Attractive, masculine hands, as handsome as his face. His gaze had not left her, and the shifts regarding what he looked at had been subtle but unmistakable. Not only her face had been measured. She did not think she had been as closely examined in her life, let alone by a man such as this one.

She was not an inexperienced young girl. She recognized the purpose of that gaze, and could imagine the thoughts that occupied part of his mind. A small part, she hoped. She trusted at least some of what she had said took root amidst his masculine calculations.

In a different circumstance she might be flattered, but the bawd's words made the attention dangerous. He did not appear of a predatory nature, and such a man hardly needed to take advantage of an accused man's female relatives if he wanted to satisfy carnal needs. However, she experienced some alarm and a good deal of confusion. The latter resulted from the undeniable and inappropriate low stirring his attention evoked. She did not want to acknowledge it, but it was there. He was the kind of man who could do that to a woman, no matter how much she fought it.

"You do not know the accusations, so you cannot say they are insulting," he said.

"Any accusation of a crime would be insulting to a man like my father. If you met him you would understand what I mean. Hadrian Belvoir is the least likely criminal in the world. Truly."

The smallest frown flexed on his brow. His atten-

tion shifted again, to the inside of his head. She ceased
to exist for a long moment. He stood abruptly. "Excuse
me, please. I will return momentarily."

Then he was gone, his midnight banyan billowing
behind him.

Hadrian Belvoir.
   Ever since his visitor introduced herself, an in-
definable something had nudged at Ives. The pokes
implied he should know her, yet nothing about her
was familiar.

Hadrian Belvoir. That name did more than poke.

He strode up to his private chambers, to a writing
desk there where he dealt with personal letters. He
rifled through a thick stack of old mail, discarding it
piece by piece, frowning while he sought the letter he
wanted. Finally he found it.

He flipped it open and held it near the lamp. There
that name was, buried amidst a casual communica-
tion. *You can expect to be asked to be prosecutor for a
Hadrian Belvoir, once his case is brought forward. It
would please us if you accepted.*

He checked the date. This had been written a month
ago. No wonder the name had not been in the front of
his memory. If Mr. Belvoir resided in Newgate Prison,
why had this informal approach not turned into a formal one by now? It was possible his victims had hired
their own prosecutor, of course, but if that were likely,
these sentences would never have been written.

It would please us if you accepted. Considering who had written this, it went without saying that acceptance was assumed, and would indeed be given.

He would have to inform Miss Belvoir that she must look elsewhere.

He returned to the office and the bright-eyed Miss Belvoir. He had realized, while she talked and talked, that her eyes sparkled even when she did not cry. He had also calculated that if she stood, she would be willowy and long limbed. An idle curiosity had crossed his mind, about what it was like to take a woman who was a good match for his own height. His mind had pictured it, making the necessary adjustments . . .

No sooner had he walked into the chamber than she began speaking. "I think you can see that a great injustice will occur if my father does not receive your help, sir. I beg you to consider accepting his case. I am prepared to pay you whatever fees you require."

Not likely, from the looks of that dress and spencer. "Miss Belvoir, allow me to explain that no barrister will accept financial remuneration from you for defending in this matter."

She went still. Her lips parted in surprise. He felt bad that his refusal shocked her, but there was nothing else for it.

She looked up at him, confused. "Are you saying you will do it for free?"

"I am saying that barristers do not get paid by clients; they are engaged by solicitors who take care of such things. Barristers will be insulted if you offer to pay them like they are tradesmen."

"So I must first find a solicitor and have him ask you. Instead of one lawyer I must hire two."

"You must find a solicitor to investigate, but I will not be the barrister he engages to argue the case in the courtroom. I cannot be the defending lawyer. When you mentioned your father's name, I realized I have already been approached to serve on the other side."

"Other side?"

"Prosecutor."

She absorbed that. Her full, deep rose lips mouthed the word.

She stood, which brought her close to him. Her crown reached his nose. Yes, she was unusually tall. The scents of Newgate no longer cloaked her. Rather that of lavender wafted subtly, as if by force of will she had conquered the ill effects of the day. Since the glint in her eyes no longer came from tears, he guessed she had, in many ways.

She strolled away, thinking. She moved with notable elegance and a subtle sway. She wore her unusual stature the way a queen might wear a crown.

She turned and faced him. He pictured her in a white diaphanous gown that flowed down her long body, one bound under and around her breasts in imitation of the ancient deities. Only, from the expression she now wore, she might also wear a helmet and shield, like Athena, goddess of both wisdom and war.

"This is awkward," she said. "However, it is not without value to speak with you."

"Since I have not even seen the brief, there is nothing to learn from me."

"It is always useful to meet one's adversary. Had I not made the error in coming here, I doubt I would have had the chance. I would have arrived at the trial, with you a total stranger."

"I am not your adversary, Miss Belvoir. You are not the one who will be on trial."

"We will have opposite goals, so I think the word is accurate."

"I am sure you will find a worthy lawyer to take up this case for you, as you intended."

"Having met you, I am not sure I will find one worthy enough. I dare not leave it all in another's hands now."

Her gaze penetrated him. He had the sense of his soul being searched by an intelligence as sharp as any he had ever met. Whatever she found, it lightened her expression. Softened her. The unusual beauty that had drawn him into this chamber became much more visible. The sparkles in her eyes implied humorous conclusions.

He knew what she had seen. An acknowledgment of it passed between them in an instant of naked honesty. Hell, yes, she was sharp. He had been nothing but restrained. A bishop could not have hidden his sensual speculations better, but she had still sensed them in him.

She turned those eyes on him fully. Ives recognized

the expression of someone about to offer a bribe. A few had come his way in the past. He waited for hers.

Resolve flickered. Boldness flashed. Then, in the next moment, both died.

"I am sorry to have taken your time, and at an unsuitable hour at that. I will leave you to your evening." She walked toward the door.

"I will find out about the charges," he said. "That way you will know what he faces, at least. Leave your address with my man, and I will make sure you are informed."

She turned. "Thank you. That is very kind, coming from someone I must now see as an enemy."

"I am only an enemy if the truth is, as well."

That amused her. "Noble words to soothe the helpless woman's fears, sir? That is generous of you. However, truth depends on the equation, too, doesn't it? Different variables yield different solutions."

CHAPTER 2

By the time Padua slipped through the garden behind the house on Frith Street, the last of dusk's light showed. High-pitched voices leaked from the building's second storey, where the girls ate their supper. If she moved quickly enough, she could take her own chair in the dining room without attracting much notice. If she were very lucky, Mrs. Ludlow would be none the wiser about Padua's activities today.

She did not fear Mrs. Ludlow, the gentlewoman who owned this building and school, and in whose hands rested her ability to support herself. Generous to a fault, and as warm as a mother, Mrs. Ludlow suffered from a level of absentmindedness that made her quite benign. Learning one of her teachers had left the property would distress her, however, and Padua did not want to do that.

She checked the garden door, and was relieved to find it still unlocked. She strode through the back sitting room, removing her spencer while she walked. She rolled it up and tucked it behind a chair in the reception hall before mounting the stairs.

Assuming an expression of confidence, she entered the drawing room that now served as the dining room for Mrs. Ludlow's School for Girls. She made her way to the head table and slid into her chair. She drew no particular attention from the others already into their meals. Only Caroline Peabody's gaze followed her conspicuously, first with a little frown, then with visible relief. Caroline was one of three girls Padua tutored in higher mathematics. Those lessons were not part of the curriculum, and took place late at night after Mrs. Ludlow retired.

She enjoyed the extra work, because it meant these girls could discover what their minds could achieve. She found contentment in doing for them what her mother had done for her. The pay at this school might be low, but it was a respectable living, one for which she held excellent qualifications. The employment also permitted her to squirrel away some money for the plans she had.

"Miss Belvoir." Mrs. Ludlow's address drifted down the table, past the other teachers. "Please join me in my chambers after dinner. I would like a word with you."

Padua finished her meal while the room emptied. She then made her way to Mrs. Ludlow's chambers. The door to the sitting room stood open, as it usually did in the evening. Once she entered, however, Mrs. Ludlow closed it.

Padua loved the sitting room. Small and tidy, its upholstered chairs and patterned carpet created a cozy den. She and Mrs. Ludlow sat near a low fire, in two of those comfortable chairs, with a small table between them. On the table sat a tiny glass of sherry, which Mrs. Ludlow indulged in "for her health." The chair, of decent size for a person of Padua's height, almost swallowed short, plump Mrs. Ludlow. If not for a footstool, her feet would have dangled.

Fifty and filmy-eyed, with a cloud of fair hair that resisted taming, Mrs. Ludlow forever appeared perplexed. Indeed, the world confounded her on a regular basis. She lacked constancy as a result, which Padua at times found exasperating, but often also found useful. The school had many rules, as schools do, but Mrs. Ludlow could be swayed by tears or promises from the girls, or threats from the parents upon whom her fees depended. Or logical persuasion from her teacher, Padua Belvoir.

"You left the premises today." Mrs. Ludlow spoke an observation more than an accusation while she bent to tuck a throw around her feet. Contented with the result, she sat back into the fat embrace of the chair's cushion, and reached for her sherry.

"I had a family matter to attend to."

Mrs. Ludlow sipped, then cradled the fragile glass in her fingers. "I do ask that you inform me and receive permission. Those are the rules, Miss Belvoir. Without rules, where would the world be?"

"As you know, I think that, as an adult, I should not need permission. None of my classes or charges were neglected, and I returned before nightfall."

"Barely. Had you walked in ten minutes later—" The very thought had Mrs. Ludlow flustering. "What would the parents say if they learned my teachers went abroad in town at night alone? I would be entertaining a long line of them as they came to get their girls. Really, you must see that." She flushed, and patted her hand on her heart. "Why, we would all be ruined, Miss Belvoir. Ruined. I would have been forced to release you, in an attempt to stave off the worst."

"There is no reason for any parent to know our business, unless we lack discretion," Padua said. "Yes, the world needs rules, but as independent women, we should make our own, and ensure they are practicable."

"Make our own? Oh, dear girl, that is rich. And so like you. As for discretion, allow me to enlighten you on the limitations of that. I needed to speak with you tonight about more than your absence today—and, truly, Miss Belvoir, I cannot have it, you know I cannot."

Padua avoided making any promises. The situation with her father prevented that. "What other matter concerns you?"

"I have received a letter today, from a parent, complaining."

"Not about the lessons, surely. Your curriculum is far superior to what is normally found."

"As it happens, that was the complaint." Mrs. Ludlow sighed, then sipped again. "This father expressed dismay that his daughter wrote to her brother like a braggart about her lessons in geometry. It appears the boy has not yet mastered that at the same level, and he is a year older."

"We cannot be blamed for either the brother's lack of ability, or his tutor's lack of attention."

"Quite so, quite so, and yet—this man had not expected such a thing. Well, they never do. Sewing, drawing, music, French, basic ciphers—you know the sort of lessons he wants." She looked over, all confusion and little confidence. "Perhaps he is correct. Maybe—I am not sure. It is so hard to know. There can be no harm, I think, then I receive such a letter and . . . " She looked around her sitting room as if expecting some figure of authority to emerge from a wall and tell her the best course of action.

The parents expected the curriculum the school had before Padua arrived. She had quickly convinced the impressionable Mrs. Ludlow to allow a few changes. Now she wondered if she would be reduced in the future to teaching basic arithmetic to girls who could do much more.

"His objection to the mathematics only served as a prologue," Mrs. Ludlow continued, her hand flashing gestures of distress. "After that, his letter became much more pointed. Indignant, he was. Aghast. His girl, it seemed, also wrote to her mother, this time about a fascinating pamphlet a teacher had loaned her. She encouraged her mother to find it and read it for herself."

Padua wished she did not know what was coming. Only she did. "She asked to borrow it. I told her not to let anyone know."

"Oh, dear. I had hoped . . ." Mrs. Ludlow patted her heart again. "Did I not tell you that you must not teach your ideas about women's rights to the girls? I am sure I did."

"I have not taught the girls anything. I have not openly discussed such things, although for an educated female to be ignorant of such arguments is comical. However, I have kept those ideas out of the schoolroom."

"But not out of the school. You must do so in the future."

What a bizarre suggestion. The ideas were in her head, and she was in the school. There was no way to keep the ideas out of the school, unless . . . Better not to point out the obvious. Mrs. Ludlow was a dear woman, and good at heart, but she was also afraid.

"She saw the pamphlet among my books. She asked to borrow it. I allowed it, but warned her to be discreet."

"Hence my first words, about the limitations of discretion," Mrs. Ludlow said sadly. "I would be sorry to lose you, Miss Belvoir. Most sorry. However, those pamphlets must be locked away, so the girls cannot see them. And you must obtain my permission before leaving the school in the future, and explain your purpose in doing so, lest I get more letters."

Padua bit her tongue. Of course she could not tell Mrs. Ludlow that she intended to leave again tomorrow, to bring food and clothing to her father *in prison*. If Mrs. Ludlow learned of his situation, she would surely send Padua packing by morning. She would have no choice.

Padua did not argue. She excused herself and retired to her chamber. Jennie waited for her there.

"Did she let you go?" Honest concern showed in Jennie's blue eyes. A young widow of good birth, Jennie was as dependent as Padua on her situation at Mrs. Ludlow's. Handsome, blond, and well-bred, she taught the girls comportment and etiquette. Her relatives may not give her a penny, but Mrs. Ludlow liked dropping their names to parents of prospective students.

"No. She said she does not want to either." But she would, if necessary. Padua knew that.

"Then you must not do this again. Where did you go?"

Jennie was the closest thing to a friend that Padua had, but they were not so close that she would admit to Jennie that her father was in prison. "I thought I knew where to find my father, so I might see him."

Jennie shook her head sadly. "He avoids you so he does not have to give you any money, Padua. I have told you that."

It was why Jennie's family avoided her, so she assumed it was a rule that governed all lives. "I know he has nothing to give. Anyway, I had to try."

Jennie turned to the door. "I must go. I am going to

tell those girls not to sneak in here tonight, for those extra lessons. You do not want to risk forcing Mrs. Ludlow into making a choice, Padua."

"Skipping a night or so might be wise."

After Jennie left, Padua knelt beside her bed. She reached under it for a valise she stored there. Opening it, she removed a little purse that held her money.

These coins had a purpose, but she doubted now that she would ever save enough to pay for her passage to Italy, and to her namesake city, where her mother had studied and her parents had met. Not when these coins were required to pay for the lawyers to help her father now, and to procure him what little comfort she could while he lived in his current abode.

She had saved almost enough once before, when she was younger and teaching at the school in Birmingham that she had attended as a student herself. After three years of scrimping, she had the passage. Then she had met Nicholas and fallen in love. Beautiful, glorious love. The kind of love her mother and father had known, and about which poems are written. She had loved totally, freely, and without guilt or worry.

Three months later Nicholas was gone, with her money in his pocket.

She stared at the coins. Her father had been cold to her for ten years, ever since her mother had died when Padua was fifteen. He had sent her away to that school then, at a time when she wanted to be with what family she had left. She had only seen him a few times a year since then, even after she moved to London in order to be closer to him.

He did not want her help. He did not even want her company. She should just leave, and go to Padua and apply to the university and make her mark if she still could. Papa might even respect her then.

Her mother's voice came to her, frail and trembling from the consumption taking her life. *He is like a child, Padua. You must promise me you will watch over him, as much as he will allow. For a man who has traveled extensively and read the great books, he knows almost nothing about surviving in the world.*

A long sigh escaped her. *Oh, Mama, what a promise to demand*—to care for a man who did not love her. To demand a place in his life when he would prefer she had none.

She thumbed fifteen shillings aside, then returned the rest to the valise.

G iven a choice, most lawyers would never sully themselves with criminal law. The result was those who did usually were the lawyers who could not find something more lucrative to do.

Ives was a rarity, a lawyer who argued criminal cases out of a sense of duty. There was no criminal bar, and his colleagues in the endeavor consisted of a motley assortment of lawyers whose primary work involved other courts and pleadings. Like him, only on occasion did they arrive in regalia at the Old Bailey or other criminal courtrooms to lend their eloquence and legal knowledge to the deliberations therein. Solicitors, sergeants—there was no limitation on who appeared to defend.

If one saw a trained barrister in the Old Bailey or Newgate Prison, most likely he served as prosecutor, either one hired by the victims or by the state. Some judges now allowed the accused to have lawyers, too, but not all did. In many cases judges held to the tradition that a defendant could provide his own defense by simply speaking the truth.

Today Ives entered Newgate by way of a door through which most of those other lawyers were never received—that of the house of the gaoler, Mr. Brown. Being Lord Ywain had its privileges. Within minutes he was sitting in Mr. Brown's office, explaining his purpose.

"Belvoir is being held here, while further investigations are pursued," Mr. Brown confirmed. "He has been here going on four weeks."

"If charges have been laid or are imminent, I would like to know what they are."

"Coining, it was. It will be the noose for him, or at best a life on the hulks."

Ives was not sure what he had thought the crime would be. Something political he supposed. As an intellectual, to hear his daughter describe him, Mr. Belvoir was the sort to take to radical ideas and company, and get swept into some misstep against the laws in place to control that sort of thing now.

"What is the evidence?" Coining, or counterfeiting

money, was among the most serious offenses. Counterfeiting undermined the health of the economy, and
was viewed as a type of treason.

"Caught him red-handed, is how I hear it," Brown
said. "Found the bad money in those rooms he keeps
on Wigmore Street."

This was not looking good for Hadrian Belvoir.
Ives expected he would dispatch the entire trial in less
than an hour. "What has he said for himself?"

"Well, now, that is the rub. He hasn't said anything.
Magistrates and others keep asking him, and he refuses
to cooperate. Unwise of him, isn't it? He might garner
some mercy if he turned on his colleagues in crime.
You know how that works, sir."

He did indeed. Criminals laying down information
about other criminals was the oil that made the wheels
of the criminal courts turn.

"We even showed him the old press in the yard, to
frighten him. Usually the mere threat of torture works
wonders," Brown said. "With this strange one, nothing.
If anything he became more stubborn."

"Strange, you call him. Is he perhaps demented?"

"I wouldn't say so. As for strange, well, come see for
yourself."

The gaoler rose. Together they walked into the prison
proper and its long corridors of cells, or wards.

Enough of a breeze penetrated through the small windows today so it did not smell as bad as it might. Still,
when hundreds of people crammed damp cells, the mere

odors of humanity's existence became concentrated and offensive. The smell of human waste alone overwhelmed the senses. Add to that the effects of unwashed bodies, rotting food, and the almost sweet odor of illness, and it produced a mix strong enough to leave men retching.

As they approached a crossway in the corridors, a woman sped past on the other path. Padua Belvoir, tall and proud, walked with determination toward the exit, a handkerchief to her nose. She headed down past wards holding women, some of whom mocked her with lewd calls and cackles. Ives paused in the crossway and watched her run the gauntlet.

"That is his daughter, or so she says," Brown commented. "Showed up yesterday, asking to see him. She brought him some food, clothes, and books today. Them that care about Belvoir's case were very interested in this woman's sudden appearance after all this time. I expect they are hoping she was sent by those he worked for."

"She really is his daughter." Ives spoke with more authority than he could claim. He hardly had proof of the fact. Yet there had been very little dissembling, and considerable concern, in the woman who intruded on his evening. Should she cajole her father into cooperating, it would be a good thing. That she had now attracted the attention of the authorities alarmed him, however.

After a few more turns, Brown stopped in front of a cell. Like many of the others, it held at least twenty men, all of whom lived, slept, ate, and wasted away in it. For a price a man could have better lodgings. The wretches here could not afford it.

"That is him, in the corner."

Ives did not need the gaoler's direction. The man in the corner stood out from all the others. Although he sat against the wall, with his manacled ankles pulled close to his body, one could tell he was very tall and very thin. He wore a waistcoat and frock coat that, while disgusting and dirty now, had once been those of a gentleman. Presumably there had been no beard when he entered that cell, and his steely gray hair had been better groomed too.

The most notable thing about him, however, was not his appearance, but rather his activity. In his corner, beside his hip, stood a little stack of books. Belvoir read one so intently that he did not notice the gaoler and Ives peering through the door's iron grate.

Beside the books rested a wrapped package, and a small basket of fruit. The other men in the cell eyed the last item with lust. Ives assumed Belvoir would soon be relieved of the fruit, and perhaps the package of clothing. No one would want the books.

"When he first came, and I took down his information, he identified his occupations as teacher, scholar, gentleman, and mathematician." Brown found it amusing. "Funny how they never say forger, coiner, murderer, or thief."

Ives looked at those books. Hadrian Belvoir would not even notice his surroundings until they were all read, he guessed. Then read again, if no new ones were brought by his daughter.

"That daughter, if she is a daughter, wanted to buy him a better place," Brown said. "She had the coin for it. I said I would check to see if that is allowed. My guess is they want him here, and as uncomfortable as possible."

Ives did not think it would matter now. Anyone who saw him could tell that Hadrian Belvoir had entered a different world from the one in which he sat. His mind had been freed even if his body still suffered.

Padua pushed through the crowd waiting to hear the news from the Old Bailey's trials. She found a spot near the end of the building, where she could pause and compose herself.

She would never grow accustomed to seeing her father in that place, but his condition was not what agitated her. Rather she carried a deep anger away from her meeting. She had brought him some items to relieve his suffering, at notable cost to herself, only to have him once more reject her help. Oh, he had taken the food and books, but there had not been one word of thanks, and he had once again ordered her not to return.

The only reason she had not lost her temper and upbraided him was the way he looked at those books, and then at her. His relief had been palpable and his eagerness visible. When his gaze rose to hers again, she discerned some gratitude, and also embarrassment. Then he had flipped through them hungrily, and almost smiled when he found the paper and pencil secreted inside one of them.

Other than that vague expression in his eyes, had he acknowledged her love and concern, though? Not at all. And his words had been cruel and sharp. *I said not to come here again. Do not disobey me this time as I say it again.*

"Miss Belvoir." The call came from the other end of the building, from beyond the line of people waiting to petition to see their relatives. Her gaze snapped to a waving hat, and a man on horseback. Ives. He had given her leave to think of him by that name, and she had taken to doing so most of the time.

He trotted toward her, and the line split like the Red Sea to permit him to pass. Fifty yards from her he dismounted, and approached on foot with his steed in tow.

Decked out like the wealthy aristocrat he was, Ives proved quite a sight. In the sunlight his face proved no less impressive, but the raking illumination showed the fine lines on either side of his eyes and mouth. Laugh lines they were called, yet they made him appear less friendly not more so, and gave his classic beauty a hard edge that the soft haze of candles had not revealed.

"Miss Belvoir, it is fortunate to find you here." He made a little bow. "I have learned a few things that you should know. Walk with me, and I will tell you all."

Of course she walked with him. Together they strolled along the edge of the square.

"You visited him again today," he said. "Did you learn anything?"

"If I had, it would be unwise to tell you."

"Anything he says in his own defense will aid him. The Crown is not without mercy."

"Do you have reason to think he will need mercy?"

He stopped walking and faced her. "I regret that I do. It is worse than I thought, and I think worse than you feared. The pending charge is for coining. It is very serious, and the evidence is solid."

Coining? Her father? Hadrian Belvoir? She could not keep a laugh from emerging. "That is ridiculous. He has no sense of money, and little use for it except to buy paper and books. Anyone who knows him would know—"

"The counterfeit money was found in his home. They have him dead to rights. He is only in prison, instead of tried and convicted, because they hope to get him to reveal the rest of the scheme. No one counterfeits on his own. It is a complicated procedure that requires specialized skills."

"If there was bad money in his possession, he probably received it from some shop and was not aware it was bad."

The less friendly aspects of his handsome face hardened. "Do not assume the law is upheld by fools. A few pounds do not a counterfeit charge make. If they have him in prison, a good amount was found in his possession, Miss Belvoir." His expression softened. "You must prepare yourself."

Prepare yourself. It was the kind of thing said to relatives of the dying. She stared at this man who would be the agent of her father's destruction. Fury at her father collided with fury at him.

"How kind of you. How sympathetic. You lower your voice and pretend concern, but when his trial opens you will be there in your wig and robes and convince the jury to convict him and the judge to damn him. His life will be over for a small crime barely worth noting."

His countenance turned very hard indeed. "Miss Belvoir, I am truly sorry for you, but not for him. Counterfeiting is not a minor crime. It is never small. It is normally undertaken on a large scale, because it requires significant skill and investment. If your father did this, as it appears he did, I will indeed convince the jury to convict him. My sympathy is for you, as it is for all relatives of criminals, but to expect sympathy for the criminals themselves is expecting too much from me or anyone else."

His words sliced like so many lashes from a whip, inflicting pain the way uncompromising reality can. She glimpsed a terrible future for her father, and an ignoble end. Her dismay must have showed, because he stepped closer to her. His hand came to rest on her shoulder in a gesture of comfort that dismayed her all the more.

"The gaoler said that you wanted to see him moved to a better ward. One with some privacy and less damp. I will see what I can do about that if you want."

What a voice he had when he spoke like this. Low and resonant, the tone alone seduced one to listen and want to hear more. That and his proximity tempted her to pretend the gesture of comfort came from a friend. It would be blissful to have someone share the burden if only for a few minutes.

She sniffed back the tears threatening to fall. "First kind, then cruel, then kind again. What kind of man are you? I do not want to be indebted to your whimsies of generosity. I want to be free to hate you."

His hand fell away. "I will look into it anyway. You will owe me no thanks."

She did not think her composure would hold. Without another word she hurried away, so she did not have to acknowledge his offer.

CHAPTER 3

Padua did not ask the most likely man to refer her to a solicitor. While Ives no doubt knew the best of them, she could not count on his impartiality. A different option occurred to her as she blindly walked the streets near Newgate after leaving Ives. Before returning home she visited the gaoler's office again, and requested names of him.

"You cannot count on the judge allowing it," Mr. Brown said. However, he provided three names of solicitors whom he thought to be honest and smart. Two days later she again slipped away from the school and made her way to the Inns of Court to call on one of them.

Mr. Notley listened to her tale of woe, his sharp, dark eyes peering at her over his broad, empty desk. She suspected him to be one of those people who required exacting order in his life if he managed his affairs with so little evidence of industry. His attention to his dress gave her heart. Unlike Ives in his midnight banyan, Mr. Notley indeed wore black coats of perfect fit and had a clerk nearby taking notes.

His face indicated he was not a young man, but his hair remained as black as his eyes. Padua wondered if he did something to encourage the color. She found herself eyeing his collar, looking for dust or stains from dye.

"You say Lord Ywain will prosecute?" Mr. Notley found that detail of great interest. "That is, I am afraid to say, not good news."

"I am so accustomed to bad news that I find I greet your observation with surprising equanimity."

"He is very good, but that is not my concern. Due to his birth he has the highest connections, including a friendship with the prince regent."

"I had no idea."

"His father was the Duke of Aylesbury, Miss Belvoir, and his brother is the current one. He is asked to prosecute when the government has a particular interest in a case. We would prefer it did not have too much interest in this one."

"I see what you mean about not good news now."

"Indeed. However, at least he is honest. We will depend on that."

She hoped the repeated *we* meant he was going to help her. Mr. Notley appeared to still be thinking it over.

"If your father will not aid me in his defense, my hands will be considerably tied, Miss Belvoir. I will feel like a thief taking fees from you."

"I cannot allow him to be tried without someone speaking for him, however."

"That is understandable." He made a tent with his long fingers and pondered the point they made. "If it comes down to providing a defense based on his character, I will do the speaking. Normally solicitors do not appear in front of judges, but matters are less formal in the criminal courts. However, if information develops that brings his guilt into question, we will need to obtain the services of a lawyer skilled in the theatrics of the courtroom, one who will match Lord Ywain in ability and prestige. That will be expensive."

"Tell me how much when the time comes, and I will tell you if I have it. For now, please let me know what I will owe you."

"Normally my clerk attends to that." He looked at that clerk. The two exchanged knowing looks that said, *Such is our lot to serve such as this.*

"Two pounds for the preliminaries," the clerk said. Mr. Notley managed to appear like he had not heard.

Padua had that much on her, and more. The valise under her bed grew emptier by the day. "If I give you ten shillings more, will you look into something else for me? It does relate to my father."

Those dark eyes sharpened with interest.

"My mother passed away when I was fifteen. Soon after, my father came into a legacy from a distant rel-

ative. He used it to send me away to school in Birmingham. I rarely saw him after that. I would like you to see
about that legacy if you can. I think it was a property,
and if so, perhaps I can obtain some money out of it to
help pay the fees of his defense."

Mr. Notley jotted down some notes. "You are asking for a service that is more familiar to me than
criminal work, Miss Belvoir, and more welcomed. I
will see what I can discover."

The note came to Ives at nine in the morning, before
he had risen from bed. It was the kind of note to
get him on his feet at once. Cursing all the while, he
dressed fast and haphazardly and skipped a shave so he
could gallop through town to Mayfair as soon as possible. Arriving at the family house, he took the stairs
two at a time and threw open the door to his brother's
apartment.

He found Lance enjoying the shave that he himself
had forgone.

"What the hell has happened?" he demanded.

"What are you doing here?" Lance asked. "I did
not expect you until afternoon."

*"Come immediately. I need you to serve as my second
for a duel.* That is what your note said."

"Well, yes, but I did not think you would read it until
noon, so then you would arrive around one."

"Some of us rise earlier. Now tell me why you need
a second and, by Zeus, your story had better show

you the victim of some fool in his cups, and not the instigator of a challenge."

The valet scraped the last of Lance's beard, then laid a warm, damp towel over his face so only Lance's dark hair showed. "I had no choice," came Lance's muffled reply.

"So you did issue the challenge."

"Had to."

"Damnation."

The towel was lifted. Lance removed another one from around his neck. "You would have done the same. There was nothing else for it."

Ives paced the chamber. "I *would not* have done the same thing, because I would not be in London. I would have listened to my brother, whose advice on such matters is sought by the highest of the high, and kept my ass in the country."

The valet began tidying up the dressing room. Lance led the way to his sitting room.

"Why did you call for me to be your second?" Ives demanded. "Why not one of your friends in crime?"

"I thought your eloquence might be useful. I had to issue the challenge, but it would be better if we did not fight. I don't want to kill another duke." He caught himself, and laughed. "By another, I mean one other than myself, of course. Not one other than Percy."

The explanation made Ives pause. "You did not have to explain the distinction to me, Lance. Surely you know that."

Lance said nothing. Weariness marked his dark eyes.

Being suspected of his own brother's murder was taking its toll, despite his claims otherwise.

"Just which other duke is it?"

"Middleburrow. It was about Percy, of course. He was drunk, and lost a small fortune to me and could not resist thrusting a few daggers at my reputation out of spite. I could not let it stand."

No, he could not. But a duel, let alone with Middleburrow, would do nothing to keep the hounds at bay. "I will find a way out of it."

"He will have to apologize. Nothing less will do. I set the meeting for two o'clock, in the hopes of giving him a chance to sober up."

Ives began planning how to affect this miracle. "If I succeed, you must promise me to go down to Merrywood again. I'll not be fixing disasters for you over and over."

Lance's deep scowl reflected what he thought of that condition.

"Give me your word, Lance, or you can find someone else for the meeting."

"Fine, damn it. You have my word. I will rusticate until I am gray and feeble and until a silken noose appears a mercy, if you want."

Ives would have liked to reassure him that soon the current burden would be lifted, but in truth he saw no end in sight. When he left, Lance had begun cleaning his dueling pistols, should eloquence not avert the duel after all.

Ives had planned to go riding this morning, but by

the time he left his brother, there was not enough time to go out of town and return in time for the meeting. He instead returned home to complete the grooming barely begun, then rode back to Mayfair in the afternoon.

The Duke of Middleburrow's second appeared relieved when Ives explained that Lance felt an indiscretion blurted while drunk should not lead to a man's death. They spent an hour negotiating the language of the apology that Middleburrow would make. Knowing Lance's mind, Ives insisted it not be so qualified as to edge into ambiguity.

Lest Middleburrow balk, they also made arrangements for a duel should that be needed. Ives trusted those details would encourage Middleburrow to swallow his pride, claim incapacity due to spirits, and back out with grace.

The entire endeavor took most of the day. The intrusion on his time left Ives irritated. He returned home, determined to spend the morrow out of doors, on horseback, free of all obligations.

As he sat down with his book that evening, the paper with his list of mistress qualifications caught his attention again. He read it, too aware that abstinence was becoming a nuisance. With each item on the list, a face took clearer form in his mind. Dark hair. Sparkling eyes. Determined expression. Uncompromising loyalty.

Hell.

He tucked the paper away again.

CHAPTER 4

I ves entered the Home Office in Whitehall, too aware
that this was the third day of his precious respite that
he would spend on what he had come to call Miss Belvoir's Dilemma. Pride prevented him from including
yesterday, too, even though while finally enjoying a
good country gallop, he found himself mulling over
Hadrian Belvoir's case. One thought had led to another,
and soon he was imagining Miss Belvoir's dark eyes
alight with pleasure and her tall, lithe body naked and
bending to his erotic lessons.

The fantasy had been so engaging that he had not
relinquished it easily, and suffered last night from its
insistent presence.

He had been involved in enough dealings with the
Home Office that almost everyone he passed greeted

him. More than once in his career he had undertaken tasks for the Crown that might best be described as extralegal. A friendship with the prince regent had first brought one of these little investigations his way, as a favor. Success at that turned him into the man the royal family called on when an awkward problem arose that needed someone to ferret out a few facts discreetly, and perhaps bend a few ears. Or arms.

That he might on occasion do such favors did not mean that he approved of an entire government apparatus doing the same thing. That was what the Home Office had become under Viscount Sidmouth, the secretary of state for the Home Department.

As the political situation grew more tense in the country, this branch of the government had resorted to domestic spying and even agents to infiltrate and disrupt what its leaders considered potentially treasonous activity. The French excesses of thirty years earlier were never far from the minds of some of Ives's social equals, and the calls for reform and other radical notions sounded far too dangerous to them.

And so while he walked the halls of the Home Office as a friend, there were those within who knew he fully expected to one day serve as prosecutor when they themselves stood trial.

That was not the case with Ivan Strickland, whose office door he opened. Strickland remained a sane voice that argued against the more serious invasions of old-fashioned British liberty. Ives believed he could trust Strickland if he could trust anyone at the Home

Office. They sometimes did favors for each other, so they shared a history of mutual debt.

Strickland was a hearty, fair-haired fellow who possessed the kind of strength that could turn soft if not kept in check with regular exercise. He greeted Ives enthusiastically, and they enjoyed catching up. Strickland of course wanted to know whatever Ives would share about the untimely death of Ives's eldest brother Percival the prior spring, and the suspicions still surrounding his other brother Lance, who had now inherited.

It was not until a good half hour into the visit that Ives broached his reason for coming.

"I received a letter from the prince regent a month ago," he said. "You were not in town then, I think."

"Up north," Strickland said. "That business in Manchester. What a hellish mess. Try as we might, we will not be able to make it what we want. History will damn us."

He referred to the deaths at a large demonstration of workers in Manchester, a disaster now popularly called Peterloo.

"In that letter he made reference to a case I would be asked to prosecute. A man named Hadrian Belvoir."

"Belvoir?" Strickland's brow furrowed in thought. "Ah, now I remember. Coining, it is. Have you found it interesting?"

"It never went beyond that letter. He has not been brought to trial yet. Nor does it appear he will be soon."

"I know how you feel about men not getting speedy trials. Don't lecture me on it. I seem to remember the magistrate said they intended to use this fellow as fish bait to catch a whale."

"The gaoler at the prison said counterfeit money was found in his home. Anything else?"

"Printing press and such? No. Just bad money."

"Who laid down information on him?"

"Some thief who with an eye to burglary broke in and saw enough to bargain for his lover's reprieve from the gallows, as I remember it."

It all made sense, yet Ives's instincts kept waving at his mind.

"You know a lot of particulars about Belvoir, Strickland."

Strickland beamed a smile. "Well, that magistrate was the loquacious sort."

"I don't suppose he explained just how big a whale he hopes to catch with his bait."

"Let me think about that." Strickland pondered. "More a giant octopus, actually. All those arms going this way and that, if you understand me."

Ives understood well enough. Someone thought Belvoir could lead them to a criminal involved in much more than this incident of counterfeiting. If Strickland knew so much, the Home Office was either involved, or monitoring the situation closely. And if the Home Office showed this much interest, they probably thought this octopus was dangerous, and had an arm or two tied to political radicals seen as threats to the realm.

"I trust the magistrates, or whoever is investigating, are being thorough. I have seen the man, and he is an unlikely culprit. I would not want another case like Waverley's."

Strickland's face fell. His gaze shifted. "That was unfortunate."

"It was not unfortunate. It was a tragic miscarriage of justice."

"You really need to forget about him. Mistakes happen."

"I sent an innocent man to the gallows. That is not something one forgets."

"*You* did not send him. The process sent him."

"Carelessness sent him. Settling for the easy solution did, and indifference to finding the truth did." He heard his voice rising. *Let it go?* He would forever regret that day in the Old Bailey. "If I learn Belvoir is being sacrificed to the Home Office's notions of expediency, there will be hell to pay."

"This is not like that," Strickland said. "There's no politics here. As I've heard, it is counterfeiting, and other normal sorts of crimes."

"If you have only heard, you do not really know. If others in this building are crossing legal lines, they would not inform you." Ives conquered the anger that had gripped him. It had been unfair to throw that burden at Strickland, who had not even been involved in Waverly's case. "They cannot hold Belvoir forever without trying him," he said. "He is a citizen and does have his rights."

"I expect you will be meeting him in the Old Bailey within the month. According to that magistrate, of course. Although if you are so suspicious, maybe you should not prosecute. You can still beg off."

He grinned when he said it, because of course Ives could not beg off. When the Crown indicated it wanted one to serve as its prosecutor, one did it.

They turned the conversation to other things, but all the while Ives calculated the ramifications of Strickland's confidences. Padua Belvoir had better find that lawyer she sought, and quickly. And if she were not careful, she might end up needing legal counsel for herself.

P adua strolled between the tables, looking over the girls' shoulders while they worked on their geometry lesson. The few who showed the worst mistakes were not the ones who lacked the ability to learn mathematics. Rather they were the ones worldly enough to know that no matter how well they mastered the subject, no one would celebrate their achievement.

Padua's efforts to encourage learning for one's own satisfaction made little headway with some of the girls once they became distracted by thoughts of parties and suitors.

Before the hour ended, Jennie, whose lessons on comportment and etiquette the girls never treated as useless, came to the classroom's door.

"You have a caller," she said, after drawing Padua aside. "I will take over here, so you can go down."

"I am amazed that Mrs. Ludlow allowed me to be pulled away from my duty to receive this person."

"I'm not. Go and see why."

Stepping into the reception hall solved the mystery. Mrs. Ludlow herself already sat with the caller, in a little chamber off the hall decorated with frail gilt furniture and a nauseating combination of pink and rose fabrics. "Ah, here is Miss Belvoir now," she chirped when Padua entered the room. Mrs. Ludlow's high color blotched her cheeks, and she all but giggled when she gestured at Padua with a silly flourish.

Her caller was none other than Ives. Padua suspected his calling card would sit in the salver in the reception hall until it turned yellow from age.

Mrs. Ludlow appeared at cross minds regarding leaving the chamber. Padua smiled at her reassuringly. The chamber had no doors, for heaven's sake, and its interior was in full view of the hall. Nor, at twenty-five, did she require a chaperone, especially with this man.

After Mrs. Ludlow left, Padua turned expectantly to Ives. "How did you find me?"

"You left your address with my man that first day. Remember?"

She did now. She sat on a little silk-covered bench. He took the only decent-sized chair.

"I apologize if my arrival will create difficulties with your employer," he said.

"I do not expect any problems. She is probably eavesdropping right now, so I will even be spared her curiosity."

From out in the hall, very close to the entrance to the sitting room, a sharp intake of breath could be heard. Then very light footsteps, receding in sound.

"Expect her to tell parents that you visit frequently, have relatives here, and patronize the school with donations," she said. "She is a sweet woman, and essentially honest, but this is her livelihood, and there is much competition."

He smiled. He appeared quite kind. But then the light was soft here, due to northern-facing windows and the early hour.

"*Did* you come to patronize the school?" she asked, when he did not explain why he had called.

Was that a slight flush she saw? Goodness, perhaps he had forgotten himself, quite literally.

"I have come to give you some names of lawyers who would serve your father's interests well." He reached into his coat and extracted a small sheet of paper.

"Thank you, but I have already engaged one."

"May I ask which one?"

She considered not telling him. It was none of his business, at least not until the trial.

"Mr. Notley."

"That is not a bad choice. Notley is diligent, sober, and honest."

"I thought so."

"However, he has little courtroom experience, being a solicitor. He can serve in that capacity in the criminal court, but he would be wiser to engage a barrister."

"So he explained. We will do so, if it is necessary. He also said that if you were asked to prosecute, it meant very important people had an interest in the case. Is that so?"

His gaze locked on her. "Often."

"Your brother the duke?"

"No."

"Of course not. What possible interest would he have? I can think of no one else who might make a claim on you, however."

"Honor makes a claim. Duty makes a claim. Above all else, justice does, Miss Belvoir."

If you care about justice, refuse to be a part of this. She bit her tongue. It would be foolish to antagonize the man whom her father would face in court. "Why did you come here? What do you want of me?"

He walked over to the entrance, and peered out into the hall. Then he came and stood near her so he could speak quietly. "I have come to warn you. You must not go to Newgate again. You should remove yourself from this entire process. Allow Mr. Notley to work in your stead if you must, but tell him to do so discreetly and as counsel to your father rather than in your service."

She did not like being talked down to, literally. Nor was she in the mood to take direction from Ives. She stood so she might better look him in the eyes. "Much as I would like to believe you have my best interests at heart, I am sure you do not have my father's interests in mind at all when you issue this warning. As a prosecutor you will be an opponent to his interests. Without me, he will be easy pickings for such as you, especially if I remove myself."

His head cocked to one side. His lids lowered. "Are you insinuating that I fear your involvement because it will cause me *to lose*?"

"It will certainly make your winning less assured."

"Miss Belvoir, I am not here for anything having to do with me. I am concerned for you. There may be more to all of this than either of us knows."

"Obviously there is. I have said from the start that my father is not the sort to be involved in such a crime. A monstrous mistake has been—"

A firm slice of his hand through the air cut her off. "That is not what I mean." He sighed with exasperation. "Listen to me now. And believe that I am not speaking as a prosecutor, but as someone who knows more of this part of the world than you ever will."

She sat again, to listen. Not because he commanded it, although her own will had little practice in meeting the challenge of one of similar mettle. She sat to listen because he was no fool, and his expression and voice convinced her that whatever he had to say must be heard.

He pulled a chair very close to hers, again so eavesdroppers might not overhear. Their knees almost touched. She found it very difficult to deny the power of this man's presence with him so close that he wrapped her in it. There was something compelling about him, as if he intruded on her spirit somehow. How inappropriate, outrageous even, to react to him that way, when he would play such a horrible role in her life.

"Your father had become involved in something that may be far bigger than he knows," he said. "I have cause to believe that the government has taken an interest in him, and in that bad money they found in his rooms on Wigmore Street, and in his associates. If so, someone thinks this is not a simple crime, but part of a conspiracy."

The word *conspiracy* sent a chill down her spine. The word got bandied about a lot these days, since the end of the war caused disruptions in the economy that had sent workers into the streets, and given leave to radicals to restart their campaigns for major changes in society and politics. Ever fearful of the upheavals such unrest can cause, the government had passed laws to make conspiracy harder to concoct.

"He is not political," she said.

"He does not have to be if his associates are."

"Who are these associates? Is that known?"

"They expect to learn that from him. However, right now, there is curiosity about one associate who has recently come to light. You."

Another chill.

"You showed up after almost a month. You visit him daily. You bring him books and paper. What does he in turn give to you? What do you say to him? Such are the questions being asked. The gaoler even questioned if you are really his daughter."

"Who else would I be?"

"An accomplice."

"That is insulting."

"See it with their eyes. You must stop going to Newgate. You have done your duty as his daughter. His lawyer will do the rest."

"I cannot do that."

"You must." His demeanor showed he expected obe-
dience.

She owed him none, but she did not want him to
think her foolhardy either. She would explain herself
once, but no more than that, so perhaps he would understand she did not reject his advice due to mere stub-
bornness.

"You said there were claims on you. Well, there are
some on me too. I also have duties, and one is to make
sure my father is not left to his own poor devices. I promised my mother I would. She did not mean I should
make sure his shirts were clean or his cravat properly
tied, I realize now. She meant watching over him if something like this happened. Papa's head remains in his
numbers and abstractions. He will prove hapless on his
own in such a complication of suspicions and conspir-
acies."

He appeared to understand, but he did not like it. He
gazed at her much as a strict tutor might look at a student who offered a good reason the lessons had not
been done. Acknowledging the excuse was valid did not
solve the problem of lessons not learned.

"Promise me at least that you will not return to Newgate," he said. "If you send food to the gaoler's office,
it will be brought to your father. I will make the arrangements."

She wished he would stop helping her. Did he not see a contradiction in doing things like this when he fully intended to lower the wrath of justice on the same man?

"I cannot promise. However, I will not return unless I believe it to be necessary that I do." She lost little ground in agreeing to this. Her father did not want her there, and refused to speak to her. Perhaps Mr. Notley would have more success.

Ives smiled. He appeared pleased. She could not understand why. He glanced around the chamber, and it was as if his gaze penetrated the walls and saw the rest of the building too. "Do you teach here?"

"I do."

"Which subjects?"

"Mathematics and natural science, although I can cover most everything else taught here too."

"Mrs. Ludlow is lucky to have you."

Padua had to laugh. "I do not think she would always agree. I am, however, useful and inexpensive. If I left she would have to replace me, which for mathematics most likely means having to pay a man much more."

"Did your father school you in mathematics?"

"Everyone assumes that, but he did not. My mother did."

She enjoyed people's surprise when she said that. Ives was no different. Curiosity entered his eyes.

He would have to wait to have it satisfied. Familiar footsteps heralded the return of Mrs. Ludlow. A servant followed, carrying a tray. "Lord Ywain, would you honor us by joining us while we partake of some coffee?"

He graciously accepted. Padua noticed the tray had only two cups and saucers. Mrs. Ludlow's "we" had been the royal one.

"Miss Belvoir, should you not return to your classroom? The younger girls are waiting for you now."

Padua excused herself. Ives managed to appear welcoming as Mrs. Ludlow turned an ingratiating smile on him, but Padua thought she glimpsed a few seconds of pain first.

Well, if the man insisted on interfering, he had to expect a little discomfort every now and then.

L osing hours and days to Miss Belvoir's Dilemma was bad enough. Now Ives found himself subjected to Mrs. Ludlow's social blandishments. She spent half an hour talking about her educational endeavors.

"We do our best here with the girls," she confided after treating him to a description of her school. "As well as possible, I like to think, considering their backgrounds." She lowered her voice. "Most of their fathers are in trade, and if ever the results of breeding trump those of money, it is in young women like these."

"How long has Miss Belvoir taught for you?" he asked. "I sought her out today on a matter concerning relatives of hers, and do not know the particulars of her own situation."

"She has been here three years. She came with only one reference, and a qualified one at that. I took her on with some risk because she can teach subjects it can be hard to staff. I do not deny her qualifications, and I enjoy her company. However, I find her opinionated and proud at times too. She is given to radical ideas, I regret to say, enough that I have debated asking her to leave."

Ives would have preferred the word *radical* not be associated with Padua Belvoir, under the circumstances. He hoped Mrs. Ludlow only referred to those reformist ideas that he knew about.

"I trust she does not advocate eliminating all the aristocrats," he said with a little laugh.

Mrs. Ludlow thought that very funny. They chortled together at the absurd notion. "No, she is not that kind of radical. Goodness, if our parents ever thought that." She patted her heart, as if in danger of fainting. "She has some inappropriate ideas about women, however. You know the sort I mean. All that boring Wollstonecraft sort of thing. Her own mother attended a university abroad that allowed women. With a mother like that, you can imagine the strange notions Miss Belvoir has inherited. Our parents would not find it amusing." She looked at him like he were an old friend worthy of confidences. "Am I remiss in keeping her on? I go back and forth on the question."

"It cannot be easy to find a teacher of mathematics who will take employment at a school for girls. If Miss Belvoir is competent in the schoolroom, I do not think you are remiss, or need to rush to send her away."

Mrs. Ludlow looked at him with gratitude. "How good of you to advise me. You are correct, of course.

Unless she does something that will harm the girls or the school, I can overlook her way of thinking."

It seemed an excellent time to take his leave. He did so, believing his good deed for the day done several times over. Miss Belvoir would keep her employment, and would make herself scarce at Newgate. With luck, anyone following her father's case would lose interest in her in a week or so when she no longer made her appearances at his cell.

He would not mind being done with Hadrian Belvoir completely for the time being, but one more thing needed his attention. He knew from sorry experience that sometimes magistrates, eager to identify a culprit, overlooked inconvenient evidence that might call a person's guilt into question. It sounded like they had Hadrian Belvoir tied up in a neat package, but before he prosecuted, he wanted to make sure.

CHAPTER 5

More had been achieved by Ives's visit than Padua's reluctant agreement to no longer visit her father. Of more interest to Padua had been Ives's reference to her father's rooms on Wigmore Street.

Her father's use of a mail drop all these years had been especially wounding. She now knew where he lived, however. She hoped this was the property he had inherited too. If so, she would not need to pay Mr. Notley ten shillings to locate that legacy. And if her father used only some rooms in the building, perhaps that meant he let out the other rooms, and it served as a source of income.

She had to wait three days before she was able to leave the school with Mrs. Ludlow unawares. Fortunately, Mrs. Ludlow had a ritual of social calls every Friday afternoon. She always took Jennie with her because Jennie's connections, severed though they might be in reality, enhanced Mrs. Ludlow's social standing and even opened a few doors.

Padua bided her time until then. As soon as the hired carriage bore them away, she donned her spencer and bonnet and let herself out the garden door.

Time would be short today, so she hired a hackney and gave the driver the name of the street. She hoped it was not far away and she could walk back. It surprised her when the carriage stopped on a street near the northeastern edge of Piccadilly. She paid the fare, stepped out, and took a good look at her surroundings.

There was nothing fashionable about Wigmore Street. The houses appeared solid, and she guessed many of them contained several homes. Since she did not know which was her father's, she asked at a grocer's on one corner. She did not have to describe her father in much detail for the proprietor to recognize the man she wanted. He pointed her to a brick house on the next block that stood three stories tall over its raised cellar.

A blond woman sat at the window of the first storey. Padua asked after Mr. Belvoir.

"He lives above," the woman said. "He is not there now. Hasn't been for some weeks."

"Does he own this building?"

The woman laughed until she cried. "That odd duck own this building?" She wiped her eyes with the edge of her apron. "What would he know with owning a building. Nah, he lets his rooms same as I let mine, thank you."

Padua opened the door. She mounted the stairs leading to the next level.

As expected, the door to her father's rooms had not been locked. Hadrian Belvoir would never bother with such practicalities. When she entered, she had to admit there would be little purpose in doing so anyway, because he had nothing to steal.

A monk might live like this, in chambers crammed with books that overflowed the cases into stacks on tables and floors. A writing table, all but barricaded into a corner of the sitting room, held a heap of papers. Padua made her way to it and examined those pages. Few words had been written. Most of them carried numbers and mathematical notations. Her father had long been in search of impossible proofs. He would not be the first man to spend his life in such pursuits, only to fail.

She looked around, wondering where all this counterfeit money had been stored. From what she could tell, there was no room for it. She wandered into the bedchamber. There she found a conspicuous void near one wall. It appeared a trunk once stood there but no longer did. Its outline could be traced on the floorboards by the absence of any other items.

She had hoped to find proof no large stash of money had been here, so the conspicuous void disheartened her. Her father clearly lived here, but why? If he had inherited property, why would he not live there?

Unfortunately she suspected she knew the answer to that. He had probably sold that property long ago. She would not be surprised if someone had cheated him by paying too little, or even not at all. It would be just like her father to sign over the deed and forget to collect the payment for it.

Discouraged, she returned to the sitting room, and began choosing books to be delivered to the prison. She had withdrawn two, when a small volume bound in red caught her eye. She pulled it out. It was one of the schoolbooks she had used as a girl. It touched her that Papa had saved it.

She flipped it open to see if her childish signature still marked its first page. A banknote fell out and fluttered to the floor. Twenty pounds. She picked it up, then fanned the pages. No more money.

Her gaze went to the books, searching. She spied another thin red binding. She checked that book, and found another ten pounds. Excited, she looked again, and saw a third book.

She pushed the piles of journals and pamphlets off a table, in order to make room for her schoolbooks. Her excavations revealed a wooden box beneath one pile that distracted her. She remembered it from her childhood. Her mother had kept this box in her dressing room. Seeing it again called forth memories and feelings, all of them warm and nostalgic.

Back then it stored gloves. It did not store gloves now. Instead a stack of letters filled it. The letters carried her mother's scent, she was sure, and their mere existence entranced her. She set the schoolbooks down, to be dealt with later, and stuffed the banknotes in her bodice, to get them out of the way too. She dumped books off a chair and sat.

The letters were mostly in her mother's hand, but her father had written a few. The dates indicated these were old, from before Padua's birth. Her heart trembled while she looked at her mother's handwriting. Finally, she unfolded one of the letters and read it.

L ance agreeing to quit town for Merrywood was not the same as Lance actually getting in the coach and leaving. Ives visited for breakfast, dawdled in conversation up in Lance's dressing room, and generally remained underfoot until Lance, with annoyance, told his valet to pack.

"I expect I will see you next week," Lance said just as the coach began to roll.

"Damnation, don't you dare come back that quickly."

"Not here. In Merrywood." The vehicle jostled forward.

Ives had no intention of spending the last part of his precious respite entertaining Lance in the country. "Do not count on it," he called after the coach.

Lance stuck his head out the window and looked back. "A fine brother you are. Gareth brings his bride home from their travels and you do not bother to come down to greet them."

Ives called for the coach to stop. He paced to that

window and peered in. "Gareth is returning next week?"

"Did I neglect to tell you that?"

"You did."

"I received a letter two or three days ago. Maybe four." He pondered the detail as if it mattered.

So much for week two of unencumbered freedom. "I will be there, of course."

"We will go hunting."

"Wonderful." He tapped the coach, to signal the driver to continue. The coach rolled.

A head appeared at the window again. "Did I also neglect to mention she is with child? Eva, that is."

The coach turned onto the street. The head disappeared. Ives wondered just how drunk Lance had been the last fortnight.

I t was past three o'clock before Ives made his way to Wigmore Street. He tied his horse near the crossroads and approached Belvoir's building on foot.

He noticed two things as he walked. The first was a fellow dawdling several doors down from Belvoir's. He managed to appear busy without actually doing anything. Ives thought it likely a watch had been set on Belvoir's abode. That was not something that a magistrate had the resources to do, which would mean the Home Office had involved itself far more than Strickland would ever admit.

He then saw an unexpected face from the past. A

woman with an elaborate style to her brassy hair sat in the window on the first storey. When she looked out as he approached, Ives recognized her.

She pasted on a smile, but her gaze carried unmistakable hatred. Ives could not blame her for her reaction. Two years ago her common-law husband, Harry Trenholm, had been transported after a trial in which Ives prosecuted. The charges had been arson and sedition, for burning down a factory near Liverpool, one owned by an industrialist who had contributed plenty of fuel to the confrontation that ended in those flames. As for the sedition—Trenholm had cloaked his act in political rhetoric to justify himself.

The fool hired to defend failed to make sufficient use of that factory owner's provocations, or of the fact no one had been injured. Ives artfully did instead, thus keeping this woman's husband from the gallows. She could be excused if she did not appreciate the effort. Her man disappeared anyway, and was dead to her for all intents and purposes.

He paused on the building's stoop. "Mrs. Trenholm. It is always nice to see a familiar face when on a strange street."

"The pleasure is all yours, I am sure."

"How do you fare these days?"

She gritted her teeth behind her smile. That made her already prominent chin cut forward more. "Life goes on. What brings you here? Not the sort of street that sees many of your sort, or carriages like that one down there."

"I am seeking the home of Mr. Belvoir."

"You, too, eh. Well, up one set of stairs and there you are. What's he done to make you interested in him? He must be in gaol. That explains why it is so silent up there these past weeks, doesn't it?"

"Do you know him well?"

"He's a strange one and keeps to himself. I figured he mighta died up there. I've been waiting for the smell to tell me so. I've no time for crazy men like him. I work in a flower shop now, and I've a new gentleman in my life, so I am not here most days."

"I am glad to see that life indeed goes on for you. Tell me, what did you mean when you said, *You too*? Has someone else visited Mr. Belvoir's rooms?"

Her eyes looked upward. "A woman. She's up there now. She has been for over an hour."

"An attractive woman with very dark hair?" *And porcelain skin and star-filled eyes with lashes thick and dark?*

"Attractive? Hardly. She is freakishly tall. That is all one notices about her, how she is as tall as some men."

What a ridiculous description of Miss Belvoir. Anyone with a discerning eye could see that her height gave her elegance, distinction, and presence. She pulled it off so well because she did not try to do anything in the false hope it would make her appear smaller to stupid women like Mrs. Trenholm, whose flamboyant hair and painted face marked her as without taste.

He let himself in, and walked up the stairs. No sounds came from above. No steps on the floorboards. Perhaps

Mrs. Trenholm was wrong, and Padua Belvoir no longer remained in her father's chambers. A note of disappointment played in his head, surprising him.

The door to the chambers stood open. He looked in. Padua had not left yet. She sat on a wooden chair. Beside her, on a small table, lay an open glove box.

She read something. Whatever it was had transfixed her, and affected her entire being. Her face appeared very soft and young and vulnerable. The chamber's dusty light bathed her and made her skin luminous. Not merely attractive. Beautiful.

It seemed a cruel intrusion to interrupt whatever thoughts her mind contained. So he remained across the threshold, waiting for her to return to herself.

CHAPTER 6

Padua read the letters one by one. Not just normal letters. Love letters. Beautiful, passionate love letters. She almost put the first one away when she realized that. Her mother's voice moved her, however. In her mind she heard the words spoken as she read. She continued so that she might preserve that vivid memory for a while.

In doing so she learned her father's appeal to her mother. In a world that laughed at her ambitions, he loved her for them and encouraged her ever higher. Together they were poised to join the pantheon of Europe's most celebrated minds. Fame waited, and royal patronage and a future free to devote to investigations of the natural order of the universe.

Then disaster struck. While her father enjoyed a

special appointment at Oxford and her mother held dazzling salons, a child had been conceived. In the last few letters, written while her father sought a living anywhere, practicalities replaced dreams and passion. There were no letters after she was born, or at least none that found their way into this box.

Padua folded them all and replaced them in the box. She did not regret reading them, even if the last ones left her sad.

No wonder her father did not love her. She had ruined his future and forced the most ordinary of concerns into his life. As for her mother, who had sacrificed much more . . .

A floorboard squeaked. She looked in the direction of the sound. There, outside the doorway, stood Ives. He kept turning up like a bad penny, except—his green eyes held dark depths right now, and his expression showed subtle sympathy, as if he read her thoughts.

"You mentioned the street," she said. "It was not hard finding these rooms once I knew that."

He entered the sitting room. "Have you found anything of use?"

She shook her head. "Only some letters from long ago. I had hoped to discover some documents he should have, or anything that might explain why that money was found here."

He glanced around at the disorganized papers and books. "It is a wonder anyone could find anything at all."

"Including counterfeit money. Unfortunately I think

I know where it was." She rose and walked into the
bedchamber. She pointed at the void in the floor. "I
think a large trunk used to be there."

"It would appear so."

"Is it not careless to store a large amount of counterfeit money in one's own home? I would expect the
criminals to have a less incriminating place to put it."

"If your father was no more than a tool, he *was* the
less incriminating place."

"My father is so distracted when solving mathematical mysteries that he could have served as a tool
and been unaware of it. Look at this place. Someone
could have put that trunk here, covered it with books
and papers, and he might have never noticed."

"You should share that theory with Mr. Notley."

"I think I will tell him to ask you about it at trial. You
yourself said it was a wonder anyone could find anything here. I think it would be beneficial if you were
asked to repeat that in court."

"It was a very large trunk, Miss Belvoir. One that
could not be overlooked by your father. However, if
asked I will answer truthfully." His fingers flipped the
edges of a sheaf of papers on the bed. "You are very sure
you found nothing of interest to his case here? Something you have squirreled away in that reticule you are
carrying?"

"Very sure." She left the chamber and returned to
the table with the glove box. She began choosing a few
books for her father. "You said the gaoler would deliver

items I bring. I will keep it small, so I do not appear to be taking advantage of anyone's generosity."

She plucked a few books off the shelves and made a little stack. She wished she could check more of her schoolbooks, but that would be stupid with him here. She tucked the banknotes deeper into her bodice, lest they fall out. Behind her back she could hear Ives moving around, shuffling papers and opening drawers.

"Don't you believe me?" she demanded, turning on him.

He bent to pull a drawer set low in a cabinet. "I think you are inexperienced, and would not recognize useful evidence if you found it."

"The magistrates would, however. Are you determined to find more nails for his coffin than they already claim to have?"

"My only goal when I prosecute is for justice to be served. I would be delighted to find something that supports your father's innocence. I am not so coldhearted that I am eager to see him convicted. Now that I know you, rather the opposite."

An arch response popped into her head, but her voice would not work. That was due to the way Ives looked at her. Not angrily. Not kindly either. His eyes carried no disapproval or pique. Rather he looked at her with a man's calculation. The hardness emerged, but not due to displeasure. The considerations she had suspected that first evening in his office now showed more explicitly.

He appeared devilishly handsome with that look in his eyes. Wickedly dangerous. It should incite the urge to flee. Instead she could not move at all. She could only look, while a brief gaze alone sent tremors down her spine.

He broke the spell, and looked out the window. She thought she saw confident satisfaction flash before he masked himself.

"It is getting late," he observed.

Reality banished the thrills. The light outside the window had dimmed considerably. She would be unlikely to return to school before night fell.

"I must hurry." She looked at the glove box. "Would it be acceptable for me to take this with me too? As I said it is only old letters. I would not want them lost or destroyed if—if he does not return."

"It would be yours anyway. Take it for safekeeping now if you want."

She lifted the books and box and clutched them all to her body. Ives strolled over.

"You are very sure that you found nothing important?" he asked.

"I said as much. Why do you ask yet again?"

He looked down at her. "Because you are crinkling."

"Crinkling?"

He picked up a piece of paper and crushed it in his fist. It made a distinctive sound. "Crinkling."

All kinds of paper made that sound. Like banknotes stuffed in one's bodice. She resisted looking down at herself.

He did not. His gaze settled right at the level of her breasts. If she were not holding the books, he would be peering at her body most inappropriately.

"I am thinking I should make very sure that you are not secreting documents or evidence out of this chamber," he mused.

She wanted to clutch her stack even tighter, only she feared she would crinkle again. "You have my word that I am removing no documents or evidence, sir."

"Can I trust the word of someone who has declared me an adversary?"

"As a gentleman, you have no choice. Unless you think to search my person, which I do not believe you are bold enough to do."

"Not your entire person. Only the area where women are known to hide things."

To her horror, his hands reached toward her. But he was only lifting the books and box out of her arms. She dared not breathe, lest she begin crinkling again.

"Let us go," he said, holding out his arm toward the door.

He did not hand the books over, but carried them out as he walked behind her. She kept her back very straight so the banknotes might not move at all.

He handed her down the stairs, and escorted her from the building. He remained by her side as she strode down the street.

"My carriage is here. I will bring you back to Mrs. Ludlow's, so you are not walking London's streets alone at night." He gestured to the fine carriage up ahead.

His offer would help a lot, but a little caution sounded in her instincts. "Mrs. Ludlow will probably ignore my escape if you are my escort," she said. "She is the sort to assume your sort should have their privileges, and our trust."

"She is? How convenient." Charming creases framed his smile.

"All the same, it would be better if I found my own transportation."

"I will not hear of it."

He opened the carriage door and handed her into the carriage. He set the glove box beside her after he settled himself across from her, and the books next to himself. Seeing the box took her mind back to the letters inside. She set the box on her lap and tipped the cover up on its hinges.

A few trinkets had been left inside with the letters. She poked down and pulled a small handkerchief out. It was her mother's. She lifted it to her nose, and a familiar scent filled her head. Memories popped up, all from her childhood, when she was still of an age that a mother holds and embraces one for no reason other than love.

She had not expected a handkerchief to move her so deeply. Did her father sometimes of a night hold this so he could smell her again? Her eyes blurred and stung.

She stretched toward the books on Ives's bench, reaching. He moved to aid her at the same moment, and his hand came to rest on top of hers. He did not lift it, but kept her hand under his fingers.

He angled much as she did, toward her, until their faces were mere inches apart.

"You are weeping." The thumb of his free hand brushed at a tear. "Why?"

She opened her other hand to reveal the handkerchief. "It was my mother's. I recognize it. It still . . ." Her voice caught. "I thought I would slip it inside one of the books, for him to discover. I thought it might give him comfort."

Without releasing her hand, he pulled out the top book, and opened it. He offered it to her. She placed the handkerchief inside. He closed it and set it aside.

"Your loyalty to him is impressive, especially considering that he all but abandoned you, from what you have said."

"I have been angry at him for that. I read things in these letters that explain some of it, however. I had forgotten that he was not always the strange man that you see now. When I was young, he still showed the remnants of ambition and potential. Had the drudgery of life not been forced on him—on both of them—who knows what might have been."

"I think that you consider yourself part of that drudgery. I hope not."

She could not reply. Tears choked her too much.

His hand took hers more completely. With the other he crooked a finger under her chin and tilted up her head. "What a loss if you have not been born, Padua. To the world, but mostly to them. He would have had no one fighting for him now. Your mother would have had no one to charge with his care, and would have passed less peacefully. And I would have never met the rarity that is Padua Belvoir."

His gaze mesmerized her. His words moved her deeply. She could barely breathe. She waited, and knew a shocking anticipation. A reckless hope.

The slightest movement, as if he pulled away an inch. That disappointed the magical excitement in her heart and head. And so it still surprised her when he leaned just far enough to kiss her. A sound kiss, not some brief connection of pity or kindness. A kiss of unmistakable passion. The excitement in her body began a pagan dance.

She should not allow it, but she did. There could be no logic to this man wanting to kiss her, yet it felt inevitable that he did. That kiss gave expression to an intimacy that had arched between them from the first, and right now, with her emotions raw from those letters, she needed to feel close to someone.

It did not last too long, even if it seemed it went on a good while. Long enough for him to cup her face in both his hands. Long enough for the kiss to turn into more than a gentle press. She did nothing to encourage him, but nothing to stop him either. She accepted and allowed the riot of emotions he evoked to have their way.

She realized the coach had stopped. The kiss did too. He continued holding her, his firm hands angling her face up toward him. He gazed deeply into her eyes, then released her, opened the carriage door, and hopped out.

She stepped down. They were a block away from the school. He reached in and retrieved the glove box and books and handed them to her.

"You are in time, I hope," he said.

She walked toward the school, in a daze, noting with unseemly specificity the various ways in which that kiss had aroused her. He escorted her, not speaking either. When they parted in front of the house, he gave her the lightest kiss on the cheek. She felt it on her skin the whole time she walked around the building and into the garden.

"W ait here," Ives told the coachman upon walking back. "I am going to take a turn."

He headed down the street in the direction opposite the school. The last light of evening still streaked the western sky with blood orange hues, but night had fallen on the streets. He worried that Mrs. Ludlow would catch Padua returning, and wondered what would transpire if she did.

Try as he might to occupy his mind with such concerns, the effort proved futile. Rather his thoughts veered to the impulse that led him to kiss Miss Belvoir, and the other impulses that he had, just barely, suppressed while he did so.

It had been mad. Stupid. Unworthy of him. He did not impose on young women. He did not steal kisses.

He arranged that part of his life with discretion and measured care. Not for him the seductions of virtuous females. His women were experienced and willing, and all had been mistresses to other men before him. He did not lead them into the life, and as far as he knew none of them wanted a different one.

And yet this evening—he should be calculating how to make amends, and forming words of apology. He sure as hell should not have this spring in his step. The smile he could not get off his face would be damning if anyone saw it.

It would never do. She would never do. He would never do for her. Even if this business with her father would not make a muddle of anything further—and there could be nothing further, would not be, of course, *definitely*, he swore—she was not the woman for him.

Yet he had enjoyed that kiss far more than he had enjoyed a first kiss in many years, and now allowed himself some prolonged delight in its fresh, clear pleasure while he circled several blocks, castigating himself to little avail.

Padua noted with dismay the lights coming from the upper windows. When she pushed open the garden door to the house, she paused and listened for sounds that might indicate some of the girls had already finished their meal.

"I thought this might be how you would return."

The statement made Padua stiffen. She clutched the

box and books to her chest. Mrs. Ludlow stepped into the chamber, carrying a candle. The light made her face look like that of a sad, plump ghost.

"I had family matters to attend to again," Padua said, hoping she sounded innocent.

"I expect you did." Mrs. Ludlow set the candlestick on a table. "I have been looking for you, to talk about that family matter that occupies you these days."

Padua's heart sank. "What do you mean?"

"I think you know." She sighed, then came over. "I received a letter from Mr. Peabody. He is a solicitor. Did you know that? His daughter often speaks of you, and the name Belvoir thus garnered his attention when he learned of a man of that name who has been put in prison, to be tried for counterfeiting." She dabbed at her eyes with her handkerchief. "Please tell me this is not a relative. If you only say it is not, I will believe you."

Padua set down her books and box, and took Mrs. Ludlow into her arms. "I will not lie to you. I had hoped, until the trial, there would not be too much notoriety."

"Oh, dear. Oh, my." Mrs. Ludlow wept. "I dare not— I am sorry but—"

"I will leave at once. Tonight."

"Tonight! I hope I do not have to throw you onto the street at night." She sniffed. "Do I?"

"It might be best."

"Where will you go?"

"I will find someplace." With thirty pounds in her dress, she expected she could find someplace. Thank goodness Papa had hid that money. Thank goodness she had found it.

"No. I'll not have it," Mrs. Ludlow said, collecting herself. "Tomorrow is soon enough. You will sleep here, and eat breakfast, and we will tell the girls then. You will say good-bye, and if Mr. Peabody does not like it, that is too bad. This is my school, not his."

Padua kissed her forehead. "You have always been kind to me. I thank you for that." She picked up her books and box, and went up to her chamber.

She began packing, telling herself that all would be well. In truth she felt sick. The future appeared to her as a vast gray ocean, with no land in sight and no hope of rescue. She had been content here. She had not been alone. Now, no matter where she went, she would not even have the home this school had been.

The door opened a crack and Jennie slipped in. She saw the valise. Her expression fell into one of dismay. "Oh, *no.*"

"Oh, yes. I will leave tomorrow."

"Why?"

Padua realized Mrs. Ludlow had not shared the story given her by Mr. Peabody. Jennie did not know yet. "She received one too many complaints from a parent. She had no choice. I would have done the same."

"Where will you go?"

"I will find a hotel or an inn."

"You cannot live in one forever, and even a few nights will cost a lot of money." She turned to the door. "I do not have much, but I will go and get it so you—"

Padua caught her arm. "I will not take it, so stay. I will never forget you offered, however."

Jennie sat on the bed. "It will be lonely here now, with you gone. You must promise me that you will take care. You must let me know where you are and that you are safe."

Padua closed the valise. She sat beside Jennie and embraced her. "I will miss you too. Perhaps you can come and see me. Mrs. Ludlow favors you, and if you ask, she will allow you to visit an old friend on occasion."

"I will find a way to see you, as soon as you send me word. I will not sleep well until you do, I fear."

"Do not worry for me. I have been on my own before. I am not afraid. I was not raised like you were."

She lifted the valise and set it on the floor. "I suppose I should eat dinner."

"Yes, come join us."

Together they went to the dining room, and took their places at the high table. Padua was glad to have this meal before the girls knew she would leave. It offered a respite of normal emotions, even if Jennie and Mrs. Ludlow had long faces to the end. Tonight her special students would visit for the math lesson, too, unaware of it being the last one.

Then, tomorrow, she would be gone.

CHAPTER 7

Ives hopped out of his carriage shortly after noon. He walked toward a figure in the portico of Mrs. Ludlow's School for Girls. "It is a fair day, is it not, Miss Belvoir?"

She looked up from where she had been poking into her reticule. A valise rested beside her feet. "Oh. You. What are you doing here?"

"I received a letter this morning, from Mrs. Ludlow. It had been sent to my brother's house, and a messenger brought it to me. She thinks I am a lawyer for your relatives, and wanted to ensure that you were not left to your own devices." It had been a peculiar letter, full of misunderstandings about his role in Padua's life. Half gossip imparting confidences, half guilt-ridden mother worried for her child, Mrs. Ludlow had been most effective in leaving him no choice but to interfere.

"She feels guilty. She should not."

"Perhaps she only felt responsible." He pointed at the valise. "Is this about last night? Did she see me with you?"

"It is about my father." She picked up her valise. "I was about to walk out to hire a carriage, but since you are here your man can take me and I can save the fee."

He removed the valise from her grip. "In the least we will take you wherever you want to go. However, perhaps if I went and spoke to Mrs. Ludlow, I could convince her to let you stay."

"Please do not. She is distraught enough that she might just agree, and the school would suffer for it. This is probably for the best. I have things to do that require me to be abroad in town now. I cannot keep slipping away. I will manage, and find other employment."

He set the valise in the carriage and handed her up. "Where do you want to go now?"

She settled in. "My father has chambers that he is not using presently. I may as well make use of them instead. The rent is paid for a while. Tell your man to take me to Wigmore Street."

He climbed in and sat across from her. "No."

"It is the most logical solution to my current predicament."

"I cannot allow it. If you take residence there, it will only continue the attention you have already drawn."

"I do not think what you would or would not allow

signifies. I hope that you are not one of those men who believes one kiss allows him to dictate to a woman."

"This is about your well-being. You invite the worst suspicions if you live in your father's apartment. Of more concern to me is that his accomplices know about those chambers, and might well visit them. You are too smart to take the risk of attracting their attention too."

She did not immediately argue against his reasoning.

"You are a very good barrister, aren't you?" she finally said. "That was neat. Very well done. I am without recourse in the discussion."

"I like to think I am persuasive when I choose to be."

"You are most persuasive. Expensively so. It appears I will go to a hotel tonight, and seek out my own chambers for the days ahead. Perhaps you can recommend a hotel that is suitable for a woman alone who is not without means, but hardly well to do."

"I know of an excellent place that will suit you splendidly for a few days at least."

She stiffened so much her head rose an inch. "Where is this *place*?"

"You will see." He turned and gave the coachman the street.

When he turned back, rigidity had left her posture.

"You worried I meant my own home, didn't you?" he asked.

"Of course not. It was only one kiss. Well, two. You would never assume I was amenable to staying in your own home after such a small intimacy."

"Only one kiss? A small intimacy? I am insulted, Miss Belvoir."

"I think you view it the same way, and were as astonished as I that it even happened."

How wrong she was. That kiss had been coming for days now. In the dark silence of the coach, its descendants clamored to be born. He doubted she experienced the same anticipation, but the mood in the small space crackled with the charged atmosphere of desire. The wicked side of him started making arguments for behaving badly.

The coach drew to a stop. She looked out the window. "This is not a hotel."

"It is a place where you will be safe and well cared for, however." He opened the door, stepped out, and offered his hand.

She alighted, and angled back her head to look up the façade. "Where am I?"

"This is my family's home. It is the Duke of Aylesbury's town house."

"It appears the size of ten houses."

"That means it has plenty of space for you." He reached in for her valise, and handed it to a footman who had come down from the door. "Come along. I will see you settled. This evening we will share some dinner. Then I will leave you to rattle around inside to your heart's content. You will have privacy. No one else is here except servants now."

She took a few steps, then hesitated. "I should insist you have the carriage take me to a hotel."

"Mrs. Ludlow made me responsible for your safety.
I would be obliged if you did not make the charge more
difficult."

"I suppose if you put it that way . . ." She accepted
his escort to the door. "I should not allow that one inexplicable kiss to make me suspicious of your intentions."

"You are too generous."

P adua agreed to accept the offer of sanctuary in part
because curiosity about the interior of the house
consumed her. Ives lived luxuriously on his own, and
she suspected his family's house would impress even
more.

The mansion did not disappoint her. The reception
hall alone could hold a good-sized apartment. A staircase towered up a well, wrapping it again and again
as it ascended five levels. Appointments and paintings
of incalculable value decorated tables and walls. She
experienced the urge to speak only in whispers, lest
she disturb the noble ghosts living within.

Ives handed her over to a housekeeper, who led her
above to a fine chamber on the third level. Almost Spar-
tan in its elegance, it suited her with its white bedcover-
ings and drapes and finely wrought mahogany furniture.

The most decorative element, with pride of place beneath a window, was a gorgeous, small writing desk
with elaborate multicolored inlaid patterns on its ebony
surfaces. It sounded a contrasting note of excess and
whimsy to the chamber's simple melody. She pictured

it covered with books. She would study them at leisure by good lamplight, instead of for an hour now and then when a stub of candle offered a bit of light at night.

A girl appeared, to help her unpack her valise and to help her wash. The servants acted as if her visit had been expected, and as if she did not appear far poorer than any of them and thus a peculiar visitor for this house to have.

When she finally found herself alone, she sat on the bed and marveled at her sudden change in circumstances. It would not last, but for a day or so she would not have to worry about where she would sleep and what she would eat.

What must it be like to never, ever have to worry about such things? She could not imagine such a life in full, but for a few moments she had a hint of what it must taste like.

That Ives had become her benefactor complicated her contentment. He had helped her more than he needed to. Perhaps he felt guilty about that kiss. Perhaps he even thought of it with regret, and felt foolish.

She was not the sort of woman he probably kissed most of the time. He had certainly concluded that wisdom decreed he should have never let sympathy for her distress over those letters lure him into comforting her in quite that way.

She was not such a goose as to put much stock in that kiss, even if it had been very nice. Nor was she such a child as to pretend it had not happened. Still, the less said about it, the better.

She would let it slide into the past immediately, so it did not inform their dealings with each other after this. Which did not mean she would not enjoy the memory for a very long time.

That evening, her servant girl let her know that dinner waited. Dressed as she had been all day, Padua descended the staircase. Ives lounged in the reception hall. She spied him before he heard her, and she paused to look at him.

He had changed his clothes for dinner. The dark coats and pantaloons and boots gave him a strong presence on that chair despite his relaxed pose. His face in repose displayed all its fine beauty, and his expression, deep in thought, caused one to want to know his mind. His eyes' expression reminded her of what she had seen right before that kiss, only now the attention went inward.

Then he directed that intense gaze toward her. Her legs turned wobbly.

He rose. "I hope you are hungry. The cook has been busy."

"I am very hungry. However, is it wise for you to be here considering your involvement in my father's case?"

"Only if I do not allow you to influence my judgment. That will be our rule at this meal—no talk of his situation. It will do you good to have a respite from that worry."

He escorted her to the dining room. The majestic chamber awed her. The table went on and on. The draperies alone probably cost more than her valise would ever hold. Blues and reds dominated, with plenty of silver and gold reflecting the large candelabras' lights.

"Goodness," she murmured, looking this way and that as she took it all in.

"It is a little old-fashioned, and perhaps too colorful," Ives said. "My late brother, the last duke, refused to redecorate until he married, which he never did."

"And the current duke?"

"Also unmarried, and not much interested in such things."

"Marriage, or decorating?"

"Both, so it will probably persist looking as it has all my life for many years longer."

"I cannot imagine always knowing this luxury. Do you lose sight of it due to familiarity?"

"I suppose I do."

He handed her to the table. Their places had been set across from each other at one end.

"At least we will not have to shout to hear each other." She took her seat. "It would have been impossible to talk much, with you down there and me here. Perhaps we could have sent messages to each other by a little dog who ran between us."

That amused him, perhaps because it became apparent no dog would have been needed, since two-legged creatures obliged them. Footmen arrived to serve the meal, which began with a fine fish soup.

"Will they stand there the whole time?" she asked when the footmen took up stations near the door.

"Only when they are not needed."

One was needed to pour a different wine. The other disappeared and returned with some lamb in a wonderful sauce. She had not eaten since breakfast, and made no effort to hide how heavenly she found the food.

"I will be spoiled by this. I am beginning to be glad Mrs. Ludlow asked me to leave."

"Her board was not generous?"

"She feeds the girls and teachers well enough. Her cook is a drunk, however, so it is rarely well prepared."

"Perhaps you should start a school with better food."

"That would be impossible."

He gave her a quizzical look.

"Mrs. Ludlow only has that school because she inherited that house," she explained. "One needs a building to have a school, a very large one if one is going to take boarding students. I could never afford a London house, so if I tried that I would have to do so in a distant city."

"Can you obtain another position teaching at another school?"

"Mrs. Ludlow might feel obligated to mention my father in her reference. However, I have an earlier reference that I can use instead. It is not unqualified, unfortunately. Also, the recent years will need to be explained. Again, if I go to a distant city—"

"That would take you too far from your father." He frowned and set down his fork and knife. "If you cannot teach, what will you do instead?"

"I have some money that I had saved for another purpose, but it will keep me if I need it to. Also, my mother used to act as an accounts keeper for small tradesmen while I was growing up. They could pay her much less than a man, so they allowed themselves to be convinced to hire a woman for that reason. If necessary, I will let my services the same way."

He reacted with an inscrutable expression. He called for more wine, then told the footman to leave the bottle. Another course arrived, of small fowl accompanied by root vegetables. She tasted hers. Pheasant. She dug in, noticing that Ives had not returned to his own meal.

He regarded her with cool assessment, much as he had that first night when she intruded on his home.

"What other purpose?" he asked. "You said you had saved money for another purpose."

She hesitated. She had never told anyone her dream. She realized she wanted to tell him, however. She was proud of her plans, odd though he may find them. "I intend to go to Italy, to study. There are several universities there that allow women to stand for examinations for degrees."

His eyebrow rose, but he neither scoffed nor laughed. "Which universities allow it? I confess I have never heard of such a thing."

"Padua, Bologna, and Pavia have given higher degrees to women. Bologna has even had women professors. I plan to go to Padua, however, because that is where my mother studied and I have names of people there who might help me." Talking about her plans brought her excitement about them bubbling up in her imagination.

"Mrs. Ludlow mentioned your mother attending a university. I had assumed she misspoke. So you will follow in her footsteps. Will you pursue a degree in mathematics?"

"Questions may come from any of the arts or sciences." She sounded mad, she knew. Even madder than he might think. She had not been studying these last few years as intensely as her dream required. The money she had, even the thirty pounds she had found, would be gone soon. She had continued honing her knowledge of Latin while at Mrs. Ludlow's, but her command of Italian, taught to her by her mother, had become very rusty from disuse.

She poked at her fowl. Her enthusiasm retreated under the weight of her plan's impossibility. "I will have a lot of catching up to do. It would be years before I could pass the examinations. It may even be too late already."

"I doubt that. But what has held you back? Have you been waiting to pursue your studies while you saved the money?"

It would be so easy to simply say yes. Perhaps it was the wine that led her to tell him the truth instead.

"I had the money once before, when I lived and taught in Birmingham," she said. "I was distracted from my goal, however. Then the money was lost, so I had to start over."

His gaze invaded her own, curious and searching.

Then sympathy touched his expression. "You spoke of a qualified reference. Was it qualified due to this distraction affecting your reputation? Were you distracted by a man?"

How had he guessed?

"Did the scoundrel steal the money? Is that how it was lost?"

Her face burned hotly. "The lying rogue took every damned penny."

"At least you knew for certain what he was. You were not left wondering, or pining."

"Such good fortune for me. I was able to console myself that I had been a thorough fool, from beginning to end. That was so much better than harboring a few decent memories that might excuse my judgment."

The kindness that could warm his gaze unexpectedly did so now. "My apologies. Of course you must have been disillusioned and hurt. I should not have attempted to pretend there was a bright side to it."

She looked down at her plate, battling the revival of the humiliation she had experienced when she indeed knew Nicholas for the scoundrel he was. *Disillusioned* did not sufficiently describe her emotions that day. She had been unhinged with fury.

"Do not apologize. You were correct. Better to know the truth."

A silence fell. She kept her gaze downcast and forced the bad memories into the past again.

"You were wrong today, about that kiss," he said. "It was not inexplicable. Surely you know that."

She looked up, surprised.

"From my perspective, *inexplicable* is an apt word," she said.

"I do not believe you are that ignorant of men, Miss Belvoir. In fact you have just admitted as much. Those bright eyes of yours see most clearly, I think."

"I am sure that you kiss many women. That you kissed *me* makes very little sense, though. Hence it is inexplicable. My person is not fashionable. Rather the opposite, in notable ways. Men do not, as a general habit, impulsively kiss me."

"How stupid of them." His eyes burned. Goodness, he appeared devilishly handsome.

He lifted the decanter and tipped more wine into her glass. "That kiss was also not nearly as impulsive as I led you to think, either. I have been wanting to kiss you since the first moment I saw you in my chambers a few days ago."

"If not impulsive, then was it at least rash?" She responded coolly, hiding as best she could how his words affected her.

"Rash? No, I would not describe it as rash." He pretended heavy thought. "Let me see—not inexplicable, not impulsive, and not rash." He quirked a naughty smile. "I think we are concluding it was a very good idea, Miss Belvoir."

"*I* am not concluding that."

"I should have kissed you longer, then."

He captured her with his gaze. He looked at her as

if he considered rectifying the mistake then and there. A delicious shiver shook her. She could not look away from the new, sensual light in his eyes.

"You are so free of convention in your plans . . . I am almost inclined to stay in this house tonight," he said.

"You are remarkably honest. And *very* wicked."

"And you, Miss Belvoir? Are you honest enough to admit you did not mind that kiss at all?"

"I am not *wicked* enough, that is certain."

"I do not believe you think it is wicked to admit it, or to enjoy it."

No, she did not. Objectively speaking, when analyzed from a distance, she did not hold with many of the notions society held about these things. She had not been raised by people who conformed by rote.

That was why she had been such easy pickings for Nicholas. Even that experience did not persuade her that the rules of denial always made sense, however.

Right now such philosophical musings did her little good. She balanced on a precarious ledge with this man. One nudge, one encouragement, and she suspected he would not leave the house. By morning she would be seduced. Inevitably.

From the looks of Ives, magnificently.

She found her voice. "My notions about conventions notwithstanding, we would both jeopardize our positions if we indulge in passing passions."

He gave her a very wicked look indeed. "Ah, you

are a master of logic. How inconvenient. So . . . were it not for our 'positions,' as you put it, do you think you would enjoy being my lover?"

What a scandalous question. Yet, the daring naughtiness of it was inexplicably thrilling.

"I expect that your lovers find you at least tolerable, and I would too."

He smiled at her prim tone. "I try to be more than tolerable."

"How generous of you."

"If my lovers are honest regarding what gives them pleasure, it is not difficult to be generous."

"Honest regarding . . . So you discuss these matters? How . . . interesting."

"I prefer a direct approach. It is mutually beneficial."

"I am astonished that the ladies of the ton talk about such things at all, let alone directly."

"I normally do not pursue ladies of the ton. I leave their delicate sensibilities to other men. My brothers, for example."

"Any lady then. Any woman. Even this conversation is, to me, astonishing in its directness, and I am in no danger of one of your seductions."

He leaned forward, engaging in the conversation more closely. He rested his hand on the table, so close to her own that she expected him to caress her. "If you are in no danger, it is mostly because I do not believe in seductions. That implies cajoling someone into something they believe they should not do. I prefer negotiations, and we have already begun those. Hypothetically speaking, of course."

She glanced down at the hand a mere inch from her own. She imagined those fingers moving slightly, and meandering on her skin. He was teasing her deliberately. There was nothing hypothetical about *that*.

"So, then, hypothetically, do you think you would enjoy being my lover, Padua?"

So it was Padua now. The first liberty taken.

"That depends on the direct negotiations, doesn't it?"

"You are a clever woman. I like that. I assume you are not referring to settlements and property, and the other things mistresses want to discuss."

"As I see it, those negotiations should come after the first ones."

"Not only clever, but wise too."

"I think—I could be wrong, but—I think you are direct for a reason. It would behoove a woman to learn why, before she filled her mind with visions of jewels and a new wardrobe."

He laughed. "You are indeed a rarity if jewels do not turn your head and take the lead in negotiations. Or perhaps you value them more poorly than other women do."

"I am neither wise nor clever, and I hope not rare. Only a woman's intuition guides me. So *you* tell *me*, sir. Would I enjoy being your lover? Or are you one of those men with peculiar notions of pleasure?"

Her own directness surprised him. For an instant he looked taken aback. *Good.*

He recovered in a snap. Of course he did.

"Since you are well read, I will assume you know to what you refer. Honesty I promised, and honesty it will be. I do not think of myself as peculiar. I am not a bishop, that is true. However, I am also not the Marquis de Sade."

"That is good to know. Within the hypothetical context of our conversation, that is."

"And you, Padua? Would you object to pleasures of a more adventurous sort?"

It was her turn to be taken aback. She sipped of her wine. The deep red liquid sloshed near her nose. Clearly she had enjoyed the wine too much tonight. Look where it had gotten her. Discussing inappropriate topics with a man who was in a very real sense her enemy.

Even worse, she was thoroughly enjoying it.

It was past time to end this.

She set the glass down. She removed her hand from the table. "Since we are playing a game, I will allow that a bishop would no doubt be quite boring. Even to one as lacking in experience as myself. But you were wrong when you said I value jewels poorly. At the moment, in my present situation, I would be foolish not to value them very highly indeed."

He regarded her closely. She suffered it, wishing his gaze did not excite her. She could not blame the wine for all the heat and tingles.

"You seem to have opened the door to a proposition, Padua."

"I certainly did not!"

He stood. Her heart pounded so hard she heard it in her ears. He walked over to her. She saw him as if time slowed.

He stood beside her chair. She felt him so completely he might have embraced her. Something in her—some recklessness she'd never known she harbored—wanted him to try it, to vanquish her good sense with one touch. She knew that was all it would take.

"I should leave now, lest I not leave at all." He lifted her hand, bowed over it, and kissed it. She felt that kiss all through her body. He did not straighten completely afterward, but hovered, looking into her eyes.

"It is hell, not getting what I want, Padua. I normally do, and right now I want you fiercely." He kissed her lips briefly, then walked away.

CHAPTER 8

Padua did not sleep well that night. Despite the wine, or because of it, she tossed in her luxurious bed. Images intruded repeatedly on her thoughts. Lord Ywain looking dangerous. Lord Ywain looking stern. Ives bowing for a kiss. Ives caressing her. Ives naked . . .

When she finally woke, her view of the prior night had changed severely. What had she been thinking? She had behaved outrageously, and she could not entirely blame the wine. Their conversation no longer appeared merely reckless, but stupid. Goodness, she would have to leave this house at once, so it did not appear she was really opening the door to a proposition.

Her servant came in as soon as she made a sound. The girl handed over a letter, then went about fixing the bed.

The letter came from the man who did not believe in seduction but who managed, with his direct honesty, to be extremely seductive.

Dear Miss Belvoir,

I trust that the servants have made you feel at home. Make free with the house as you wish. Do not rush to leave on my account, nor that of my family, none of whom intend to visit town for some time. When you decide your next destination, I would be grateful if you would write to inform me of the location.

Your servant,
Ives

It sounded as if they would not share dinners in the future. The letter made it clear he would not be visiting the house while she remained there. He offered no apology, however. Perhaps he did not have anything to apologize for.

She opened a wardrobe and removed a clean dress. The servant girl appeared at her side, took it from her, and pulled out other garments. As she stepped away to allow the girl free access, Padua noticed the stack of books on the wardrobe's floor. She needed to bring those to her father. Not today, however. Today she intended to enjoy this house, as her host had instructed.

"There is breakfast in the morning room," her girl

said. "I sent down word you were awake, so hot food should be there soon."

Breakfast first, then the library. She would make today a little holiday, and read to her heart's content. All those words and noble ideas would help her forget she had been imprudent last night. They would block out memories of how her embarrassing behavior had allowed that conversation to take the turns it did.

Before she went down, however, she sat at the lovely inlaid writing desk and found some paper in a drawer. She wrote a quick letter to Jennie, to let her know she had found a refuge for a day or two.

Or maybe three.

I ves resolved that he would not spend one minute thinking about Miss Belvoir's Dilemma the next day.

In the morning he visited Jackson's on Bond Street, where he had arranged for an old friend, Jonathan, Lord Belleterre, baron, to join him for some sparring. Stripped to the waist, fists high, they went at each other. Ives threw himself into the exercise with enthusiasm.

Punch. He'd be damned if he would allow himself to be—*punch*—distracted again. Any interest in Padua—*punch*—Belvoir was the result of unaccustomed—*punch*—abstinence. He had crossed a line—*punch*—last night that he certainly would never—*punch*—ever—*punch*—cross again. He wasn't a damned schoolboy in need of tutoring on ethics, least of all from Padua herself. As for her father, hell, the questions he had—

punch—about that case needed to be resolved before he—*punch*—found himself compromised in other ways.

Belleterre called a halt. He strolled over to a chair, picked up a towel, and mopped his dark hair. Belleterre's quickness and natural studied skill stood him in good stead in boxing, and he had achieved renown in the sport. Ives liked to spar with a man who did not require pulling one's punches.

"Who is she?" Belleterre asked, dropping the towel.

"What are you talking about?"

"You are all force and little skill today. You are showing aggression for its own sake. I think you would be happier hitting a wall."

"I don't think I was that bad. You worked up plenty of sweat."

"As I would if I boxed with an ape. So, who is she?"

Ives helped himself to a towel too. He mopped his head and chest.

"What makes you assume it is a woman?"

"You are giving in to some emotion, and it is not happiness. Since you have not been in court for several weeks, I do not think it is a pleading gone badly or a case lost. That leaves a woman. Are you still angry that your mistress threw you over?"

"*She* did not throw *me* over. Nor have I ever been angry about that."

"Perhaps it is loneliness that irritates you. Something does."

Nearby, "Gentleman" John Jackson gave a lesson to

a young man of university age. Fists and sweat flew.
Ives observed them while he admitted to himself that
he *had* been releasing emotion with his fists. Mostly
he had punched out anger with himself.

He had come damned close to offering Padua an arrangement at dinner. In the easy intimacy of their conversation, it had not even seemed inappropriate. Rather
the wine and warmth led him to consider it a splendid
solution to her sudden lack of home or support.

What had he been thinking?

That he wanted to take her upstairs to bed, and that
possibly he could.

It was the calculation of a scoundrel. A rake. A man
not only with wicked tastes—all men had those—but
also with a wicked heart. His worst side had gotten the
better of him, because she was lovely and interesting,
and, yes, damn it, vulnerable.

"Whoever she is, do not allow her to make you an
idiot. Find another if she is not amenable," Belleterre
said. "Remember Mrs. Dantoine? You had a tendre for
her once. She has returned to town."

"Has she now? It has been, what, five years." He had
had more than a tendre for her back then. Lust had
almost deranged him. She had chosen another. One
with a title and enormous wealth. She had enjoyed
carte blanche for several months, then disappeared.

"She will be at Charlene's salon on Tuesday," Belleterre mentioned, pacing back into his position. Charlene was his own paramour, who entertained friends

every Tuesday evening. "You should come. I am told Mrs. Dantoine has asked after you."

Ives stood opposite Belleterre and raised his fists. He tried to remember Mrs. Dantoine's beauty. Small, neat, and blond—his memories got that far. But while he sparred, and tried to picture her face, the mental image that kept forming was of a dark-haired woman with luminous skin and sparkling eyes.

I f one is going to live in a palace, even for a few days, one wants to show it off. Padua decided to do just that after indulging in several delicious hours in the library. So she wrote Jennie again in the late afternoon, and invited her to visit at Langley House the next day, if she could get away from school.

At twelve o'clock the next day a footman found Padua on the terrace, working up her courage and spirits to make another visit to Newgate. The footman provided a reprieve by informing her a visitor had called. At her instruction, he left and returned with the caller.

Jennie hid her amazement until the footman left them alone. Then her eyes widened. "'Safe' hardly describes your situation, Padua. Whose house is this?"

"It belongs to the Duke of Aylesbury."

Jennie looked over her shoulder, alarmed.

"The family is not here," Padua explained. "I have been put here as an act of charity for a few days, while I find other accommodations."

Jennie sat on the bench beside her. Her eyebrows knitted. "Who offered you this charity? Lord Ywain? He is Aylesbury's brother. It was odd enough he called on you at the school, but if he has now given you a home—"

"It is only for a few days."

"If you say so."

"You appear unconvinced."

"I am sure you know what you are doing. Only . . . do you? Such a man . . . his interest in you does not—"

"Does not make sense? I agree. So you can rest assured he is *not* interested in me."

"I intended to say something else."

"Perhaps you should say it, then."

Once more Jennie looked over her shoulder. Then she angled her head closer. "His interest in you does not speak of good intentions. There. I have done my duty."

Padua could hardly defend Ives, considering that dinner. "You sound as if you are familiar with his character. Have you two met?"

Jennie laughed. "I may be a gentleman's daughter, and related to a baron by marriage, but I never moved in such rarified circles. I do, however, know people who know of him."

"Know *of* him, but do not actually know him, you mean."

"Well, yes, but—after he called on you, I wrote to a friend who has not dropped our friendship despite my current circumstances. She has married very well. Her husband is the cousin of a viscount. So while she does not move in the highest circles, either, her shoulder brushes against the edges of them at times. She wrote back at some length."

Nothing but tittle-tattle, in other words. Rumors shared by women in drawing rooms when they paid calls. Nothing this friend had to report could be of any value or worthy of confidence. Padua detested such gossip and refused to participate.

Usually.

"What did she confide?"

"That he is among the most well-respected barristers in England. That for the most part his character is without blemish. That he has an income that is impressive, and considerable charm to go with his handsome face—and he is handsome, isn't he? I near fainted when I saw his face in our reception hall—that he even has a friendship with the prince regent despite their age difference."

"He sounds like a paragon."

"Doesn't he indeed." Jennie's lids lowered. "Except for one flaw, he would be perfect."

Padua waited for it. Jennie waited, almost bursting. Padua sighed. She was not very good at wheedling gossip out of people.

"What flaw is that?"

Two pink blotches colored Jenny's cheeks. "It is not the kind of thing I normally talk about."

"Perhaps you can manage it just this once, so I am properly forewarned. I promise to forget at once that you spoke of scandalous things. That is what it is, correct? Something scandalous?"

Jennie nodded.

"Recent scandal?"

"Not recent. Also not a scandal as such. But scandalous."

"How can one be scandalous without creating a scandal?"

"I suppose if one, in a private conversation, broaches subjects that are not virtuous."

Padua wondered if the conversation in question had been hypothetical. "Pray, enlighten me."

"Well." Jennie licked her lips. "My friend says that when he was younger, and pursuing a lady, upon gaining her favor but not, I think, her favors, he was very frank in explaining his preferences regarding the latter."

Padua hoped blotches were not now on *her* cheeks.

"I suppose there is something to be said for finding agreement on the expectations," she murmured.

"According to my friend, those expectations were not merely the ordinary sort. They involved things ladies do not do. Wicked things."

"If your friend knows so much, this lady must have told others and not kept her discovery to herself."

"It would be hard to keep it to oneself, what with the shock."

Padua pictured that lady enjoying the attention for a whole Season while other ladies cornered her in drawing rooms, wanting the details. Did her descriptions get specific? Unlikely. This gossip was built on innu-endos and euphemisms.

"You say it was some time ago. He was very young then."

"My friend says most ladies will not allow his pur-suit as a result. His reputation precedes him. Although one can't picture him forgoing all female companion-ship."

"I am sure he does not do that."

Jennie took her hand and gripped it. "He probably pursues others now. Actresses and such. And women who are vulnerable and in need, who can be lured to wickedness due to their poor circumstances."

Women like you.

Padua stood. "How good of you to warn me, although I am sure that, even with wicked intentions in his heart, he can do better than me. Now, let us investigate this house and ogle its riches. Wait until I show you the din-ing room. The table can hold fifty guests, I am sure."

A night of drinking and gambling with old friends took its happy toll, and Ives slept soundly, obliv-ious to the impulses that plagued him. With daylight came sobriety, however, and thoughts of Padua once again intruded.

While he dressed, he considered that perhaps he should visit a brothel, so he might avoid going around town insulting women by propositioning them. One good rut, and Miss Belvoir might cease to fascinate.

He had better do something, because if she continued to absorb his attention, he would be thoroughly compromised regarding her father.

How bad would that be? He mulled the question while he broke his fast. He was not the only lawyer who could prosecute. Let them find someone else. He knew the likely prospects. While all good men, they placed winning above fairness, just the way the courts expected. The way he used to. Justice sometimes suffered then. Rarely, but it happened, especially in cases where the guilt was not clear-cut.

Of course it was with Hadrian Belvoir. Supposedly. Only, between imagining what he would do with Padua when he had her naked, he also mulled her father's case. And Strickland's information. And that apartment on Wigmore Street. For a crime in which the man was caught with the evidence in his home, there were questions unanswered and coincidences unexplained.

He called for his horse, with the intention of riding out of town. Instead after a few blocks he cursed, and turned his mount toward that apartment.

When he stopped at the nearby corner, he was still trying to convince himself to ride on. Then he noticed the blond head at the low window. Mrs. Trenholm had not left for the flower shop yet, despite it being two o'clock.

The head disappeared. A few minutes later the door opened, and out she came. Even from a distance he could see the paint on her face.

He followed her as she walked down the street, then turned left for several blocks. She stopped and stood there. Once more he watched from a crossroads.

Five minutes later a carriage stopped where she stood. She approached the window and spoke. A man's arm reached out and their hands met. Then the carriage door opened and Mrs. Trenholm climbed in.

Ives rode back to the apartment. He could not damn the woman for lying about working in a flower shop, considering the work she did instead. Still, her presence in the same building as Hadrian Belvoir had become one of those coincidences that nudged at him.

What were the odds of two people with serious criminal activity in their backgrounds living on that street, let alone in the same building? And although Strickland thought there were no political overtones or suspicions in Belvoir's case, Ives was not convinced. So Mrs. Trenholm's husband and Belvoir may have had something else in common.

Back at the apartment, he dismounted and tied his horse. He climbed the stairs and entered the cluttered chambers. Padua said there was nothing of use here, but he did not think she had looked very far before those old letters absorbed her.

He opened a window, shed his frock coat, and began digging.

An hour later he had viewed enough mathematical notations to last most men a lifetime. He sat back in the desk's chair and viewed the chamber. He was disappointed. He had hoped—damn, he had hoped to find something that might help Hadrian, he supposed. He would bear it to Padua like a gift. And he would avoid the moment when he had to choose whether to don his wig and robe and enter the Old Bailey, or whether his friendship with Padua meant he must leave her father to his fate at the hands of another lawyer.

While his mind worked, his gaze drifted over the motley assortment of publications that filled the case of books on the chamber's wall. The collection spoke of other interests besides mathematics. He could spy history books and volumes of poetry amid the scientific titles. Many purchases had never been bound, however, and their contents remained invisible.

Just as his thoughts were leading to unfortunate introspection about the first time his instincts on a case had been proven right, but too late, his gaze lit upon a binding that made him smile. He rose and walked over. Thin, small, and red, a schoolbook for children on mathematics had been stuffed between two tomes on chemistry. His tutor had used the same book when he was a boy.

His gaze saw another one, then another, interspersed on the shelves. Padua's schoolbooks, he assumed. He pulled out the first one. Perhaps she had put her name inside. The idea of seeing her childish hand charmed him.

He opened the book, and froze. He turned the pages. Then he pulled out all the other children's books, and did the same. When he was done, he had a stack of ten little books. No, twelve, because two others had already been removed and placed on the table near the chair.

He also had a stack of something else.

Money.

CHAPTER 9

"Dear child, how often must I repeat the same thing. *Do not come here.*"

Padua hugged herself while her father scolded her. His words were harsh, but he appeared pained and his tone sounded more exasperated than angry.

The men in his cell laughed. One of them sidled over, and stuck his lascivious smile to the grate through which she saw the cell.

"Don't you listen to the crazy old man," he said. "We all like your visits, don't we? When we are out of here we all will be happy to show our gratitude." He reached over and plucked a book out of her father's arms. "More food and less of this, though, if you don't mind."

She burned the man with a furious glare. It appeared

her father had not heard the insinuations and lack of respect.

He had other things on his mind. "I wish you had never left Birmingham," he muttered, his sad eyes refusing to meet her gaze. "You are too willful by far. That is your mother's doing. That is the reason for your disobedience now. You think you know better than I do, but you do not."

"I only think you need my help, so that you have a bit of fresh food now and then, and some books to occupy your mind." She spoke quietly, praying at least half of this argument would not be heard by the whole prison.

"I don't need books to occupy my mind. My thoughts alone can do that, and I rarely can keep these scoundrels off the food, so you waste your money." He paced away, and dumped the books in his corner, then came back.

He was under duress, she reminded herself. His cruelty could not be held against him. "The gaoler said you refused to meet the lawyer I sent to you."

His heavy eyebrows joined over his nose. "He came with a clerk. You can't have confidence in a man who needs another to remember what he says."

"The clerk makes a record, for reference later. Much as a person takes notes of a lecture. Mr. Notley came well recommended. He can advise you on how to respond to the questions put to you, before and during a trial."

He dipped his head until his nose touched a bar right

in front of her eyes. "I am not addled. I can respond on
my own well enough. Tell this Nutley—"

"Notley."

"Tell him his services are not needed. Now, be gone.
Stop trying my patience with your infernal interference."

He turned away so she saw only his back. He walked
over to his corner, his manacles clanking. He sank
down against the wall, and closed his eyes.

She thought her head would explode. He had ren-
dered her invisible. Gone for sure, to his awareness. As
gone as when he sent her to that school.

If he had not walked away, she would reach through
the grate somehow, grab his coat, and force his ear to
her mouth so she could spew out the fury racking her.
Only knowing the whole prison would hear kept her
from pouring out her resentments anyway.

That he did not love her was the least of it. She could
live with that truth. Many relatives do not love each
other. That he denied her any connection to a family,
however—she had lost two parents when her mother
died, not one. The difference was that her father had
chosen to be dead to her. He *wanted* it that way.

She glared at the stack of books beside his hip. Would
he even care about that handkerchief inside the top one?
Maybe those letters had been the product of a brief,
passing tendre. He probably had not even cared much for
her mother either.

A painful fullness choked her breath at the idea he
might have spoken to Mama the way he just spoke to

her. How horrible and sad. No, surely not. Mama had always spoken of her marriage as a glorious passion. She had taught her daughter to seek the same, and never settle for less. If there had been disillusionment, she would not have done that. Would she?

She had to leave, before she lost her composure right there in front of the criminals sharing the cell.

"I will tell Mr. Notley to try again later this week, Papa. Perhaps you will feel better then. More yourself." She turned on her heel and passed blindly through the prison's passages.

The autumn air outside brought some calm. The breeze blew away the worst of her indignation, but the hurt remained a nauseating lump in her chest.

Ives had been correct. She had done her duty and all that she could. She should leave her father to Mr. Notley now, for whatever good it might do.

She looked at the low sun and experienced a moment of panic before she remembered she no longer had to answer to Mrs. Ludlow. She judged she could walk back to the house before night fell, and set off.

Two hours later, her arrival at the house raised more notice than she expected. A footman waited right inside the door, his wig visible from the street. When she entered he asked her to wait while he retrieved something for her. He returned with a letter. "It was delivered by messenger a few minutes ago, Miss Belvoir."

She carried the letter up to her chamber. A lamp cast soft illumination from its place on the inlaid writing desk. She sat and opened the missive.

One of Mr. Notley's clerks had written, asking her to call on the lawyer this evening on a matter of importance. They would remain in chambers until ten o'clock, he explained, in the hopes she could meet tonight.

She set the letter down, then removed her bonnet and pelisse. She would wash first, and eat something. Then, if there were still time left to hire a carriage to go into the city, perhaps she would visit Mr. Notley. Right now she had no inclination to do so. She did not think she could bear being disheartened even more about her father in one day.

I ves patted the flat package in his coat while he trotted through town. The mere existence of the money he carried put him in a black mood. That he now carried it into Mayfair—when he should not—did not make the ride any more pleasant.

He had told himself he would decide on the way. He had debated with himself while his horse's hooves clipped out his progress on the stone streets. Even as he turned onto the block dominated by Langley House, he pretended he still had the choice of turning around, and instead visiting the magistrate in the morning.

Curses flowed in his mind while he paused and looked at the house. Curses at himself, because he knew he was going to do what he should not do. Curses tinged with resignation. God help him, he was an ass.

All the same he began to move his horse again, but stopped abruptly. He squinted into the shadows across from the house. He was sure that for an instant he had seen a hat poke forward before being absorbed by the darkness again.

He slid off his saddle and tied his horse to a post. Assuming a casual gait, he strolled down the street toward that shadow. As he drew near, the figure of a man became more obvious. He watched Langley House so intently that he noticed Ives rather late. When he did he pretended to be scraping his shoe. He looked over his shoulder at Ives, and smiled. "Damned shit. Can't even walk on the best streets without risking your shoes."

Ives smiled back. When he came abreast of the man, he reached out. He grabbed the fellow by the collar of his coat, and swung him around. The man immediately took a fighting stance.

"I would be glad to beat you soundly, in a sportsmanlike manner, but I don't have the time," Ives growled. He hauled the fellow over to a gate illuminated by a street lamp. "What are you doing watching that house?"

"I'm not watching—"

Ives tightened his hold on the collar. "One more time. Why are you watching that house? Why and for whom?"

"You have it wrong." As he protested, the man glanced down the street. Ives looked, too, and saw the small carriage waiting there.

Ives pulled the culprit's face into yet more light. Narrow and long, the face needed a good shave. The eyes, close set and round, appeared familiar. "I know you. I have seen you before."

"That you have, milord."

"In court."

"As a witness for the Crown, I am proud to say. We were on the same side. The loyal side. Crippin's the name, milord."

Now he remembered. Crippin worked for the Home Office. A year ago he had infiltrated a radical group, and led them into acts for which they were arrested once he informed on them. The jury had shown little sympathy for radicals lured into crime by the state. Ives sorely regretted agreeing to serve as prosecutor after he learned of the government's involvement.

He looked down the street at the carriage again. "You are planning to abduct someone, aren't you? The guest in that house?"

"Not abduct. Borrow. For a conversation. You know how it is done, sir." His voice came out strangled and low. "Will be quicker this way, than your trying to pry it out of her."

"I have concluded there is nothing to pry, so you can spare her the outrage."

"I just got word she visited Newgate again today, and talked to the prisoner for some time, so there's those who don't agree with you on that conclusion. Now, if you would unhand me, and take yourself elsewhere, she will be coming out soon, I believe."

Ives did unhand him, but only to ensure he did not throttle him completely. "You will leave, not me. Nor will you return. This is the home of a duke, and no one has the authority to set a surveillance on it. Whoever sent you here will pay dearly for the insult. As will you, if I see you here again."

Crippin sighed heavily. "Maybe he who sent me will talk to that duke, and you will be the one to pay for interfering with matters that address the safety of dukes, and others like yourself."

"Do you dare to threaten me? *Leave*, before I thrash you senseless."

Crippin walked away, shaking his head. Ives waited until he climbed into the carriage and it rolled away. Then he strode toward Langley House.

P adua had no desire to ride through town again. Mr. Notley's note made her feel guilty, however, so after dinner she tied on her bonnet, donned her pelisse, and picked up her reticule. She checked to be sure she carried some coins, then headed down to the door.

"Please have a hired coach procured for me," she told the servant manning the reception hall.

He turned on his heel, and strode to the door.

He did not leave. Someone stood outside. The servant stepped to the side of the threshold.

Ives strode in. He walked right up to her, stopped, and examined her from bonnet to shoes. "Are you going out?"

"I received a summons from the lawyer. He asked that I call on him as soon as possible."

"It is very late for that."

"It is important, he says."

"May I see this letter?"

She did not like his tone. Not so much suspicious as imperious; there was a good mix of the former in it too. His expression had assumed its most chiseled countenance. His eyes pierced whatever he saw. Especially her.

She dug into her reticule. "It is a business jotting, no more, from one of his clerks." She handed it to him.

With a flourish he flipped it open and held it to the lamp on a nearby table. "This did not come from Notley, or one of his clerks. Clerks have better hands when they use a pen, and lawyers have better paper."

"If not from Mr. Notley, from whom?"

"Come with me." He took her hand and strode to the back of the house, pulling her along.

She tried to dig in her heels to no avail. Extricating her hand proved impossible. She stumbled along behind him, getting crosser, more resistant, and less balanced with each step.

He led her into the morning room, released her, and closed the door.

She set herself to rights. "Your letter yesterday implied that you would not be visiting while I am here. I am sorry to see I misunderstood."

"It is a damned good thing I visited." He stood straight and tall. He waved the letter in the air dramatically. "This was sent to lure you out of the house this evening. Men waited to abduct you."

His pronouncement inspired laughter that she could

not contain. "No one would abduct me. There is no one to pay a ransom."

He did not so much as smile. Under that dark gaze she swallowed the last giggles. "Surely you are mistaken," she said.

"Hardly, since I just sent those men packing. Nor did they seek a ransom in the normal way, although your father may have found himself bargaining for your freedom. They wanted information from you. Information that your father refuses to give them."

"Since I cannot give it, either, it would have been much drama to little purpose."

He paced in front of her, setting his boots down firmly, never taking his eyes off her. "*They* do not know that. *They* do not believe that."

"Who are *they*?"

He looked to the ceiling, as if praying for patience. "Did you, or did you not, return to Newgate this afternoon?"

She decided it was a good time to remove her bonnet. While she did she deliberated whether a small untruth would be wise. Or successful.

He waited for her answer, his hands clasped behind him, his gaze daring her to lie.

"I did."

"Did I not tell you not to do that? Did I not warn you that suspicions abounded about you?"

"Yes."

"But you ignored me, and visited his cell anyway,

bringing once more books—which are almost never brought to prisoners and in themselves suspicious."

"Why would books be suspicious?"

"It is easy to hide messages in them. If not a note, something written on the pages themselves."

She faced him squarely. "I intended to have a warden deliver them. Then Mr. Brown told me my father refused to meet with Mr. Notley. So I went myself, to convince him to make use of the lawyer I had found. I realize that you think I should just let him rot there, but as his daughter I cannot do that."

"Did it do any good? Did you convince him?"

She hated giving him the satisfaction of hearing what he expected. "No. I did not."

He just looked at her. He considered something important, from the intensity of his examination.

"Did he tell you anything useful?"

"He only scolded me for coming, as he always does."

"Nothing more? No directions, or instructions? No confidences regarding the location of his ill-gotten gains?"

"What are you implying?"

"I want to know everything you know about him, damn it. I demand you tell me anything he may have said that in any way touches on his role in that counterfeiting."

Hardness had settled on him. The famed barrister had her in the dock, and through force of will intended to make her confess.

To what?

"Do you also think now that I may be his accomplice? Do I look like one to you?"

"I would have said not. However, I do not put much trust in my judgment now."

"Why not? What has changed?"

"Damn it, you know why not. As for what has changed . . . " He walked over to the table used for breakfast. He reached into his coat and removed something that he placed on the table's surface. "You did not search his apartment much, did you?"

"Not well at all." The letters had distracted her.

"Of course, I interrupted you. Had I not, you may have found this, as perhaps he intended."

"What is it?"

"Money. A good deal of money."

She eyed that stack, wondering what size notes it contained.

"I am surprised someone in authority did not find it. I assumed they searched," she said.

"Perhaps not, having found the counterfeit money so fast. If they went farther, they missed this." He slid a note out of the stack and took it to a lamp. He examined it. "It is good. All of it is, I expect." He threw a ten-pound note on top of the packet.

She walked over to the table and lifted the little bundle wrapped in paper. "How much is here?"

"A little over two hundred."

A small fortune. She tore off the wrapping.

"These notes were hidden in books. Schoolbooks. *Your* schoolbooks."

She hoped she did not flush. "He kept those old books?" She filled her hands with the banknotes. She fanned them out.

"There were twelve of them. I found money in ten. Two others had already been searched, so I think you did find some of it, Padua."

She had no intention of confirming his theory. She much preferred being distracted by the money to looking at the severe lord hovering at her side. Maybe he thought Papa had discovered an easy way to tell his accomplice daughter where to find his ill-gotten gains.

"You did find some of the money, correct?" His voice, crisp and demanding, flowed into her ear. "Before I interrupted."

"What makes you think so?"

"Because you kept crinkling. I should have searched you after all, it seems."

She turned her head. He stood right beside her. "I do not understand why you are so angry. This is a wonderful discovery that you have made. There are funds now to pay the lawyer fees, and to tide me over until I find another situation. What is it you suspect me of doing?"

"Of not wanting me, of all men, to see the fruits of your father's crimes."

"I am sure this money is not that." She would probably not be allowed to keep it if that were the conclusion. The evidence of payment would only hasten her father's conviction too.

"It is a lot of money," he said. "More than most men

have on hand. If not payment from his accomplices, how did he get so much?"

She made a thick stack with the notes, so she could hold them tightly. "He does not use much money. You saw how he lives. Over time he probably just squirreled away the extra."

"Really, Padua." He reached for the notes.

She turned so he could not touch them. She wished she had searched all of those little red books, before he did. She should have returned and done so yesterday, instead of playing lady of the manor in a duke's house.

"The legacy. That is what this must be. Payment on the legacy, or from it. It probably pays out only once or twice a year, and he hides the money, then lives off it, bit by bit."

Despite her desperation, it sounded logical. He thought so too. He did not try to take the notes from her again.

"Tell me about this legacy."

"There is not much to tell. It came to him soon after my mother died, from a distant relative he did not know. They had never met. Lawyers had spent years tracking down an heir. He never told me how much it was. All he said was fortune had finally smiled on him and provided money to live on, and he could afford to send me to school."

I've the means to buy you an education now. I've not the patience to be a child's tutor, the way your mother was, or to have a girl underfoot, so this is the best for both of us.

He flicked the edges of the notes with his fingertip. "No one will believe that."

"And if they don't?"

"The money will be confiscated."

It would kill her to give this money up. It was unfair for it to fall from the sky like a gift from heaven, only to have it disappear just as quickly. She looked at him, searching for the kind, sympathetic lord who could appear at times. "They cannot confiscate that which they do not know exists," she said.

His lids lowered. He crossed his arms. She waited for the barrister to explain all the legalities she did not want to hear.

"I should inform the magistrate of what I found, of course," he said.

Except he had not, had he? He had brought that money here instead. She had half-won this battle before he entered the door.

"I have asked Mr. Notley to investigate the legacy," she said. "I promise I will not spend any of this until he confirms its existence." At which point, she would declare this money the proceeds. Not that she would say so now. "In the meantime, I will keep it very safe."

A final flash of indecision showed in his eyes. On impulse, she stuffed the banknotes down her bodice.

He laughed, darkly. "The fashions today do not lend themselves to that maneuver with such a large number of notes. One or two at most."

She looked down at the ridiculous bulge between her

breasts. "Still it is safe from any gentleman with inconvenient notions of duty."

"Some gentlemen would decide duty was a good excuse to pluck it back out." He came closer to her. "You have all but invited me to try."

She swallowed hard. "But you won't. Correct?"

No response came. No nod. All she received was that deep consideration to which he so often subjected her.

"I wonder," he murmured, as if to himself.

"Wonder what?"

"That first night, you came close to trying to bribe me." He tipped her chin up with his hand. "Have you been trying that, Padua, in more subtle ways? Are you attempting that now?"

"I am not the one showing up unexpectedly in *your* life. *I* have not been the one interfering. Do not blame *me* just because you—you—"

"That is true. You are blameless. I am my own undoing." He angled his head and kissed her lips, first with a gentle touch, then more fully.

She pretended to suffer it, when in truth sensual sparkles descended in a shower. She turned her head in halfhearted resistance. "Shouldn't you be showing more fortitude? Thinking of duty and such?"

"I suppose so. And yet—" His kisses enlivened her cheek, her jaw, then the sensitive skin below her ear. He embraced her, his firm arm encompassing her waist. "If I am going to turn a blind eye to one small point of duty regarding that money, I don't see why I should deny myself on another."

"I am flattered to know I am a small point."

"*You* are not. I have decided that kissing you is, though."

They both knew that was not true. She did not think he would listen to reason now, however. Nor could she muster enough sense to make the argument. The possessive manner in which he began to caress her became too distracting. Thrills commanded her attention so she could barely think at all.

Still, she really should stop this, except—a touch on her breast made the idea dissolve.

That hand just rested there, on the top of her breast, while his arm pulled her closer to his body.

She looked into eyes like faceted dark emeralds, unable to read his thoughts. Except one. He knew she enjoyed this too much to deny it. He knew he had won without much effort at all.

The light touch on her breast became a deliberate caress that made itself felt through her garments. Luscious pleasure poured through her body and pooled low in her stomach. She thought she would swoon.

"Your eyes are as bright as I imagined they would be when I caressed you, Padua."

His caress continued absorbing all her attention. She barely managed to speak. "You said you did not believe in seduction."

"Did I say that? How careless of me." He nuzzled and kissed her neck. Sensual chills enlivened her skin with a thousand streams of delight. "Although I think you have seduced me, you see. Not I you."

"You talk so smoothly. However, it is you who lure me."

"How little you know about your power, Padua." He brushed his lips against hers again. Her mouth quivered. His fingers found her nipple through her garments. The way he teased at her sent her up on her toes.

"Should I stop? I will, if you demand it."

Stop? End this bliss? Reject this transformation of her entire being? She did not want it to end, ever.

He waited for her answer. Even his caress stopped, which maddened her. She opened her eyes. His gaze contained everything she knew about him. His wicked side and his kind one. His hardness and his charm. Mostly it reflected that he knew her answer without her saying anything at all.

"Well, then," he murmured. "Let us do this properly."

Do what? The notion that she should ask slipped away as soon as it formed.

He moved her, his embrace lifting her off her feet. The chamber spun. She found herself on his lap, her shoulders cradled by his arm, her body slung across his thighs. Astonished, she watched his head lower until warm kisses pressed her neck and the skin exposed above her garments. Each one shot tantalizing streams down her body.

He turned his ravishment to her mouth. He no longer lured, but claimed. Her body responded erotically. He took advantage of her gasps to invade her mouth.

Shocked momentarily, she quickly submitted to the bold intimacy. When his caress smoothed over her body, from her neck to her knees, her consciousness submerged under a stupor of sensation striped with feral anticipation.

She felt his fingers on her chest. He lifted the money out of her bodice and dropped it to the floor. She looked down to see him unbuttoning her pelisse.

He sat her up and slid the pelisse off. She turned her head and watched it fall into a green pool beside the money.

Hot kisses on her neck reclaimed her attention. Purposeful caresses on her breasts beckoned her into delirium. Her dress was half-unfastened before she realized the hand on her back had intentions more wicked than that on her front. Even after her bodice lowered, revealing her stays and petticoat, that hand moved back there.

A thread of rationality returned. "Shouldn't we be negotiating first? You said you always did."

"To hell with that." His mouth moved to the soft skin exposed above her stays.

She felt her stays loosen. They began sliding down her shoulders, along with her petticoat. A masculine hand helped them. Through the fog of sensation, she realized she would soon be half-naked.

"I thought—" She turned her face so his kiss could not silence her. "I thought you always ensured women and you were of like mind. I thought you chatted first."

Warmth on her skin. On her breast. A new caress, a direct one, made her dizzy with pleasure.

"We already did."

"That was hypothetical, and not very detailed. We may not suit at all in this."

"You suit me fine. Chat all you want, however. I promise to listen." He even looked in her eyes, so she could see his attention.

Unfortunately, his caresses did not stop. That made forming coherent thoughts difficult, let alone speaking them. His hot gaze undid her further. She looked down at her now bare breasts and her garments bunched below them. While she did, his fingertips slid to her nipple. He began to gently rub.

The sensation overwhelmed her. Her vision blurred. She could barely sit still. The pleasure became excruciating. If he continued she would die, but if he stopped she would scream.

His breath warmed her shoulder. "You are lovely, Padua." Lower kisses, on her chest. "Perfect." Lower yet. Her breast turned heavy and full. Her breathing quickened while she waited for him to . . . She wanted, she needed . . . She arched in offering and frustrated anticipation.

When his kiss grazed her nipple, she spun into abandon. He teased at her, his hand on one breast and his mouth on the other, his teeth and tongue and lips driving her insane. A tempest of sensation built and built. Her consciousness dwelled in the center of the storm.

Of course she noticed when the sensual torment stopped. His arms slid under her body and lifted.

Through hooded eyes she saw the chamber swim by. When it settled she was looking up at the ceiling.

The table. She was on the table. On her back. She looked down her body, at her exposed breasts and bunched garments, at her long skirt. At the hips, torso, and head of the man standing between her dangling legs.

She could not bear that he no longer touched her. Her breasts had grown so sensitive that even the air teased them, making her want more. She instinctively pouted, just as her mind found some curiosity about why he had laid her here.

He reached down her body and touched one nipple. She arched. Joy poured through her.

"Do it yourself now." A caress slid up one of her legs. "I will be busy."

She frowned at his odd suggestion.

"Have you never touched yourself, Padua? Given yourself pleasure?"

Of course not. What a peculiar question.

His caress rose higher on her leg. Her hem rose too. "It is much the same. Try it. You will see."

Now? With him there? Watching?

He appeared wonderful, looking down, his gaze warm and dangerous at the same time. She saw no amusement at her expense at least.

She tentatively put her hands under her breasts, to see what it felt like. Nothing special. "You will be busy doing what?"

He raised one of her legs. The hem dropped, revealing her hose to its top, and her knee. "Just kissing you. Touching you." He turned his head to show her. She wasn't impressed. The kiss tickled a little, and was not nearly as shattering as those on her breasts.

Then he caressed down on the inside of her leg. That gossamer touch, so light it could be a feather's brush, sent a deep thrill right down to her— *Oh*.

For the first time since he first touched her, misgivings wormed through her bliss.

"I think that you are being wicked now."

His fingers continued giving her vague licks. His mouth more obvious ones. "Not too wicked. Not yet."

Not *yet*? "About those negotiations—"

"Too late." Her skirt fell more, exposing more of her leg. Almost to her—to where the pleasures he created also fell. The sensation intensified until it was far stronger than when she sat on his lap. She barely resisted the urge to raise her hips in scandalous ways. She bit her lower lip so the begging cries haunting her mind did not leak out.

He glanced at how she still cupped her breasts. "Not like that. Do it the way I did. I promise it will be extraordinary."

Too far gone to worry about how it would look, she gently rubbed her nipples. Spirals of ecstasy aimed down her body, toward those he created. They met at her— *Oh!*

"This is outrageous," she murmured. "Disgraceful." She did squirm then, but it did nothing to relieve the sensual torment that built with each moment. Her essence begged for relief, but it also demanded she flick at her nipples with the palms of her hands, to deliberately make it worse, not better.

Kisses on her knee now. Hot. Searing. First this spot then that, then lower on her thighs. Utter abandon made her lose hold of herself. The most wicked notions lodged in her foggy thoughts—to spread her legs wide, to make him kiss higher yet, to touch herself not on her breasts, but on her—and still his light caresses, those faint, fluttering touches, lured her deeper, and made a hollow need open that even the pleasure could not fill.

He kissed up her thigh, holding her leg so he could reach the softest flesh. A moan escaped her, then another. She looked down to where her skirt now bunched high on her legs. It formed a hedgerow of cloth. She realized that if he turned his head, he would see that which no one had seen before.

He did turn his head. He did see. Then the light masterful caresses moved down until he placed his fingers on the very source and center of her sexual agony.

It unhinged her. She heard her own cries sing through the air. Grateful, hungry cries that gave voice to the need consuming her. *You are wicked, wicked, wicked.*

"Yes."

I should not allow— You should not—

"Yes."

He pulled her hips toward him. She forced herself to look at him. His body lowered bit by bit as he knelt. She could only see his head, then only his crown when he kissed her inner thigh again. *Ah, ah, wicked. Too wicked.* He knelt higher, and arranged her legs over his shoulders. An extreme notion entered her thoughts. A hope but also an alarm. He was not going to— Surely he would not—

She quickly pressed her skirt's fabric between her legs and held it, scandalized at the notion. He caressed her thigh, soothing her. Only it did not really soothe. It kept the heat and sexual agitation alive and vivid.

"I have shocked you."

"Now I understand why you normally negotiate first."

Rebellions in her body created discomforts never experienced before. Disappointment made itself known in visceral ways.

He stood. "You are safe. I promise." He caught her gaze with his own and slid his hand under the fabric, beneath her pressing palm.

"I thought you said I was safe."

"From that, for now. Not from me." He wrapped her legs around his hips. "Move your hand now. I will not take you, if you worry I have put you like this for that. Unless you want me to."

She stared at him. She shook her head.

"Are you sure?"

She was not sure at all.

"Move your hand. I am good to my word."

She moved her hand.

"Close your eyes, Padua. Think of nothing."

That devastating touch pressed again, ensuring she

obeyed. Her physicality dissolved until only the pleasure remained. Amazing pleasure. Demanding pleasure. No thoughts meant no restraints. She felt as she
never had before. As she never knew possible.

He knew just what to do to intensify the madness.
She knew he watched. Wicked. Wonderfully wicked.
She knew she moaned and cried. When the pleasure
became too intense and relentless to bear, she knew she
begged. For something, anything, she knew not what.
She stretched toward it, desperate, insane and adrift in
agonizing sensation.

Suddenly it grew worse yet, wonderfully worse. Focused and deep. The locus of pleasure filled, then spread
abruptly. It conquered what was left of her separateness.
Then it burst, awing her with its perfect bliss.

CHAPTER 10

I ves pried Padua's hand off his. As her climax neared she had tried to stop him and spare herself from plunging into the unknown. He sat her up and embraced her. He could feel the echoes of her explosive finish still affecting her body like aftershocks.

Expression slack, skin flushed, she did not object to how he handled her. Perhaps she did not even notice. She set her head on his chest and rested limply against him. He pressed his lips to her crown and slowly trailed his fingers over the sheen on her shoulders.

He should not have done this, but he did not care about that right now. Later he would scold himself for following impulse. He knew the lecture well. Anger, passion, sorrow—conquering outbursts of emotion remained a lifelong effort at which he often failed.

Subtle changes in her body showed her retaking control of it. She did not move or break the intimacy of the embrace for a good five minutes, however.

"We have been bad, I think," she murmured into his shirt. "Very bad."

He'd be damned before he agreed to that. He might have been bad, but she had been glorious.

"What you wanted to do—I suppose that is why decent women won't have anything to do with you."

"One reason."

"There is more? Yes, of course there is." She sighed. "It is well that you negotiate directly, although one wonders how you explain it all. I suppose being a lawyer helps. All those fancy words you can command. I expect those pour over the women, and by the time they dig through them all and understand your meaning, it is too late to be embarrassed."

In truth his mistresses needed little explanation. They were in the business of pleasing men. He did not shock them any more than a merchant is shocked on hearing a patron wants one gallon of the best ale for his shillings, instead of two gallons of the ordinary kind.

She eased off him, and looked over her shoulder. She flushed, and groped at her garments about her waist. "I should—"

He lifted the stays onto her shoulders. He tightened and tied the laces. He stepped back and lifted her petticoat by the neckline.

"I can do it." She took the cloth out of his hands.

"Could you perhaps . . . ?" She made a twirling motion with her finger.

He turned so his back faced her. "Are you embarrassed, Padua? You should not be. Not with me."

"I am too astonished to be embarrassed, but I expect that to change. I think that soon I will conclude I have been foolish. You are a revelation to me. I assumed that a man of your standing and cool thinking would never be so—impetuous."

"I only am when I am strongly provoked."

"Are you blaming me now?"

He glanced over his shoulder. She had set herself to rights and now buttoned her pelisse.

"I am not blaming anyone." He turned and took her face in his hands. He bent and kissed her lips. "Not you, and not myself. I am saying that desire for you provoked me more than is customary. I lost my head."

Dark eyes gazed up at him with amusement and naked skepticism. "What pretty words. You do have a talented tongue, milord."

As soon as she said it she realized the allusion she made. Her expression fell in horror.

He lifted her off the table and onto her feet. She looked at the table. "Shouldn't we call for soap and water?"

"The servants will take care of that."

She glanced to the door. "They know? Or do you make use of this table for such things frequently?"

"They wash and polish the table every morning, long before anyone who uses it wakens."

"That is good to know."

He took her hands in his. He suffered all this talk of practical things because he knew she inched closer to embarrassment again. He could see the way her eyes avoided his, and how she forced the most bland expression.

"I will be warning the footmen to be alert, lest anyone try to enter this house. You must promise to wait in the house until I come in the morning, Padua."

She nodded. "I cannot remain here forever, though. I need to let chambers and do other things that require I be abroad in town."

"We will discuss that tomorrow. For now, stay here."

He released her and turned to leave. To his delight she fell into step with him. They walked silently through the house to the reception hall.

Damn it, he owed her more . . . more something. A shelter for her pride, at least, if the next hours brought regrets.

"I must apologize for my bad behavior." He hoped it did not sound as insincere as it felt. He was not one whit sorry. Rather part of his mind speculated on what he had forgone, and how to rectify the omissions.

She made a small, reflective smile. "I think you were a rung or two lower in the pit of hell than bad. If I were not still recovering, the thought of what we—" A deep flush rose on her face.

"The fault is all mine. I importuned you. It was inexcusable of me." Oh, how it all tripped out, sounding so damned *correct*. He still burned for her. He had not descended far into hell at all while she lay in abandon on that table, but he would dwell in its depths tonight.

She looked in his eyes. Her brow puckered. "It was impetuous, as I said. On both our parts. I am sure you agree that we must be more temperate in the future, if we are going to have any dealings with each other at all."

He bent to kiss her hand. "That would be wise." *And impossible.* "I will go now, and see you in the morning."

Padua made her way to her chamber. Her girl arrived and prepared her for bed. When she was alone again, she tried to pull herself out of the haze that had surrounded her since Ives had shattered her awareness into a thousand sparkling pieces.

Their conversation afterward repeated in her mind. She had to laugh at herself. A man had almost ravished her, had seen her worse than naked, had almost done a very wicked thing to her, and she could only quiz him about the condition of the table that had served as her bed? She laughed until tears flowed. *Oh, you are a very sophisticated woman, Padua. This aristocrat has not seen the likes of you before!*

The rest of their conversation had her sober in a snap. The apology. The attempt to take the blame. He had to say that. Did he mean any of it? Or did he really think he had gone to a great deal of trouble and had little to show for his efforts?

They could never do that again. They could never

do anything like it. She was not that kind of woman. Surely he was not the kind of man who lured women to their fall either.

Or was he? Either he had few scruples in such matters, or she truly had overwhelmed his better nature and provoked impetuous behavior.

Had she?

What an odd notion.

Surely not. She definitely was not *that* kind of woman either.

However . . . if that were the case . . . might she nudge him toward handling her father's case a bit differently than he would otherwise? He suspected her of possibly trying to bribe him. Should she?

She almost slapped herself for entertaining the idea. How unworthy of her. How manipulative. Disgraceful, really.

And yet . . . if a daughter had that power, shouldn't she use it? Would it not be a bigger sin to turn away from a chance to help her father? In the least shouldn't she give it serious thought before throwing the opportunity away?

She rose and removed her dressing gown. She snuffed out the lamp, climbed into bed, and tucked the bedclothes around her. She stared up at the shadowed billows of the bed's drapery.

As soon as she closed her eyes, memories deluged her. Ives commanding her body with his mouth and hands . . . Ives driving her mad with a hundred feathers on her inner legs and thighs . . . Ives holding her close while profound pleasure eddied through her.

I ves went in search of Strickland after leaving Padua. The night was still young, and there was the small chance that if he occupied himself now he might eventually throw off the frustration and erotic energy that had his teeth grinding.

He found Strickland at Damian's, a gaming hall. Strickland liked to play faro and vingt-et-un, and many nights could be found doing so in one of the town's haunts, sipping brandy while he avoided the wife he had never loved.

Strickland spied him approaching and hailed him enthusiastically. Ives assumed that meant Strickland was up for the night.

"Damned glad you are here. You can admire my good fortune," Strickland said, casting a gloating glance at the man beside him at the vingt-et-un table. "Take a chair. Join us."

Ives did not gamble much. He had never developed the taste for it. All the same he sat beside Strickland and called for cards.

"I saw Crippin tonight," Ives said after they passed some small talk. "You remember him, I am sure."

Strickland shook his head. "Hell, yes. I did not realize he was in town. I thought he was up north. That is where he gets his nose into trouble."

"He goes where he is told to go. Apparently he was told to come to London."

Strickland peered at his cards. "I don't know anything about that."

"I hope not. I've a mind to thrash someone, and I would not want it to be you."

Strickland looked over, alarmed. He threw in his cards. "You are in a mood, I see. Let us get some air."

Together they repaired to a small terrace attached to the gaming hall. Strickland offered a cigar. Ives declined. Strickland lit one for himself. Positioned out of the light, he puffed away. With each inhale the burning end of his cigar made tiny orange highlights on his face.

"Why do you want to thrash someone?"

"Crippin has been keeping watch on Langley House. He stands in the shadows across the street and spies on its occupants."

The glowing tip stopped moving. "Surely not. No one would be so stupid as to set him on your brother's house. Aylesbury could break any man in the Home Office."

"And yet someone has done it."

"Zeus. Is your brother residing there now?"

"No."

Puff. "Are you?"

"No."

"Is anyone? If not, it makes no sense at all."

"Hadrian Belvoir's daughter is currently using the house, at my invitation. Her father's situation led to her losing her place at the school where she teaches."

"Ah. I see. Unfortunate for her."

"I could hardly leave her destitute and without shelter."

"No gentleman could do that." *Puff.* "It goes without saying."

"Crippin was told to watch her, and abduct her."

"Abduction now! What for?"

Ives explained his conversation with Crippin. "He implied I should help, so she can be questioned."

"Do you think she is an accomplice? If there is any chance of that at all, perhaps you should arrange it so those questions can be put to her."

"Of course she isn't an accomplice."

Strickland paced in a circle, smoking and thinking.

"Why do you know of course she is not? Have you been investigating her?"

No, damn it. He had taken her at face value, hadn't he? Because he wanted her. Today and tonight he had realized just how much he had accepted on faith.

He still did. A few questions had arisen, however. Small ones, but they had lodged in his head beneath the desire. They were why, he supposed, he had not taken things further tonight when he knew he could.

"That position she had at that school left her no time to be an accomplice to anything or anyone. Nor was she recognized by another resident of her father's building when she first visited."

He had no trouble giving a list to support his claim. He had parsed through it all many times. Yet, despite these pieces of evidence, the prosecutor in him could not eliminate those small doubts, nor the tiny suspicion that Miss Belvoir might have been leading him in a dance ever since she intruded on his peace that first night.

"Ah, well, if you *just know* . . ." The cigar's glow made an arabesque in the air as Strickland gestured.

"I did not seek you out to discuss *her*. I want you to deliver a message for me to your colleagues."

"I am not going to like this, am I?"

"Say you saw me tonight and I was looking for blood over the insult to my family. Tell whoever is behind this that if I see Crippin within a mile of that street again, I will tell Lance, and he will take it up with the prime minister and the regent and inform the other lords."

Strickland sighed. "I would rather you wrote a letter. There is this problem with being the messenger of such a threat."

"I count on you to make sure the threat is heard. Someone went too far, Strickland. A duke's home, no less. The lowest baron will feel the insult worse than Aylesbury. Tell them to call Crippin and his sort off, or the House of Lords will demand that heads roll."

CHAPTER 11

Padua faced the morning in a muted mood. There were those who claimed sleeping on a problem brought clarity, and her view of the last evening's events loomed awkwardly lucid in the light of day.

Besides concluding that years of abstinence had made her a sitting duck, she drew no conclusions and placed no blame. She did, however, admit that she had to leave Langley House.

At least she had some money now. She had promised not to use the money found in her father's apartment yet, but spending her own savings would be easier now that the other money resided in her valise. She enjoyed one more elegant breakfast, nostalgic already for the luxury. For a brief while she had felt important and notable. Just walking through these spaces made one stand tall and proud.

She asked to eat in the dining room. She took her time, then went to her chamber and called for her servant. At her instruction, the girl began folding up the few garments.

They were almost finished when the door opened. Ives walked in. Padua wished her heart did not jump at the sight of him, but it did.

No wonder she had been so reckless yesterday. He exuded a masculine power that demanded compliance with whatever he wanted. She had always been at a disadvantage, and fighting a rear-guard action against the effects his presence had on her. It would only be worse now.

He saw the valise, and the stack of clothing beside it, on the bench near the window. "You are almost packed, I see. Good. I came up to tell you to do so at once."

She asked the girl to leave, then began stuffing her garments into the valise herself. "How gracious of you. I suspected your glib words about taking all the blame were just polite cant, but I did not think you would throw me out like so much bad baggage."

A touch on her shoulder drew her attention. She conquered her humiliation before looking at him.

"I am not throwing you out, but you cannot stay here. I have no guarantee that you will not be followed, or interfered with, as was tried yesterday."

"I trust you warned them off?"

"I did. Both the man who lay in wait and his masters."

"Then I am sure no one will interfere with me." She returned to her packing.

She wished he would go. Vivid images from yesterday evening invaded her mind while he stood there. Knowing that he harbored more erotic pictures made it worse. How did people have conversations after indulging in such intimacy? It was all she could do not to choke on her own breaths.

"I disagree," he said. "It would be best if you left London so the trail goes cold."

"If necessary, I can go to Birmingham." At least she knew that city. She would not be lost in it.

"That will not do. I need to keep an eye on you. I am taking you to Merrywood Manor, Aylesbury's country home. We will leave at once."

She stopped packing. She stood frozen with comb and brush in hand. He had issued a decree, not a request.

"I will be in the way there."

"You will not be."

"Is it unoccupied, like this house?"

"My brother is there. I must be too. Our other brother will be returning from a tour of the Continent, and I should welcome him and his wife back."

She tucked the comb and brush into her valise. "I will definitely be underfoot, then."

"A person could live her life in that house and never see another soul, Padua. Isolating yourself will prove very dull, but you can do so if you want."

She peered into her valise, at the old garments she knew too well. "I will have to. I have nothing suitable to wear at a duke's table."

"No one will care about that."

Oh, yes, they will. Even he had noticed how poorly she appeared when she first called on him, although he would never admit it. She noticed him taking in every sad inch of her dress and pelisse and bonnet. *I will care too.* She did not want to suffer the pity of this other brother's wife. It was one thing to be a woman of modest circumstances, and another to be the intruding, dowdy guest.

She would indeed isolate herself, and not obligate this family to pretend they entertained her sort all the time.

"I will wait below for you." He turned to go.

"Where did they travel? The brother and his wife?"

He shrugged. "Rome, Florence, Venice, and thereabouts. The Alps, I expect. France. They have returned sooner than planned. They chose to shorten the journey."

Venice? Florence? Padua reconsidered her resolve to be invisible. She supposed she could suffer a little pity if she learned about the sites and environs of those cities. Her mother used to reminisce about her visits to Venice, and it would be good to learn how things had changed.

She closed her valise after Ives left. Before she went down, she jotted quick letters to Jennie and Mr. Notley, to let them know she was leaving town but that mail sent to her at Langley House would find her.

*   *   *

I ves spent the better part of the journey to Merrywood up beside the coachman. The alternative, to sit
inside with Padua, promised to cause him nothing but
discomfort. Far better to face the autumn wind than
her palpable fear.

The expression on her face when she left Langley
House had not been companionable. At the inns she
retired to her chamber and took her meals there. Only a
fool would not recognize the signs of a woman keeping
her distance.

She thought he would seduce her if he had her alone
again. Finish what he had started. Pass the long miles
dallying the best way one could find. He had sworn to
himself he would not do that, but he guessed the odds
were at best even that he could resist the temptation if
he met it.

Therefore he kept his distance, too, up on the board.
He took the reins at times, so his mind would not dwell
too much on the woman out of sight a few feet away.

The reception at Merrywood involved only servants.
Ives watched Padua escorted away by the housekeeper
while he went in search of Lance.

He found his brother in the library, wearing riding
clothes that displayed a good deal of autumn mud.
Lance's acknowledgment was a gesture toward the
brandy and a raise of his own glass.

"Have Gareth and Eva arrived yet?" he asked Lance.

"Tomorrow. He wrote with their plans two days

ago. They made a stop at Langdon's End first, then at Birmingham."

"I trust that means Eva is in good health."

"He did not say she wasn't."

Ives threw himself into a chair. "Did you just get back from riding?"

Lance shook his head. "I returned at least an hour ago. It was a most peculiar ride."

"How so?"

"I came upon Radley riding too. He joined me. I spent the next two hours in his company."

Sir Horace Radley was a magistrate. He had occupied himself for half a year now trying to prove Lance had murdered their eldest brother, Percy.

"Did he question you yet again? I will lodge the strongest objection. Enough is enough."

"I said it was peculiar, not typical. He might have been my best friend, he proved so jovial. His only comment about my unfortunate dark cloud was to say, and I am quoting him now, *I've cause to think an error has been made, and I shall address that soon.*"

"Odd."

"Isn't it. I have spent the last hour contemplating how odd. He did not say, for example, *I have concluded you are innocent and much maligned*, did he? It was more ambiguous than that."

"Yet his friendliness would imply—"

"Nothing at all, perhaps."

Ives wished a more optimistic reason were at work.

He hoped this peculiar conversation heralded the end of the matter.

"I should probably tell you that I did not come alone. I brought a guest," he said.

"So the footman whispered when he hurried in here to inform me of your arrival. A woman, he said. A Miss Padua Belvoir."

"I am sure you will like her."

"Do you? Like her, that is? You must, if you brought her here. You have never done that with your actresses and opera singers before. Nor do your mistresses usually call themselves Miss anything."

"It is not like that. It is not what you think."

Lance stood and ambled over to the brandy. "What do I think?"

"She is not my mistress, or an opera singer, or an actress."

Lance took that in with a vague smile. He returned to his chair, stretched out his legs, and gave Ives the kind of focused attention that he rarely showed these days. "Then what is she instead? If I am to be her host, I should probably know."

"She is—was—a schoolteacher. She got sacked, and needs a bit of help until she decides her future course of action."

"Is this the same woman who was my guest at Langley House the last few days? The butler does write to me when interesting things happen. Perhaps you did not know that."

So much for simple explanations. Ives cleared his throat. "I came to know her because of a case I am involved in. Upon learning of her dire straits, I could not just leave her destitute and homeless."

"Of course not. That would not be chivalrous. However, you could have left her in London, at Langley House, rather than journey several days in her company, and bring her here. You could have found her other lodging, at an inn for example."

He cursed Lance under his breath. He had grown accustomed to his brother lacking interest in anything, and had counted on that. Instead, for some reason, Lance kept digging. The hole was getting very large.

"I did not think it wise to leave her in London."

Lance just looked at him.

"Here is the thing. I have some reason to think she is in danger of abduction by agents of the Home Office. It was best to get her out of town."

"So this woman had drawn the attention of the Home Office, and you concluded she should leave London. You then decided to bring this troublesome baggage with you to this house, so the Home Office could wonder even more what our involvement with her might be. Do I have that at least half-right?"

"At least half."

"Did it not occur to you that there are already too many clouds gathering here?" Lance speared him with a very direct glare. "You surprise me. You are supposed to be the sensible brother. The lawyer, by God. And you take up with a schoolteacher who is under suspicion by the Home Office, and decide to hide your paramour here."

Was Lance scolding him? That took some gall. "I have not taken up with her."

"Haven't you now? That is good news, I suppose. You are supposed to be sensible in that regard too. Not for you the bored wives, as with Gareth. Not for you the whoever catches one's eye, as with me. I trust you ensured that she brought a woman with her, if it is *not like that*."

Ives sipped some brandy.

Lance threw up his hands. "Not like that, hell. Well, I forbid it. While this schoolteacher is in this house you are not to seduce her. I won't have it."

Ives laughed. "Are you the vicar now?"

"Someone has to serve as this poor schoolteacher's chaperone, since you brought her here all alone. The poor woman is probably terrified, having guessed your bad intentions."

"As you presume to know them, you mean?"

Lance stood and set down his glass. "I know *you*. That is all I need to know, because your intentions are in your eyes when you speak of her. Normally it is some actress who inspires those fires. I will meet her at dinner, and give her what reassurance I can with my ducal presence."

Ives laughed hard this time. "You have never reassured women that their virtue was safe, Lance. Duke or not, your presence does not inspire that confidence in them."

"Then I will be explicit, that as an innocent she is under my protection in my house." He walked to the door. "Now, since we have a guest, I should dress."

Ives threw back the rest of his brandy. What an inconvenient time for his undisciplined brother to decide to become a stickler on society's rules.

Padua had intended to take her dinner in her chamber. Her very luxurious chamber. It made the one in London pale in comparison. This was more an apartment than a chamber, since it had its own big dressing room. In particular she loved the tall windows that looked out on the rolling estate of Merrywood Manor. Pale green and rose colored the drapery.

The note from Ives, brought by a footman, dashed her plans. The Duke of Aylesbury expected her attendance at dinner, so he could welcome her.

Aided by a servant, she dressed as best she could, which was not well at all. Even in her best dress, a simple affair made of yellow muslin, and the blue wool wrap she inherited from her mother, she cut a poor figure. Hopefully the duke would conclude she added little to his table and not demand her presence again.

Ives arrived at her door while she tried to settle her nerves. "I thought you might like an escort."

"Thank you. That would help."

He tucked her hand around his arm and guided her to the stairs. "He is only mildly eccentric. Should he start waxing eloquent, let him talk his fill. Do not worry that you are expected to contribute, or even agree."

"I do not know why he insisted I join him."

"He is curious. He is your host."

She rather wished he were an absent host, as he had been in London.

What a rude thought.

As soon as she entered the dining room, she decided perhaps this would not be too much an ordeal. The duke had already arrived, it being an informal night. He subtly examined her during their greeting.

She examined him in turn. Although handsome like his brother, the duke's deep brown eyes and black hair increased the darkness of his appearance. A scar marred his cheek, forming a fine, pale, irregular line that lent harsh drama to his person. The intensity she at times saw in Ives seemed a permanent state for the duke. She had no trouble picturing him at dawn, stripped to his shirtsleeves, facing another man to duel with sword or pistol.

The places had been set for intimate conversation, with Ives and her facing each other and the duke at the table's head.

"Ives said you are a schoolteacher," the duke prompted.

She treated him to a full accounting of her work in Birmingham and London. He at least pretended to be interested, although she noticed him send Ives a glance or two. She talked too long, but she feared the void when she stopped.

"I must apologize," she said upon concluding. "It is

such a treat for me to converse with adults that I sometimes speak too much."

"I like knowing all about the people who take residence at Merrywood."

"I will not be here long. I am not really taking residence."

"You are welcome to stay as long as you desire. I insist you remain while Eva is here. She is my other brother's wife. She will be glad to have another woman about, so she does not have to suffer our company alone."

The duke turned his attention to Ives and asked after matters in London. The two brothers conversed in the casual, unguarded way of relatives. She ceased to be the center of attention. That suited her. She focused on the delicious meal, even better than the one she enjoyed at Langley House.

"Do you ride?"

The question intruded on her admiration for a cake festooned with Chantilly. She wanted to jump into the cream and eat her way out.

The duke had her in his sights again.

"I have never had the opportunity."

"Then you must while you are here. It is the only way to properly see the estate. The chestnut mare should suit her, don't you think, Ives?"

"Very well, I would say. I will take you riding tomorrow."

This was exactly what she expected to happen if she spent any time with this family. Her circumstances normally did not embarrass her, but over and over she would find herself begging off their generosity.

"That is kind of you. However, I do not own suitable garments for riding. I will appear comical enough on a horse without adding to the ridiculous image with my attempts to maintain some modesty while attired in a day dress."

Both gentlemen appeared at a loss for words.

"Of course if you have never gone riding you would not have riding garments," Ives finally said. "You should have thought of that, Lance."

Now they were all embarrassed. Deciding to put them out of their misery, Padua stood. "I hope you will not mind if I retire and leave you to your port and conversation."

They both rose to their feet and bid her good night.

"She is very . . . tall." Lance offered his first words on Miss Belvoir while he and Ives strolled through the garden.

"Distinctively so," Ives agreed.

"*Distinctive* is not the word I would guess she has heard most of her life regarding her unusual stature."

Had she heard unkind words instead? What idiots people were. What blind fools. "I think it is a very accurate word."

His brother glanced at him through the dark. "It will make things difficult. Finding her riding garments, for example. I doubt she can wear Eva's, or whatever is left here from our mother's days."

"I will take her on a tour of the estate in a carriage instead. She does not have to ride."

"You alone with Miss Belvoir for hours in a carriage . . . How thoughtful of you to take care of our guest. I trust you won't find it too dull."

"If I do, she will never know. I try to be polite that way."

"Do not try to kiss her until you are on the way back. That way, when she rejects your advance, there will not be too much time left before you can both escape."

Ives resisted pointing out that Miss Belvoir had already not rejected him. Far from it. He also avoided the invitation to protest the assumption he would try to kiss her again. He had not decided about that. Not entirely, at least.

"What chamber did the housekeeper put her in?" Lance asked.

"What does it matter? They are all presentable."

"I want to know. I think you can tell me. You found out yourself, didn't you?"

"Only because I escorted her down to dinner." He heard himself sound like a boy making excuses for a perceived transgression. "It is the chamber with the green and rose drapery."

"It is a fairly plain chamber. I expect the housekeeper thought Miss Belvoir would be overwhelmed if asked to live surrounded by silks and ornament. It has a dressing room, however, so she will not feel as though she had been housed with the servants." He paced on awhile. "Or did you ask to have her put there in that chamber?"

"Why would I do that?"

"Whenever you answer questions with questions, I know you are avoiding the truth. That chamber is not far from *your* chamber, that is why."

"Isn't it? I'll be damned."

"Play your game as you choose. I believe your dishonorable intentions will only bring you frustration."

"You are sure you know my intentions, do you?"

"Having seen her, and seen you watching her, I am sure that my earlier suspicions were correct. However, I do not think you will be assaulting that particular tower tonight, and tomorrow Eva arrives. I will charge her with acting as Miss Belvoir's chaperone."

"Miss Belvoir does not need a chaperone. She is at least twenty-five, and a woman who knows her own mind. She is well educated, and probably smarter than you are. Furthermore, all of this interference is absurd coming from you."

"I am only following my lawyer's advice. Remember? I should be a paragon within the county, at least for a while. I should avoid drunken revelries, or having women in this house for erotic purposes. I should even avoid going to where such women can be found in their own abodes. I must ride out on the estate like a good lord, and be generous in my dealings with all I meet. I must even suffer the company of Radley for half a day, knowing all the while that he is trying to get me hanged.

So, if I must do all of that, I'll be damned if you get to pursue a woman under my own roof while I have to be a monk."

"You are going to create trouble for me merely because I gave you very sound, very reasonable advice? This is the thanks I get for keeping you out of their clutches?"

"I am doing this because following your advice is *driving me mad*. I have no intention of suffering alone. You forced me back here, you insisted I leave town, so you can damned well suffer too. If I needed to forbid Gareth from enjoying his wife's favors while he visits, I would."

"You *are* mad."

"More than mad. Insane from boredom. Deranged by abstinence. Unhinged due to—"

"You are too dramatic."

"Try to seduce Miss Belvoir, and see just how dramatic I can be."

They let the topic drop, and chatted about other things while they walked back to the house. Lance's peevish demand for a fellow sufferer did not leave Ives's mind, however.

Lance had all but thrown down a gauntlet. Ives would be damned before he allowed his brother to dictate like this in any matter, let alone this one, and least of all because Lance was in a fit of pique over his own restrictions.

Pride practically dictated he seduce Padua now, should he choose to listen to that voice.

CHAPTER 12

Padua made it a point to finish breakfast before the brothers came down. She enjoyed a walk in the morning garden, then returned to her chamber with a book she requested a footman find for her in the library.

She did not want to be visible when the third brother, Gareth, arrived. She heard the coach outside near noon, however. With its approach the house came alive. Setting aside her book, she crossed to another chamber so she could look down on the welcome.

She identified Gareth at once. He resembled his brothers enough to make his familial connection unmistakable. He appeared a little younger than Ives, but not by much. Dark haired and dark eyed, he shared his siblings' height and good looks and, she noticed, possessed a very charming smile that carried a hint of mischief.

He helped his wife down. Padua deduced at once that Eva was pregnant. The day's fashions hid that fairly well, but Eva's stance spoke of a woman about halfway along.

The welcomes flowed noisily and casually. They all seemed to like each other. Hugs, laughter, a few arm punches, and other masculine play ensued, then slowly they all entered the house.

Eva looked up just before she disappeared under the portico's roof. An attractive woman, but not a great beauty, Padua observed. Average in size, with brown hair and a pleasant face. Padua felt bad for how that relieved her. Had Eva been a stunning woman, this all would have become even more awkward. Rather this woman appeared about her own age, and not at all conceited.

She returned to her chamber, and to her book. Eventually she would have to go down, but for now she would not intrude on the family reunion. Today she would meet this third brother and his wife and be a guest. But starting tomorrow she intended to make herself scarce.

"I ves brought a visitor," Lance said. "A woman."

"You will meet her at dinner." Ives intended to move the topic aside for now.

"What woman?" Gareth asked.

"Just a woman," Ives said. "A friend who needed a respite from town."

Gareth waited, curious. He looked at Lance. He looked back at Ives. "I have never heard of you bringing one of your mistresses here."

"She is not my mistress."

"That hardly kills my curiosity. Rather the opposite. Why is she not down here now, so I can get a good look at her? I hope you did not tell her we would mind her presence when we arrived," Gareth said.

"She chose to remain above. You will meet her at dinner, but I do not think she intends to make herself a part of our group too often."

"Why not? Is she inappropriate in some way?"

"I would never bring an inappropriate person to Merrywood."

"So why—"

"He does not want to talk about it now," Eva said with exasperation. "Do you, Ives? Men are worse than women, I am convinced. *I* know not to pry. At least not yet."

"Thank you, Eva. Your return is all that matters now, not curiosity about a visitor, curiosity that will be satisfied in a few hours when you meet her. We want to hear about your journey. Was it all you had hoped?"

Eva was a sweet, sensible, gentry-born woman. Ives liked her, even if he still found it remarkable that Gareth had married her. Gareth had cut a notorious swath through the wives of the peerage before meeting Eva, and anyone could be excused for finding theirs a peculiar match. And a love match at that.

Eva had seen the better man in Gareth, he supposed.

She might be the only person who really knew his bastard brother, aside from the duke's mistress who had given Gareth life.

"It was glorious. Far better than I dreamt. I have dozens of paintings, and books of sketches," Eva said. "The month in Florence studying with Signore Rosselli, going into the Tuscan hills—I will remember it forever."

"It was too bad, then, that you had to cut your time abroad short," Lance said.

"It was for the best reason." Her hand instinctively moved to rest on the swell under her breast.

"Ah. Of course. I did not realize that was the reason," Lance said. "I trust you are in good health? Nothing is amiss, I hope."

"She is in fine health. We merely thought it best to wait out the last months here in England," Gareth said. "You really are ignorant of such things, aren't you?"

"I have no understanding whatsoever of the condition."

Eva laughed. "I will soon become a little clumsy. It would not be a good idea to take sea voyages in that state, if it can be avoided. I did not mind coming back. I wanted to see my sister, and all of you, of course." She stood. "Now, I will rest until dinner. That is another feature of the condition, Aylesbury. Women like me need a lot of rest."

No sooner had she left than Lance stood, went to the desk, and removed some papers. "Gareth, I want you to know that the last of the paintings were removed a week ago. Here are the receipts we had them sign."

Lance referred to an investigation Gareth had embarked on in the spring involving a large cache of stolen paintings. He had become involved at Ives's request, only to end up far more entangled than anyone wanted.

"Took him long enough," Gareth said while he examined the receipts.

"Thanks to Ives, your name was kept out of it to the end. As were all the names of any other members of the family. As expected, when those gentlemen were told all their treasures had been found safe and undamaged, no one cared too much how the paintings happened to end up in a cottage down the road, or where they had resided during the intervening years since their disappearance."

Gareth looked over at Ives. "It is finished, then."

"Yes, finally, it is finished," Ives said.

A faint rap on the door captured Padua's attention. She opened it to find Eva standing there.

"I hope I am not disturbing you," Eva said. "I am Eva Fitzallen. I wanted to meet you, and welcome you to Merrywood."

"That is kind of you. Won't you come in?"

Eva made herself comfortable on a chair. She had removed her bonnet and pelisse and swathed herself in a long Venetian shawl. "Ives said you did not choose to join us today when we arrived. I hope you do not worry about interfering."

"It was a family time. My presence would have only added a pause now and then."

"Perhaps so. Actually, mine does, too, when the three of them get together. They are obligated to be on their good behavior. Left alone, they are much like boys tumbling down a hill."

"Still, you do know them. My acquaintance even with Ives is recent, and not deep."

Eva's eyebrows rose the tiniest fraction. "Is there any way I can make your stay more comfortable? Anything I can tell you about the family?"

"Since you are kind enough to offer—I was surprised to hear your name is Fitzallen."

"Ahhh. Ives did not explain. That was careless. Gareth is a bastard. His mother was not the duchess, but the duke's longtime mistress. I suppose you surmised that during the last few minutes since I arrived, however."

"There was one more brother, was there not?"

"Percy. He was the eldest, and the last duke. He died unexpectedly in the spring. I am not speaking out of turn if I inform you that there are those who suspect Lance of having a hand in that. You are sure to hear allusions to it when they talk, and if you go anywhere in the county it is common gossip. There is nothing to it, of course, but these things have a way of lingering on."

"It is a complicated family."

"No more than mine was. And perhaps yours too? I will not ask why Ives brought you here. Not for the grand seduction his brothers suspect, I think. He hardly needs to transport a woman to Merrywood for that, and I expect this house is the least convenient place for it."

"No, I am not here for that." *He brought me here because my father is in prison and the authorities think I am an accomplice.* She wondered how this sweet woman would react to hearing that.

"All the same, should he turn his mind in that direction, you must let me know. If you want it to stop, that is. Otherwise, feel free to hold your own counsel."

Well, that was blunt.

Eva looked Padua over from head to toe. "I hope you will forgive me for being forward, but—Ives said he expected you to avoid our company. You are free to do so. However—perhaps I am assuming too much because not long ago I would have reacted this way—I hope you are not thinking you will be uncomfortable because you do not have an appropriate wardrobe."

Padua could not believe how quickly Eva guessed that part. "I told Ives I did not, that I would appear out of place and worse than a poor relative. I do not mind my circumstances normally, but I do not visit a house like this normally either."

"What did Ives say to that?"

"He said no one would care."

"The point is that *you* will care. Just as if he entered one of his clubs dressed like a rustic, he would care. Men like Ives make high-minded claims that such things do not matter, but they expect women to appear fashionable and well turned out anyway. They have known nothing else in their lives except women with wealth, after all." She narrowed her eyes on Padua. "We will see what we can do. Your height will complicate it. I cannot just lend you some of my wardrobe right out of the trunk. However, the servants here know how to ply a needle to make alterations, so perhaps we can come up with a few ensembles so you are more comfortable at dinners at least."

"I do not know what to say." She really didn't. Eva's thoughtfulness touched her. "You guessed right away too."

Eva took Padua's hand and clasped it in her own. "When I met Gareth, I had one chair left in my house. I had not had a new dress in six years. I did not mind my circumstances either, normally. But there were times when I felt them keenly." She pushed herself to her feet. "Now I must rest, the way I claimed I would. Gareth will scold if I spend the whole afternoon chatting, although I would not mind doing so."

Padua wore her yellow muslin to dinner again. Thanks to Eva's perception and reassurance, she did not feel too out of place. She remained an observer for the most part, however. This was a family reunion still, and the members of that family had a lot to say to each other.

After the meal Eva removed herself. Padua followed her out of the dining room.

"I am going to retire," Eva said once they were alone. "Why don't you take advantage of the library. At dinner you expressed a strong interest in the towns we visited on our tour. I am sure there are books here with engravings of the views. I know that there is one with drawings showing the compositions of the art to be seen, including the paintings by Giotto in the town that is your namesake."

"My mother told me about those. I will look for that book."

"I will show you where it is."

Eva took her to the library. Once Padua saw its impressive size, she doubted she would easily find any particular book for a good while. Eva went directly to one case, gazed at its shelves, and reached up. She pulled out a large, heavy tome about Renaissance art, set it on a table, then took her leave.

Padua sat at the table and turned the pages. The paintings she sought were near the front, since Giotto had painted them two centuries before the Renaissance proper began. She examined an engraving of the exterior of the chapel and imagined her mother approaching it. Her mind filled in the missing colors and landscape.

She turned a page to see the chapel's interior, then another. Each page now held engraved images of each scene in the fresco cycle. Looking at them called forth her mother's voice. She succumbed to the nostalgia, and allowed her memories to give her a tour.

"Disgraceful excess." Gareth muttered the criticism while he looked over his shoulder.

He, Lance, and Ives stood in the night in the family

graveyard. At their feet, all but invisible in the dark, lay a simple rectangular stone marking their father's grave. They had come out to raise a toast to him.

The object of Gareth's scorn stood ten feet away. A behemoth of a sepulcher, it rose fifteen feet high, its white stone glowing in the moonlight. In that particular grave lay their eldest brother, Percy. No one had suggested they raise a toast to him too.

"I have rebuilt the cottage that he burned down," Lance said. "There are tenants in it now."

"And the empty cottage nearby?" Gareth asked.

"I visited, after it was empty of its recent holdings. I discovered that our brother used it as a private lair. There was evidence that he indulged his appetites there."

"A rendezvous for discretion's sake? And here I thought he never partook of amorous pursuits," Ives said. "I thought he chose to be virtuous, to be better than us." He looked down at his father's grave marker. "To be better than him."

"I suspect that his desire for privacy involved much more than discretion," Lance said. "I do not choose to say more than that. Just that there is much about our brother that we did not know. I for one would not mind leaving it thus."

They began strolling back to the house.

"She is very tall, isn't she?" Gareth asked.

Ives sighed. "You are speaking of Miss Belvoir, I assume."

"I am certainly not speaking of Eva, who is average sized."

"I agree she is tall. I do not know why everyone is obligated to comment on it. While it gives her a distinctive elegance, it is her least notable quality as I see it."

Gareth paced along on his right, and Lance on his left.

"Of course she is much more than her height," Gareth said in a musing tone. "It is just upon seeing her, her height is a little startling. Then one starts wondering."

"Wondering?"

"Imagining."

Lance laughed lowly.

Ives glared at Gareth's shadowed profile. "Imagining *what*?"

Gareth shrugged. "She is taller than most women by almost a head, so one can't help but imagine what it would be like. Calculate the difference it would make."

Ives's jaw tightened. His fists clenched.

Gareth walked on, unaware that he was in danger. "For an average-sized man, it might prove awkward, but for a tall man, there could be benefits."

"For certain positions, that is true," Lance offered.

Ives snapped his head around and glowered through the dark at Lance.

"Yes, that is what I mean," Gareth said, warming to the topic. "For example, standing, it probably would prove impossible if one tried to raise a woman that tall, but since one might not need to do that, other options come to mind."

Ives's head felt explosive. That he had immediately wondered when he first met Padua did not mean other men should presume to do so, let alone his brothers. "I cannot believe that you are speaking so outrageously about this woman who is a lady and our guest."

Gareth turned his head at the outburst. He leaned forward and spoke to Lance. "What is wrong with him?"

"There is nothing wrong with me. I am shocked, that is all, that you are speculating about her when she has given you no cause to do so, other than being by nature tall."

"I am not imagining *her*, but the idea. The woman in my wondering is anonymous. Although I don't understand why you are cross. We always wonder and speculate. You have never objected before," Gareth said. "Unless—ahhh. My apologies, Ives. You said she was not your mistress, so I assumed—I did not realize that you had a tendre for her."

"I do not have a tendre for her."

"He does not have a tendre for her," Lance echoed.

"It is not like that."

"It is not like that," Lance repeated. "Miss Belvoir is just an acquaintance. A *friend*. A woman in need of sanctuary. Isn't that right, Ives?"

"I think I will thrash both of you right now."

"Quick-tempered, isn't he?" Gareth asked.

"Miss Belvoir is a ticklish subject."

"I suppose that means she won't have him."

"That is my conclusion. At least she won't so far. Nor will he have her, while they are here. I have forbidden all such activity under my roof."

Silence fell. They walked on. Ives tried to shed the anger that had him in its grip.

"Just so I understand," Gareth said. "Did you forbid *it* only with them, or is this a new house rule?"

"The No Sexual Congress at Merrywood edict applies to everyone," Ives said. "Lance is damned annoyed that he has to behave, so he has decided no one will have pleasure if he cannot. You are forbidden too. He just neglected to tell you up to now."

"Don't be an ass," Lance said. "His wife is in the family way. I did not need to forbid him. Nature has done it for me."

Ives looked over at Gareth. Gareth smiled so broadly that moonlight reflected off his teeth.

They separated once inside the house. Lance retreated to his apartment, as ignorant as ever about women in Eva's condition. Gareth went in search of his wife, presumably to have some forbidden pleasure with her, edict be damned. Ives decided a spot of brandy was in order, and repaired to the library.

To his surprise, he found Padua there. He thought she had retired like Eva.

She sat at one of the library tables, reading a large book. The lamp near her head cast a soft golden glow over her profile and the bodice of her yellow dress. She did not hear him enter. Her thick lashes remained at half-mast over her reading eyes.

He stayed near the door and admired the picture she made. Her long, lithe body angled over the book, but

her back remained straight. Whatever she read gave
her joy. The smallest smile lightened her expression, as
if she listened to a friend speaking.

He should leave her to whatever engrossed her, but of
course he wouldn't. Couldn't. *I did not know you had a
tendre for her.* Perhaps he did. Desire alone would be
simpler. He knew how to take care of desire.

Not for the first time since he had met her, he ignored the better sense that told him to walk away, that
warned getting entangled would mean compromise at
best, and scandal at worst, that suspected none of this
was unplanned by her, and that she might be pulling
the strings while he danced to her purpose like a puppet.

Right now all that mattered was that she was lovely,
they were alone, and he wanted her.

CHAPTER 13

Padua realized she was not alone a moment after she congratulated herself on translating an Italian inscription in one of the engravings. Not a sound had been made, but she recognized the presence in the room from the way the air changed. She knew who it was too.

She did not look over. She dared not until she calmed the reaction that spread through her. Delight. Excitement. Anticipation. None of those involuntary emotions boded well for her.

He walked toward her. She had to look then, and acknowledge him.

"You are deeply into that tome," he said, looking over her shoulder. "What is it?"

"Eva showed it to me. It is full of engravings of paintings and buildings from the places she visited."

"The places you want to visit too?"

She nodded, and turned the page. "I expect you have been to most of them."

"Not as many as you may think. Like most men my age, a grand tour became difficult with the war. I did go over after it ended. I visited Venice and Florence, but I did not go to Padua, for example."

"I still envy you."

He reached around her and turned another page. "You will get there. I do not doubt it."

She did not see the new picture. His closeness distracted her. His confidence that she would achieve her dreams touched her. She wished she had such faith in herself. He could not know how for a woman the passage of time alone eroded one's self-confidence.

His breath warmed her neck and shoulder when he reached to turn the page again. She controlled the way her body trembled only by drawing on all of her force of will.

She closed the book and turned in her chair. She pulled her blue wrap tighter. "I think I will go to my chamber now."

"Not yet." He held out his hand, to help her to stand. "Sit for a while, and reassure me that my family did not overwhelm you."

She should go. Every instinct shouted that she should.

She accepted his hand. He led her over to a divan. She sat. He sat beside her.

The pulse of her heart seemed to throb out of her and right into the air. What had already occurred between them existed in the small space that separated their bodies, begging for attention. Even at fifteen she would have felt the lure Ives had become since he joined her in the library, and she was far older now, and hardly ignorant.

"I enjoyed our little dinner party," she said. "I was not overwhelmed. Eva has been only kind, and it is a revelation to see how three brothers treat one another when they are not being watched by anyone who matters."

"I will not accept your description of yourself."

"I meant that no serious guests were present, to interfere with your camaraderie and jokes. You all could be as outspoken as you wanted. I doubt you behave the same when you are among your equals at London dinner parties or balls."

"I suppose we did let our guard down, despite your presence. We have not all been together in some months."

"I am glad no one stood on ceremony. If conversation had remained formal and steady, I would have wondered if it was because of me and felt bad for robbing the reunion of its joy."

He turned toward her. His arm rose to rest on the back of the divan. "They are all curious about you."

"What did you tell them?"

"Nothing about your father. I explained that you are a damsel in distress who needed to leave London for a while. I also told them that you are not my mistress."

"Wouldn't they recognize your mistress?"

"Not currently, since there isn't one."

She took more pleasure in hearing that than she should have.

His gaze shifted to the top of her head. She felt vague movements in the hair on her crown, as his fingertips toyed with some curls. The small stimulation sent happy chills down her spine.

"They also wonder if I intend to seduce you."

"Don't they know you don't seduce?"

"It is not something I have explained to them. Even if I had, bringing you here would make them speculate. Lance is suspicious enough that he has forbidden it."

"I am trying to picture him saying that." She laughed. "I suppose if the duke forbids it, I am safe."

He leaned forward and kissed her cheek. "I don't think so." He kissed again. "I do not indulge Lance during his fits of hypocrisy."

She did not pretend she did not like those soft kisses.

She imagined where this could go if she did not stop it. She reacted with less alarm than good sense would dictate. That was probably because her body sabotaged her by purring deeply at the notion she might know the peak of sensual pleasure again.

"I suppose if you were of a mind for that, this chamber would be ideal, assuming no servants or family entered," she said nervously. His breath warmed the skin on her shoulder. "You are clever at using tables, and that table where I read is large and sturdy, for example. Without the lamp it would be shadowed but not too dark in here too. Not that I am suggesting we repeat our last indiscretion. We both agreed that would be ill-advised." She forcibly stopped the nervous flow of words from gushing forth even more.

At the same moment, he turned her head and silenced her further with a kiss on her lips.

"Remember how we agreed to that?" The call to his conscience squeaked out, an irrelevant question now.

He took her face in his cupped hands and kissed deeply. The intimacy undid her. She grasped his arms and kissed too. Their tongues battled and he won. His kisses dominated her, claiming with no quarter. Her breasts and thighs turned so sensitive he might have been licking at her skin the way she wished he would.

If she raised her lids she could see that library table. *Yes*. She wanted him to touch and kiss her until she was insane again and cried from the intensity. She wanted those feathers on her inner legs making her throb.

The kisses stopped and she gazed into eyes severe with thought mere inches from her own.

Yes. A calculation. A decision. *Yes*.

He stood and pulled her to her feet. "Go up now. Quickly."

She did not move for a few moments. Surely she heard wrong. She did not want to go. Couldn't he tell?

He turned his back on her and stepped away.

Embarrassment and frustration crashed together. Dazed, she stumbled away. At the door she looked back. He stood there, arms folded, gazing at nothing, his profile set like it had been carved of stone.

* * *

You are supposed to be the sensible brother.
Hell, yes.

Ives paced his apartment like a caged animal. Sitting proved impossible. Nothing could distract him.

He had behaved most sensibly with Padua. Honorably. Did he now enjoy the peace of the virtuous?

He wanted to punch the wall.

Not for you the bored wives, as with Gareth. Not for you the whoever catches one's eye, as with me. No, indeed. That was too messy. Inefficient. Contracted mutual pleasure made much more sense. There could be no misunderstanding, no dramatic partings, no anguished poetry. Also no lies and no regrets. And precious few infuriating nights like this one after the bargain had been struck.

Not for him the bored wives, and definitely not the daughters of prisoners in Newgate. He avoided itemizing yet again just how stupid it would be to take up with Padua Belvoir.

Nothing but trouble there. Damnable trouble. Whether she was the innocent daughter or the conniving accomplice did not matter. He would regret it. He already did.

He paused his prowling in the middle of his dressing room. A sliver of ruthless clarity entered his fevered mind, and he grabbed it for closer examination.

He acted as if he would face future choices, but the choices had already been made. He was in deep already. Whether through design or accident, whether due to desire or negligence, his position regarding the Belvoir case had been compromised. He lied to himself if he pretended otherwise.

Which meant he had nothing to lose.

P adua prepared for bed, then sent the servant away. She moved the lamp to a table in her bedchamber, wrapped her blue shawl over her nightdress, and opened a book she had brought with her from the school. A novel by Miss Austen, which she had salvaged from the rubbish after Mrs. Ludlow confiscated it from one of the girls and declared it scandalous. Padua had not found those parts yet, and was losing hope there would be any.

She remained unsettled by Ives's kisses. She was grateful he had sent her away. Wasn't she? She did not really want an affair with Ives. Did she? She was fortunate one of them had behaved with sense and honor. Not her. No, she sat with a book on her lap, trying to ignore the excitement and arousal that still simmered, trying to convince herself she was relieved, not disappointed.

She could not lose herself in the story the way she had yesterday. What attention she could give it only made her cross. Mr. Darcy was in the process of making the worst proposal any man could. It was the sort of proposal Padua Belvoir might receive in the unlikely event she ever heard one.

The lowest rap sounded on her door, so low she

almost did not hear it. Wondering if perhaps Eva had seen the light under the door, she went and opened it.

Ives stood there in his shirtsleeves. No coats, no cravat. No pretense.

He did not say a word. He did not have to. He announced his intentions with his mere presence, and through the way he looked at her. She sensed a tautness in him, much like that in an animal right before it released its physical power.

Her mind spun with a hundred thoughts jumbled together. She should think about her reputation. She should pretend joy and triumph had not rung like bells in her head when she saw who it was. She should not allow his beauty to sway her, but, oh, his appearance awed her now worse than ever before.

The suspense in the air heralded pending disaster or victory. The excitement in itself mesmerized her, but he did too.

"You should not be here." It breathed out, barely a whisper.

"No." Nothing in his expression changed. Not the set of his jaw nor the fire in his eyes. "You can close the door if you want."

She gripped the door's edge. She *could* close it, of course. And she should.

His gaze locked on hers. He looked for her decision. He saw it before she knew it herself.

With one step he was over the threshold and she was in his arms. Passion crackled through him, silent lightning in a palpable storm. He lifted her, kicked the door closed, and swung her around. Breathless and unsteady, she found herself pressed against the door. His body imprisoned her there while he claimed her in a furious kiss that made the world spin even more. He dominated her, and commanded her response with searing kisses to her mouth and neck.

The arousal she had carried to her chamber, which had distracted and taunted her, surged in a wave of sensation. His heat and strength titillated her whole body. The feral energy he exuded as he handled her incited erotic stirring low and deep. When she clutched his shoulders desperately, to hold on to something tangible and real, he would have none of it. He captured her hands in his and forced them above her head, so she could only submit to the sensual chaos. Submit she did, to the kisses coaxing her primitive self, to the ache throbbing between her legs, to the body so close it became the focus of all her senses.

He stripped away the shawl from her shoulders and neck, and it floated out of sight. Kissing her hard, he pulled up her nightdress impatiently. Air cooled her legs, then her thighs and hips. He pressed his knee between her legs, raising her so she rode a hard ledge pressing up against her vulva. Her toes barely scraped the floor. The pressure aroused her, thoroughly. Deep, dark tremors of pleasure overwhelmed her.

"Enough of this." He released her hands and peeled up her nightdress. A cloud of white cloth engulfed her head. Then she was naked, her body inches from his, waiting for the torture his caresses could create.

He looked down while his hands moved up her legs and thighs. He paused, briefly, to slide one thumb between his knee and her mound. He pressed with precision on the very spot she kept moving to relieve. Her deep moan brought wicked lights to his eyes.

"Beautiful," he murmured, while he watched his hands slide up her body. "You are elegant. Sinuous." His hands cupped her breasts. His thumbs grazed her nipples. Tantalizing excitement streamed into her blood. "Kiss me now, while I drive you mad with pleasure."

She circled his neck with her arms and kissed him hard, as best she knew how. She tried using her tongue the way he did, and her teeth. All the while his hands teased at her breasts, forcing the pleasure higher until that special madness did close in. The erotic torment left her whimpering within the kisses, and gasping out urging breaths.

His hands left her. She wanted to scold him, until she saw him strip off his shirt. He pulled her into an embrace so their bodies met with no interference. Holding him like that, feeling his skin beneath her hands and arms and against her breasts, enthralled her. The pleasure changed in that instant. Even his kiss felt different. A new intimacy touched her, and she could not ignore its power.

He lifted her in his arms and carried her to the bed. He laid her down and started to remove the rest of his clothes.

In a slice of clarity, she saw where she was, what he was doing, and what would happen. Her nakedness felt stark. Scandalous. More than when she was on that table, even if she had been equally exposed. She instinctively covered her breasts with her arm and her mound with her hand. When his trousers lowered, she looked away.

Warmth beside her depressed the mattress. Intimacy descended on her like a mist. His scent, his skin—

"Do not be shy with me now, Padua." He lifted the arm from her breast. "You were not before."

She had not been so naked before. So vulnerable. She had not been in a bed either.

He banished her misgivings with a kiss that sent her reeling. Pleasure abolished hesitation and shyness. His kiss commanded that she not only acquiesce but also participate. While the fever took control again, he came over her so his body covered hers. He pushed her legs apart so his hips could settle between her thighs.

Another shard of reality broke through the sensual fog. "Are you going to . . . ?"

"Not yet." His arms slid beneath her torso. "Soon."

His embrace made her arch so her breasts rose higher. He tasted her shoulder, then moved slowly down her skin. She arched more, offering, urging. Anticipation made her wild and so aroused that her hips rocked.

"Very soon, if you do not stop that." He kissed the tight tip of one breast, then the other.

Stopping her hips meant suffering without that small relief. Flicks of his tongue sent currents of exquisite torment down to the sensitive, weeping void where all the sensations pooled and waited.

He aroused her until she could barely see, barely breathe. She thought she might die from it, or scream. She held on to him, hard. Her body moved again, without her direction. Her knees pressed his side, and her hips insisted on that slow rock.

He had given fair warning. Now she learned why. Restraint fell off him like armor dropping. He commanded a new wildness in her with scorching, biting kisses and the most possessive caresses. His hand slid down between them and pressed her mound, then ruthlessly sought the places that made her cry. He forced her higher, to the peak, and with one devastating stroke sent her careening into the glory of completion.

No slow recovery this time, however. No floating in a cloud of perfection. Another touch, lower, deeper, sent shudders into her contentment. He shifted, and raised one of her legs onto his hip. Within the tremor a fullness filled the ache of want that had tortured her.

More fullness made her gasp. His strength hovered above her, taut and hard while he thrust deeper. She welcomed the relief but feared it too. He both awed and frightened her.

He took her then. There was no other word for it. Too ignorant to take, too, she could only wonder at the power controlling her. Engulfing her. Her past did not prepare her for this. For him. The sensation of his movements made the echoes of her completion go on and on until at the end, deep in her mind, she cried out yet again.

* * *

When something close to clear thinking began
returning—and it took a good while to do so—
Ives experienced a curious moment similar to what he
knew after thrashing a man after succumbing to an
abrupt outburst of anger. His sensible self tapped his
current self on the shoulder and asked, *What in hell
are you doing?*

*Enjoying the rarest peace with a lovely woman.
Go away, you self-righteous idiot.*

Unfortunately, he could not avoid thinking forever.
And so amidst the tangle of limbs and sheets he made
with Padua, a few solid ideas made their way into his
head.

Being with a tall woman indeed had its benefits.

He had ravished her. He had not intended to, but
there was no other word for it.

She had not been a virgin. That she might be had
entered his mind rather late, when he was long past
caring too much about it. He doubted that thieving
rogue had had her more than a few times, from her
ignorance, but at least Lord Ywain Hemingford had not
just assaulted an innocent.

She lay beneath him still. He looked down at her
long, white, shapely leg sprawled to his side. He raised
himself up on his arms and gazed at her face. Her thick,
dark lashes feathered her snowy cheeks, and her lips
remained slightly parted. Deep breaths did not sound

like those of sleep, but of someone recovering from extreme exertion.

You ass. Look at her. What in hell were you thinking?

He had been thinking nothing at all. He had left rationality in his own chambers. He had been little more than a chaotic collection of hungers and raw need when he came to this door. If she had sent him away, he probably would have howled like an animal.

Only she hadn't. And he had repaid her generosity by battering her like a whore.

He eased off her. Her lids fluttered when he withdrew, but she did not open her eyes. He settled beside her, propped on his arm. He caressed her cheek with two fingertips.

"I hurt you."

She shook her head. "I am not frail. Far from it." Her lashes rose and she looked right into his eyes. "I liked it."

Now, that was interesting. "And here I was forming an apology."

"Please don't. That would make it sad." Her lids lowered again. An impish smile curved her lips. "If I am going to be scandalous and irresponsible, I would prefer passion to politeness. I would prefer the wicked Ives to the upstanding Lord Ywain."

Even more interesting.

Absolved of his bad behavior, he pulled her over and tucked her against him. She required no apology, but the upstanding Lord Ywain sat on his shoulder, reminding him of other matters that should be addressed. *Not now.* He shrugged the inconvenient ideas away.

"Do you think to do this again?" she asked.

"Not for half an hour."

Her head jerked around and she looked up at him. "Oh."

"Ah. You did not mean now."

"No."

"I think the future is up to you."

"Not entirely."

She did not mean it was up to him too. Like most women she probably assumed men would take pleasure if they could get it. Which was true. She was thinking about the reasons they should not even be enjoying one night.

"It is a choice to be made in the light of day, I think." He thought himself damned noble saying that. In truth he wanted to establish his rights clearly and unmistakably while she was too sated and dazed to know better.

"Probably so," she murmured, her head now resting on his chest. "No negotiations, however. No jewels and such."

She would not agree to be his mistress, she meant. She would not be one of *those* women. That was something best left to the light of day too. If she held to it, he would find ways to take care of her that did not reek of her being bought. Right now she needed someone looking after her, whether she accepted it or not.

He drifted on the edges of sleep. The little conversation repeated in his head many times. The notion joined them that the light of day might bring decisions he did not like. One impulsive, insane, ill-advised night might be the sum of their affair.

The lawyer in him began marshaling the arguments he would use to convince her otherwise. The rogue in him imagined all the pleasures he might never know.

"No negotiations, you said."

Her crown moved as she nodded.

"Good." He lifted her shoulders. She blinked, confused. "Here. Like this." He guided her until she straddled him, sitting on his hips, looking down. Her dark hair fell in a tumble all around her face and shoulders. "Stay like that."

He could see her clearly this way. He watched her while he caressed her. Her expression displayed her reactions to what he did to her. She watched, too, from beneath lowered lids. Her lips trembled when he slowly teased at her dark, erect nipples. His erection swelled and prodded against her bottom.

He pulled her down over him so he could use his mouth the way she liked. Trembles of pleasure shuddered through her, into his hands, where he held her waist. Her faint cries rained down on him. He pushed her further, until she whimpered with need.

He set her back, upright. She was wet now, and lost in her abandon. So beautiful in her abandon. "Up." He urged her to her knees so she towered over him, her white body and lovely limbs open to his gaze and his hands.

He slid his fingers between her thighs and stroked. A thousand stars glinted in her eyes. He explored the folds of flesh and watched desire overwhelm her. She swayed, unsteady, unable to control what the pleasure did to her. A primitive wildness entered her eyes.

She surprised him then. She turned her body so she faced away from him. Her lovely back and rounded bottom enticed him. He caressed her cleft in a long path that ended again at the hot velvet of her swollen lips. As he did, he felt her take his cock in her hands.

It could not last long, their mutual pleasure. His arousal took on an edge he knew too well. He grasped her waist and lifted her enough to slide out from under her.

She looked over her shoulder and began to turn.

"No. Stay there."

She looked over her shoulder again, confused. He pressed her shoulders down. She looked back once more, but this time she understood.

She hugged the mattress while on her knees. Her bottom rose, round and taut. He caressed its swells, and her hips circled subtly, tantalizing him.

He rode the erotic torment a little longer. "What do you want, Padua?"

Her bated breath told him. The small of her back dipped, raising her bottom more. He reached low and caressed her. "This?"

She cried out and nodded. "Yes, please, yes."

He kept his hand on her until she moaned, then begged. Head hot and jaw clenched, he replaced his hand with his cock and pressed slightly, so its head entered her. He paused and sought an anchor in the storm breaking in him.

"Yes," she whispered. *"Yes."*

He thrust into her, stayed to savor the sensation, then

withdrew. She moved her bottom, impatiently. He thrust again and she cried out.

The storm claimed him then. He let the fury rule and let the pleasure own him, until the excruciating tension snapped in a profound relief of sensation.

In the sensual stupor afterward, he bent and kissed the small of her back. And while he did, he used his hand to send her to her own ecstasy, one that left her screaming into the sheets.

CHAPTER 14

Standing beside the bed, Padua looked down on the evidence of the night. The bedclothes appeared as if marauders had fought in them. Half the pillows lay in the wrong places. Ives, sound asleep, lay naked, sprawled in abandon. She reached for an edge of a sheet and dragged it, so he might be covered from the waist down at least.

She donned her undressing gown and padded into the dressing room. The sky outside had lightened to a dark silver-gray.

The servant girl scratched on the outside of the dressing room's door to the corridor. That had never happened before. Yesterday when she heard Padua up and about, she just came in.

Padua wondered if the woman suspected there was

a naked man in the apartment. If she did not, she probably began wondering when Padua would not let her in, and insisted she would do for herself this morning.

She pried the pail of hot water out of the servant's hands and shut the door. She gave herself a thorough washing. Ives had affected her body enough that she still felt as if he were inside her. If she closed her eyes, she sensed the echoes of his thrusts still making her throb.

She had been very bad last night. Self-indulgent and irresponsible. She might well regret every minute one day. Right now, however, she did not. Could not.

The light outside had turned from gray to gold when the door to the corridor opened again. Eva walked in. She wore a morning dress and a cap festooned with lace. She carried a stack of garments in her arms.

"I saw your maid near the stairs, so I knew you were awake. I am grateful someone else is." She set her burden down. "I always rise early now. It can't be helped. Lying abed becomes uncomfortable."

Padua casually positioned herself between Eva and the bedchamber door. "What have you there?"

"Three dresses, a spencer, and two pelisses. This red pelisse was purchased in Florence for my sister, who is taller than I am. Not as tall as you, but it will still be easier to alter. This overdress is fairly long, and with some nimble sewing should appear correct if used for the same purpose for you. Then over here are some embellishments, lace and feathers and such, that I pulled off some old clothes that the last duchess wore."

"They are all *lovely*," Padua exclaimed. Loudly. She

held up each one, and went into raptures of excitement. "This fabric is *perfect*." She twirled around in a little dance, thumping the floorboards. Noisily.

"I had hoped you would be pleased. Your enthusiastic appreciation gives me heart," Eva said. "Now, slip on this wool so we can see what must be done."

Padua slid the green wool dress over her chemise. Eva stood back and peered at it. She glanced to the windows and shook her head. "This will never do. We will have to fit it in the bedchamber, where the light is stronger." She lifted all the fabric, and clutched the sewing basket's handle.

Padua backed up and positioned herself at the bedchamber door. "Will that not be inconvenient? Pins and such should be in the drawers here, I think."

"I have my basket," Eva said. "It contains all that we need." She heaved all of the fabric onto her left arm, and reached for the door latch with her right.

Padua braced her arm against the jamb, to form a physical barrier. "I would prefer you did not go in there."

"Why?"

"I made a mess last night. So bad that I did not want my maid to set it to rights, and I have not had the chance yet to straighten it myself."

Eva laughed. "Do not worry about that with me. I doubt it is too big a mess. What can one woman do in one evening?"

"Still, I would prefer if—"

"Oh, nonsense." Eva grabbed the latch, turned, and pushed.

Padua felt the door open behind her. She knew Eva could see the whole chamber, even if she remained blocked from crossing the threshold. Eva's attention focused on Padua, however. She frowned suspiciously, as if their entire exchange had suddenly struck her as odd.

Then Eva's gaze shifted to the space behind Padua's shoulder. Her eyes widened.

"You certainly did make a mess, Padua. It will take some doing to put to rights."

Padua almost fainted with relief. Ives must have heard the conversation and slipped out of the chamber.

She turned to lead the way in. And groaned inwardly.

Ives still slept. He had moved just enough to uncover one finely formed leg, up to the hip. An arm crooked behind his head made his torso very taut.

Padua closed her eyes, mortified.

"Oh, my," Eva said. "He is sleeping very soundly. If that is his habit after—well, *after*, he should have left last night."

Padua could not remember any decision being made about that.

"I suppose those women he normally takes up with are not too particular about such things. They probably sleep until noon, too, and their households would know the arrangement." Eva slipped past Padua and set her armful of garments down on a chair. She began sorting it out.

Padua inched into the chamber. "Are you going to fit this dress while he is right there? What if he wakes up and sees you?"

"What if he does? I am not naked. He is. If it will embarrass him, he should have thought about that several hours ago." Eva shook her head. "I do not know what happened to him while we were gone. He was always so sensible, at least when he was not angry."

"Perhaps I should wake him, so he is not sneaking back to his chambers in dishabille when the entire household is up and about."

Eva held up a dress and scrutinized it. "That might be wise. Rumor has it Aylesbury has issued some ridiculous edict. It would not do to find out if he is actually serious about it."

Padua walked over to the side of the bed near Ives. She jostled his shoulder.

His lids rose. He looked over, confused, then smiled. His arm circled her neck and he eased her face down toward his lips.

Padua squirmed to avoid being dragged into a kiss, and heaven knew what else. "Uhh, Eva is here. Look."

Ives's expression fell. He looked down the bed and through the chamber, to where Eva continued to debate the dresses. He grabbed a knot of sheet to cover himself better.

"Eva." He laughed a little, very awkwardly.

"Good morning, Ives."

"You are up early."

"You are not."

"No. Quite." He looked at his situation. His gaze slid to where his clothes were heaped on the floor. He looked at Padua helplessly.

"Perhaps you would return to the dressing room for a few minutes, Eva," Padua said. "Then Ives can get out of the bed and dress and leave."

Eva faced them. Her gaze skewered Ives. "I am waiting for him to request my discretion, Padua. You do want that, don't you, Ives?"

"Of course." He cocked his head. "Are you angry with me, Eva?"

"I think I am. Padua is not an opera singer."

"I know that."

"Then do not be so careless with her reputation in the future, please." Eva marched into the dressing room and closed the door.

Ives threw off the bedclothes. He went to his garments and pulled them on. "She is right. I was careless."

"I just woke ten minutes ago," Padua said. "Day has barely broken."

"I should have left last night, or at least woken you with kisses if I indulged myself by sleeping with you in my arms." He came back to her and embraced her. "We will tour the estate this afternoon, if you like. By then I expect you will have decided if you are angry with me too."

He gave her a kiss, and walked out the door.

L ance had finished his meal when Ives entered the breakfast room. He sat at the table drinking coffee while he flipped through the mail.

"You are up early," Lance said without looking up.

"As are you. Is this a new habit?"

"It is the result of unending ennui. I sleep early to escape it, only to have more hours in the morning to suffer it." He paused over a letter, and raised an eyebrow. "Miss Belvoir has mail. Sent here by Langley House. Two letters." He set the one in his hand upon another over to the side. "One from a friend, and one from a lawyer, I would say."

Ives cast his gaze on those letters. While he did, Lance paused again, frowned, and reached for the opener that the butler had placed on the table.

Ives ate the hearty plate he had put together. He had woken hungry on several counts. That of the stomach he could at least sate. As to the other—he imagined taking Padua away to a cottage where relatives did not feel free to intrude on a bedchamber at ungodly hours of the morning.

He expected the entire household would know by noon. Eva might be discreet as she promised, but it would not matter. The maid would see that bed and know what had occurred. His manservant would report Lord Ywain had not slept in his own bed. Gareth would guess just from looking at the two of them, assuming Eva's discretion included her husband, which it probably did not.

The only person who might remain ignorant was Lance, and only because his self-absorption these days blunted his normally sharp insights into people.

He could not take Padua away to a cottage, but he could remove her from this house for a few hours. He had amends to make, for the embarrassment of Eva finding him in that bed. He also had things to say. Just what things he did not know for certain. Normally he said whatever needed saying before he took a woman to bed, not after. Usually all he did was create a contract for pleasure.

But this affair with Padua was not normal. Hence the dilemma.

Lance's nose still resided in the letter he had opened.

"What is that there, which requires you read it three times?" Ives said.

"A very curious letter. From Sidmouth. He never writes to me. Actually, I don't think the Home Office secretary has said ten words to me in my life." He waved the letter. "But suddenly I am his good friend, with whom he communicates at length."

Ives stood. "I will leave you to it. I think a ride is in order. The day is fair."

"If you could wait a few minutes, I would be grateful. I think you can shed light on this peculiar missive, you see. You are mentioned several times." He set the letter down and gazed up.

Ives had no idea what Sidmouth had written, so he had no intention of leading this conversation.

"You mentioned when you came that you were worried Miss Belvoir had attracted the attention of the Home Office. Did you suspect that because you thought she was being watched while in my home?"

"Yes."

"And did you send word up the ranks of the Home

Office that if they did not call off their watch, you would
see to it that I—how did Sidmouth phrase it?—raised so
much hell in the House of Lords that the peers would
insist that heads roll?"

"I was sure you would not tolerate such an insult to
yourself and to the entire peerage."

"Well, that explains this." Lance tapped the letter.
"It contains a cryptic apology from Sidmouth, something about a hired man not understanding his mission, and ends with a jovial assumption that I would
not put too much stock in any tales you might tell."

"I am glad he took it seriously."

"I am sorry I did not, when you first mentioned the
Home Office. What does Sidmouth want with Miss
Belvoir? Is she some radical? A revolutionary? A crimi-
nal?"

"She is none of those things." He would swear to it.
He just had no proof to support his conviction.

"You are sure, are you?"

"Damned sure."

"Then why did Sidmouth set a man on her?"

"It has to do with her father, and a misunderstanding of her loyalty to him."

"So her father is the criminal, radical, or revolutionary."

"Yes."

"Which is it?"

"The first, as best I can tell. Possibly the second, but
it is unrelated if true. Unlikely for the third, but . . ."

"But you really can't be sure."

"Correct." He shared the story of Hadrian Belvoir and the counterfeiting, and of Padua's visits to the prison and the hope of the Home Office to have a minnow lead them to a whale. "It is a matter for the magistrates, if they only think it was counterfeiting. The interest of the Home Office implies someone thinks the bad money funded something disloyal," he concluded.

"So you brought her here where no agent dare trespass."

"And where I could keep an eye on her, while I visited. If you think her presence compromises you, we will leave today."

Lance rose and paced to the window. He looked out while he thought. "Zealots cannot be trusted. Everyone knows Sidmouth's agents cross too many lines, and create as many problems as they solve. The lords do not stand up to him and end it because they are afraid these radicals will start a revolution and our heads will be on the block."

"We can still leave, to spare you trouble. As you said, there are enough clouds here already."

"Not political ones." He turned, a glint of amusement in his eyes. "I think I will enjoy this. For once I will relish having the title. *Being* the title. Lord Lancelot Hemingford might have garnered suspicion, but Aylesbury? Never. No one would dare." He picked up the letter. "I must respond. Graciously, of course. I will express dismay at the insult to my position as reported by my brother. I will be forgiving, but in a most condescending way. I will imply that since Sidmouth was only recently made a viscount, and a newly minted title at that, he can be excused his error this once."

Glad that was settled, Ives rose again to take his leave.

"As for Miss Belvoir," Lance continued, "I trust you will watch your step. As you admit, you can't really be sure about her."

"My better judgment usually stands me in good stead where people are concerned."

"As it does in all things, to the family's everlasting benefit. If I believed your better judgment were at work with her, Ives, I would have never said a word."

I ves tucked a blanket around Padua's legs and lap. That charmed her, as did the cushion he had insisted be put on the board where she sat. The day was not really cold and her pelisse would be sufficient, but she did not object to his efforts to make her comfortable in the simple open carriage they would use for this outing.

He climbed up and took the reins. Their horse paced out of the yard and aimed toward the lane.

The day shone fair, but a crisp breeze kicked dried leaves all around the gig. The horse made a fast trot down the lane. Halfway to the road, Ives pulled on the reins and stopped. He turned and pulled Padua into a long kiss.

"That is to make up for what I could not do this morning," he said, snapping the reins again. "I apologize for the embarrassment, and for a bad end to the night."

"It was not as bad as it looked. I discovered that

embarrassment has a limit. Once you reach it, things do not get worse." She laughed. "Eva had said she would come in the morning to see about altering some garments, but I never thought she would arrive at daybreak."

"I daresay she will never enter a visitor's chamber again without sending a note first, after this."

"It could have been worse. Had I not pulled the sheet over you, she would have seen much more. I doubt even Eva could have remained so blasé then."

Padua could not resist making the face of astonishment she thought Eva would have shown. They shared a good laugh over that.

Padua wiped tears from her eyes. "She did not say anything the whole time we fitted the garments. I think she will be as discreet as she promised."

"Except with Gareth. She told him."

"Do you think so?"

"I know it. I saw him right before I joined you and the smile he gave me was unmistakable."

"A congratulatory smile, no doubt. That is how men would think of it for you."

She received an odd look for that. Once again he stopped the gig. "Padua, I will not pretend that I acted honorably last night. Such considerations did not exist. The only thought in my head was that I wanted you. I did not give you much choice, either, and that was not fair."

"I was not importuned. Overwhelmed, perhaps, but not treated dishonorably. I am not a schoolgirl."

"You are not very worldly either."

"Not an opera singer, as Eva said?"

"Definitely not."

She did not care for the awkwardness descending between them. She feared, she realized, that Ives was going to decide to be honorable in the future. "I do not regret it, if you are wondering about that. I am not angry or think you took advantage. Perhaps I should be, but I am not."

He aimed the carriage down a hill toward a small chapel set among a stand of oaks. As they moved past it, she saw the graveyard to its side. A sepulcher dominated it, standing twice as high as any of the other memorials and dwarfing the small tombstones.

"Is that your father's tomb?"

He shook his head. "My brother's. My father's is very modest."

She turned and looked back at the graveyard. "How odd."

"Not at all. A man who achieved something does not need any mark on his grave to be remembered. A man who accomplished little that is good can leave nothing else to remind the world he once lived."

"You were not fond of this brother, I think."

"I hated him."

There could be no response to such a flat, simple statement.

He took the reins in one hand, and took her own hand in his free one. "I have shocked you with that bald and heartless admission. It is not something I share often. Not something I give voice to. I hope you do not think badly of me, but it is the truth. I hated him. We all did. The others had more cause than I, but he cast such a shadow over us that when he died we—well, no one mourned him much."

"If you all felt that way, there was probably good reason."

He raised her hand and kissed it, as if grateful she did not scold him. "I became a lawyer specifically to annoy him. It was a small revenge. He lectured on and on about how it was beneath us for me to do this, and I would listen and nod, listen and nod. When he learned I had discarded his advice and preference, he became a madman. I enjoyed the fit it gave him."

"Was it not reckless to goad? He became the next duke. He had the chance to exact some revenge, too, I would think."

"Only financial, but Lance and I were left portions from our mother, and my father provided for Gareth. Percy tried to use allowances to get us to heel, but we chose not to become his dependents. He would have made that hell."

"I have no siblings, good or bad, so I find it sad that you had a brother who did not know how fortunate he was. I have often regretted that I have no sister or brother. While I do not envy you your brother Percy, I get wistful when I see the rest of you together."

Again that kiss on her hand. An apology this time? Or an expression of pity? His attention remained on the horse and the road, but she wondered if his thoughts had turned to how they met, and what waited in London. She had little family, and soon might have none at all.

The lane angled up a steep hill. At the top a lovely vista waited. They looked down on an autumn countryside dotted with farmhouses. A village's homes clustered in the distance.

"This is beautiful, Ives. For someone who has only known cities, it looks like heaven. So open and so peaceful, and so very quiet."

He jumped out of the gig and tied the horse to a stump. He came around and unbundled her from the blanket, then helped her down. "We can sit here for a while, if you like."

"I would enjoy that."

He spread the blanket on the ground. She sat and he joined her. For a few minutes she just feasted her eyes on the prospect beyond and below.

"How did the dressmaking session go this morning?" he asked.

"Very well. Eva is very talented at remaking dresses." She turned her attention to him. "Did you ask her to do that?"

"That is not how I provide my lovers with new wardrobes."

"They expect better, I suppose."

"It is not a matter of expecting, so much as requiring, Eva. I am at a disadvantage with you in many ways. I dare not offer you what I normally offer, lest it offend you." The look in his eyes invited her to fix his dilemma by declaring she would not be offended and would like having a new wardrobe too.

Which she would. What woman wouldn't?

"It would be easier for you if I *were* an opera singer, you mean," she said. "Then everything would be normal. Since it is not, you do not know what to do about me now, do you?"

"No." He took her hand. "That is not true. I know what I am supposed to do. In such a situation, a gentleman offers marriage."

"I do not think I would want that." Especially if it were because he was supposed to do it. Only in her heart she truly did not want that. He would be the scandal of the year if he married a woman whose father was in Newgate for counterfeiting, and suspected perhaps of much worse.

Then there was the matter of the trial. She worried now that if Ives did not prosecute, someone less honest and more ruthless would. If there had been one misgiving last night, it had been that she did not bind him to her cause, but instead might force him to abandon the entire case.

"Ives, perhaps it would be better if we did not—"

"No. At least not yet. Of all the choices, I reject that one. Unless you insist, of course."

He expected her to choose now. Did it end here, on this hill?

She gazed out at the peaceful land. "How different this is from London. So far away from it in more than distance. I might be in a different world, that is how novel and new this place is. Magical." She looked at him. "I rather like how separate it is from what waits for me there."

There were reasons, good reasons, why she should indeed insist, but they were also far away and right now, sitting here with his strength beside her and the intimacy a recent memory, none of that seemed to weigh much.

"I will not insist, even if it would be the wise path. Of course, not succumbing to begin with would have been the smartest thing, for both of us. I will not insist. At least not yet, as you said."

Her answer pleased him.

"If you are not the kind of woman I normally have as a lover," he said, "I have concluded I have to rethink things. Do it differently. It should not be too hard."

"Do what differently?"

"I will have to leave your bed well before dawn, so you are not found with me there. No one will be fooled, but appearances matter."

He looked down to where her left hand rested on the blanket. His fingertips stroked its back. "Instead of barging into your chamber and ravishing you, I should probably seduce you."

"I thought you do not believe in seduction."

"I never thought it worth my time before."

"Does that mean we will also forgo those other negotiations that you consider so efficient?"

He looked at her hand while he stroked it. His fingers meandered up her arm. "We did not need them last night."

"I suspect what happened last night is not why you make your expectations known with those mistresses."

That amused him. "You are too clever, Padua. But I do not want to make a list with you. It seems cold-blooded, and inappropriate." He rose up on his arm, so he warmed her side. "If I request a favor you do not want to grant, you must say so. If I assume too much, you must stop me. I think you will do that, and I will never be disappointed if you do."

It sounded fair enough. She wondered just what kind of favors he required of those mistresses, however. Just how bad could he be at times?

A kiss on her shoulder distracted her from that thought. Warm breath on her neck raised trembles she knew well now. She closed her eyes so she felt each delicious shiver. His fingertips feathered along her bodice's edge, then lower until they brushed against her breast just enough for the sensation to penetrate her garments and arouse her.

"Are you practicing at seduction, Ives?" She enjoyed the little teases. She hoped he continued a long time.

His kiss warmed her ear. "It is a well-known fact that one learns from doing."

"I would say you have a natural talent for it."

"It runs in the family, I am told. It has been perverse of me to deny the legacy." He turned her head, and brushed her lips with his. Such a soft touch, barely there, but breathlessness claimed her.

"I am honored that you think me worth the effort," she whispered.

He rested his palm against her cheek and looked in her eyes. "I am the one who is honored, Padua." The kiss he gave her made her believe he meant that. It was deep, soulful, and very, very seductive.

They lay in an embrace on the blanket, warmed by the sun and cooled by the breeze. They shared the sweetest kisses and a passion different from the night. Deeper somehow, and drenched with a different intimacy. And yet, despite their interfering garments and for all of the slow building of desire, she found herself on the edge of total abandon again and wishing they were back in bed where there could be more.

As if he heard her mind, his caresses on her leg raised her dress's hem. She felt the fabric inching higher, and his palm against her bare skin. Higher yet, so that the air cooled her legs, and the dress no longer constricted her. He left her embrace and moved to kneel between her knees.

"Up." A pat on her hip showed what he meant. She raised her hips and he pushed the dress up to her waist, so her lower body was exposed.

She looked up at him. He appeared so stern in his passion, his jaw tight and mouth hard. Except his eyes showed depths and hot lights while he kept his hand on her, giving her pleasure. The mere sight of him entranced her, and she could not know any embarrassment.

He came over her, braced on his taut arms. His head dipped down and he took her mouth in a deep, tense kiss. "I am going to finish what I started in London. You did not allow it then. Will you now?"

She realized what he meant. "You intend me to have the most wicked twenty-four hours, it appears."

He just waited, persuading her with touches that left her desperately needy.

A magical place. Another world. She would dwell here for only a few days. She doubted she would deny him anything, since she had so little time.

She nodded. He lowered his head for another deep kiss. Then he moved down her body.

She looked up at the sky and clouds, at the leaves moving above her on the breeze. She became breathless with anticipation.

The touches became very specific. Devastating. Pleasure screamed through her. She clutched at the blanket, twisting her hand in its wool so she might not thrash the way she wanted to. A new stroke, gentle enough, made the sensations sharpen even more. The intensity frightened her. He bent her knees so his mouth might have better purchase.

He took advantage of her openness. She felt his tongue enter. She thought she would die from pleasure right there. She lost hold of herself after that. Her consciousness spiraled down into a single point of physical need. It became almost painful, until incendiary release exploded.

CHAPTER 15

"The women must have been sewing all day." Padua looked down at her ensemble while Eva stood back to assess it. The red overdress had been lengthened with a broad panel of lace. The cream dress beneath it sported rows of lace, too, showing below. Bits of lace had been cut and attached to the low neckline.

"It should do for dinner," Eva said.

Padua thought it would do for a ball. It was the most beautiful dress she had ever worn.

She lifted the looking glass off her dressing table and stared at herself. At Eva's instructions, her maid had dressed her hair differently. The curls did not appear disheveled the way they normally did, but instead piled artistically on her crown. Her eyes looked very big, but she suspected that was because she could not quite believe what she saw.

Eva came over. Her hands rose. "You will wear these." She attached an earbob to Padua's right ear, then moved to do the same to the left.

Padua felt the bobs. Small red jewels, their weight swung merrily when she moved her head. "You are spoiling me, Eva."

"I think you deserve a bit of spoiling. There are not many women who could even hope to bring Lord Ywain Hemingford to his knees. I confess I am enjoying the show."

"He is hardly on his knees."

"He has forgotten himself. Gareth is fascinated."

"Probably because I am the least likely woman to cause his brother to behave out of the ordinary."

"You do not give yourself enough credit. I know how that is. I was the least likely woman to attract Gareth. It took me months to realize that was the reason I did. He had grown jaded. In light of that, apparently I was actually interesting."

Padua did not think it had been so simple. Gareth doted on Eva. His love for her showed in his eyes. He did not merely find her interesting.

"I must go and see to my own dress," Eva said. "You look stunning, Padua. I cannot wait to see Ives's reaction."

After Eva left, Padua walked about to get used to the dress. She did not want to be stiff like a puppet. The raw silk of the underdress made elegant little swishes when she moved, but it fell like water around her legs.

She laughed at herself, and forced herself to sit at the writing desk in her bedchamber. She opened one of the letters that had arrived. Jennie wrote demanding to know where she had gone after sending the ambiguous note that she would leave Langley House and London for a few days. She added that Mrs. Ludlow had hired a replacement to teach mathematics. Jennie suspected the woman lacked the ability to complete even mid-level arithmetic ciphers.

Padua took no pleasure in reading that. It saddened her to know that if there were a student in the school who possessed the interest and ability to learn more, the opportunity would never be afforded her.

She lifted the other letter. This one came from Mr. Notley. Her reaction on reading it after breakfast had been confusing. It should have brought her joy. While it did, that emotion had been tempered with another. Even now as she read the few lines jotted by his clerk, a wistfulness claimed her.

He expected to have news soon about her father's inheritance, he wrote. He would contact her through Langley House, as she had instructed. As for her father, he still refused to see Mr. Notley, so the lawyer's hands remained tied.

He mentioned nothing about arranging that food be brought to the prison. Having taken on the charge, Mr. Notley did not find any need to reassure her he executed it. She did not doubt he did.

Time to go below soon. She sat, waiting. She faced the bed. Would Ives come here tonight? Probably so. They both knew their time was limited, even if they did not speak of it. *A magical place, far away. A different world.* Not her world. Not even his anymore.

"Who decided I wanted a proper dinner party?" Lance indicated his opinion of the decision with the way he pulled on his cravat's wrapping fabric. He kept sticking a finger between it and his neck, as if the binding interfered with his breathing.

"Eva," Gareth said.

"I do not know why servants immediately defer to a woman once one enters the house. I was not even consulted."

"She commanded they not bother you with such minor things."

"That is because she knew I would countermand her orders."

Ives did not join in the bickering. He watched from the chair in which he lounged in the drawing room. Most of his mind dwelled on Padua, and their time on the hill during the afternoon.

"Stop complaining like a peevish boy," Gareth said. "You have grown too comfortable with living alone, Lance. It breeds a disdain for the least formality. The butler said that sometimes you forgo a proper dinner entirely, and call for bread and cheese. If we had dallied on the Continent, we would have found a barbarian when we finally returned."

"I am not objecting to decent food. I am complaining about this damned cravat. It gave my valet unseemly pleasure to garrote me with it, and he objected adamantly when I wanted one less formal. He overdid the starch in this collar too. I will probably cut myself on it."

Gareth looked to Ives for help. Ives shrugged.

"If you must know," Gareth said. He hesitated.

"I must know," Lance prompted.

"Eva wanted to have a proper dinner because she wanted Miss Belvoir to experience one in a duke's home. The woman is your guest. The least you can do is wear a starched collar, lest she think you believe her not worth the trouble. You forget what your station means to others, and how visiting here carries certain expectations on the part of others."

Lance had nothing to say to that.

Ives roused himself. "That was very thoughtful of Eva. If a woman is a guest of a duke, she would like to live as she believes dukes do."

"Eva is nothing if not insightful," Lance said, defeated.

Gareth strolled over and sat near Ives. "The ladies should join us soon."

"I expect so," Ives said.

"You appear quite peaceful, Ives. Contented. It is good to see you without the scowl you so often wear when in Lance's company."

"That is because here at Merrywood, he cannot do the things that make me scowl."

"Ah. I thought perhaps it was more than that."

"Such as what?"

Gareth looked innocent. "The weather. The quiet. The country often brings relaxation. Contentment."

"He does appear contented, doesn't he?" Lance interjected. "You should come down more often, Ives. The country air seems to agree with you these days."

"You only want me here so you will have someone to get into trouble with," Ives said.

"As if I would be so lucky as to have you agree to that."

Gareth's attention had turned to the door. He cocked his head. "Ah, here they come."

The slightest footsteps. The barest rustle. The two ladies appeared in the doorway.

Ives's mouth went dry.

Padua had been transformed. She was always lovely, but—

He stood along with his brothers. Gareth sidled close. "Miss Belvoir looks exceptionally beautiful tonight, doesn't she?"

Ives tore his gaze off Padua and turned it on Gareth, whose own gaze remained fixed on Ives's face. "Yes."

"The red really complements her color, I think," Gareth mused. "Don't you agree?"

He nodded.

Gareth leaned in closer. "You probably should try to

close your mouth now. I don't want Eva to enjoy herself too much at your expense."

Ives finally noticed Eva. She smiled at him. Smugly. Then she spoke. "Let us all go into the dining room. We need not stand on ceremony for that. After all, we are family and intimate friends." She looked right at Padua when she said the last part. Then right at Ives, before she led the way out.

"You looked especially lovely tonight." Ives offered the compliment along with a kiss after the white light of release dissipated. Padua had joined in more this time than in the past. Emboldened, she had taken his cock firmly in hand, and experimented with giving pleasure. Her efforts had charmed him to a ridiculous degree.

"I felt lovely," she said. "It was kind of Eva to deck me out like that."

Not entirely kind. Eva's motivations reflected her view of the affair. She thought he was taking advantage of Padua. She believed he was being a rake, much as her husband used to be.

"I think," Padua murmured as she curved her body against his, "I have never felt so beautiful before in my entire life."

Her admission touched him. Of course such things mattered to women, and what they wore affected their views of themselves. That Padua carried herself with confidence even when dressed in ugly gray did not mean she did not feel conspicuous in her lack of stylish dresses.

"You should have a new wardrobe, so you always feel that way," he tried.

She did not reply to that. He cursed inwardly. It was a hell of a situation. He had bought wardrobes for women he barely cared for, but this woman would not permit it. *I am not that kind of woman.* Damnation.

She turned on her side and looked at him. "Surely you have had lovers whom you did not keep. I prefer this be like that. Did you buy wardrobes for the ladies in those affairs?"

It was his turn to withhold a reply.

"Oh," she said. "You have never had an affair like that before, have you? Just a lover, not a mistress."

He would regret this. He just knew it. "Such entanglements are full of complications."

"What kind of complications?"

"Unspoken ones. Expectations. Obligations. Sensitive topics."

"Such as the expectation that you marry, like you mentioned this afternoon?"

"In some situations, yes." Or the expectation that there is love.

"Surely that does not apply when the woman is an adult."

"If she is married, no. Widowed, no. Known to be worldly, no—"

"Worldly like your opera singers, you mean."

"Different from them. Just independent minded. More like you, actually."

"And yet you want to buy me a wardrobe. If I permit it, will that reassure you that I will not be complicated?"

If I let you make me a whore, will that make you happier? She did not say it. Perhaps she did not even think it. He could not deny the implications of the conversation, however.

"You were correct. I have not had lovers, only mistresses. However, I do not want to buy you a new wardrobe so that you can be considered the latter in my mind." He did not think that was why, at least. That he very much would like her to be his mistress was a thing apart, and had reasons other than this. He would like that because then he would know she was his, only his, for at least a while.

"I understand," she said. "Men like it when their women are lovely."

The conversation exasperated him. An innocent offer of a gift had become *complicated.* "That is not the reason either. I find you lovely all the time. I only want you to know that you are, and I am not sure that you do. If it takes pretty dresses to convince you, I want you to have them."

She went very still.

She sniffed. Hell. He reviewed what he had just said, to make sure he had not unintentionally either hurt or angered her.

"You aren't crying, are you?"

"A little." She sniffed again. "That was a sweet thing to say, Ives. I am sure no one has ever thought me lovely before."

"What nonsense. Of course they have, unless they are blind." He gathered her into his arms. Yes, complicated. She kissed him so tenderly that he decided he did not mind that so much.

She tucked against him and fell asleep. He decided to stay awhile longer, until he had to leave for discretion's sake.

L ance raised his musket. A shot broke the morning peace. In the distance a grouse dropped out of the sky. He handed the weapon to a nearby servant, who in turn handed him another one, loaded and ready.

Ives watched the brush for more birds to take flight.

Lance returned his own attention to the hunt. "Miss Belvoir received another letter today."

Gareth glanced over from where he also waited with musket at the ready.

"From the lawyer," Lance added.

Ives had not asked Padua about the letters. He had not forbidden her to communicate with friends in London, and if the letters came and went by way of Langley House, he doubted anyone would know where she was.

Mostly he did not ask her about them because if Lance thought some were from a lawyer, he was probably correct. That would be Notley, presumably. The last thing Ives wanted to do was talk about Hadrian

Belvoir with Padua. There would be world enough and time for that later, back in town.

He sometimes speculated on how that conversation would go. Not well, he suspected. Which was why he dallied here at Merrywood, while they pretended events in London occurred on another planet.

Five days they had remained here. Five days of barely suppressed desire and five nights of erotic pleasure. He would make it a month if he could. A year.

Several grouse took to flight. He and Gareth shot and brought two down.

"I also received a letter." Lance kept his gaze on the distance. "From Prinny."

That ended interest in the shooting. As a duke Lance naturally enjoyed royal favor, but that did not mean the prince regent wrote him letters. With the current dark cloud over Lance's head, the prince had kept his distance even more.

"The letter was to me, but it was about the two of you."

"How so?" Gareth asked.

"He writes to thank you both for your efforts on behalf of the lords last spring, now that the matter is finished. He asks that you call when he is in London, Gareth. He will receive you."

Gareth did not hide his astonishment well.

"As for you, Ives, he asked that I use my influence on you to ensure you accepted the Belvoir case. He depends on you to prosecute for the Crown, but has been told you might remove yourself."

"Damnation."

"Sidmouth's revenge. He tattled, and has cornered you neatly," Lance said. He turned his attention back to the field, and raised his musket to be at the ready.

Gareth cast a sidelong look at Ives. "Do not lose your temper. Neither Sidmouth nor the prince are here for its benefit."

"Lance is. Maybe I will just thrash him."

Lance looked over, surprised. "Me? I am innocent."

"Haven't you ever heard of killing the messenger?" Gareth asked.

"Kill some partridge instead. The tenants will be glad to have them for their dinner pots."

Ives managed to control his annoyance. "It is insulting for the prince to write to you about this. He is quick enough to write to me directly when he wants me to track down some woman blackmailing one of his uncles."

"He wrote to Aylesbury, not your brother Lance. He would have written to Percy if he were still alive. He is addressing the matter with the duke. The paterfamilias, so to speak." Lance aimed and shot again.

"Paterfamilias. Hell," Ives growled.

Lance handed him the spent musket and took the one resting in his arm. "Since you are not using it . . ." He turned and fired once more.

Gareth set down his weapon against the blind and crossed his arms thoughtfully. "Do you enjoy having the prince's favor, Ives? Is it important to you? He only wrote to Lance because whatever Sidmouth told him has him doubting your place in his circle."

Of course he enjoyed his position with the prince. Prinny was older, and had been a true friend of his father's. He took an avuncular tone when they talked. As for enjoying that favor—no man would treat it lightly. Even the son of a duke saw his position enhanced if he was known to have the prince regent's ear.

Gareth's gaze carried sympathy for the dilemma.

"It is a good thing I issued my edict," Lance said, while he waited for the muskets to be reloaded. "It will be easier for you to break with her now, if your better judgment failed you. Miss Belvoir, I mean."

"I know whom you mean."

"Still a ticklish subject, I see. Talk sense to him, Gareth. He long ago stopped listening to me."

He did not need anyone to talk sense to him. He had plenty of that himself. Rational, ruthless sense, and far more talk than the world needed. It was his stock-in-trade.

The Crown's friendship, or that of the daughter of a criminal. Only a fool would think there really was a choice.

Padua tucked the letter into her reticule, then put the reticule into her valise. She placed the valise out of sight. She buried the letter as if its invisibility meant she could ignore its message.

Mr. Notley had discovered her father's inheritance. He awaited her return to London before he pursued the information further.

She had to go back.

Donning the sapphire spencer that Eva had redone for her, she went down to the garden. The brothers had ridden off several hours ago, along with a retinue, to hunt. She and Eva had enjoyed some time alone, but now Eva rested and Padua had time for her own thoughts.

She paced through the garden, fascinated that time alone had become unusual. She had spent most of the last years alone. Even at Mrs. Ludlow's school, except for her conversations with Jennie, her own thoughts kept her company. Here, however, she had become part of a group. She never ate her meals alone now. Even when she read in the library, someone else often read there too.

Frequently that someone was Ives. She had spent more time with him in the last five days than she had probably spent with anyone since her mother died. She had not sought such a singular life, but she had not minded it too much. She even welcomed her isolation in the garden now, like it was an old friend.

Five days. Five nights. Different. Magical. The intimacy with Ives had transformed her. Moved her. The pleasure was the least of it. His warmth filled voids she did not even realize she had.

She was glad she had been self-indulgent and irresponsible. She did not regret allowing herself to know a woman's desire and its fulfillment. She worried, however, that she would not like the consequences.

She smiled at the memory of him on that blanket, wanting to negotiate but knowing he should not. *No.*

Not yet at least. He knew, as she did, that this affair would be brief.

She sat down on a bench at the far end of the garden, against a stone wall that held the sun's warmth. She closed her eyes and remembered the morning. He had almost been found in her chamber again. The night had been wild and erotic, almost savage, and he had fallen asleep while he held her. She could not bear to wake him or to leave the cocoon of care that wrapped her. She had feared even breathing might ruin how perfect it was.

She could tell the sun had lowered behind the house. The air carried a new chill. She opened her eyes, and began to rise.

Up on the terrace, she saw Ives. He still wore his riding coat and boots. He watched her, and his stance alone said he contemplated what he saw. Aware she noticed him, he descended from the terrace and strode toward her.

"The hunt was a success?" she asked when he sat beside her.

"Lance thinks so. His aim will feed half the tenants tonight. They will be glad for it. The harvest was poor this year."

"That was good of him. I thought it only sport for him."

"He does it as Aylesbury. He was not educated to the position, but he is growing accustomed to its responsibilities." He looked over at how she hugged herself for warmth. He unbuttoned his coat, shrugged it off, and tucked it around her shoulders.

"We will go in soon. Not yet, however."

He closed his eyes much as she had, only no sun remained to bask in. She did not need to see his expression to know he thought deeply about something. She just sensed that now. Even in the dark, while they lay together, she knew when his mind worked on something.

"Lance said you received a letter today," he said.

"The duke talks too much about matters not of his concern. This is the negative side of families, I think. Everyone minds everyone else's business."

Ives opened his eyes and looked at her.

"It was from Mr. Notley," she admitted. "He is sure he has information about my father's inheritance."

"That is good news."

"I hope so. If there is an income—just knowing there is—it changes everything." She pulled the coat a little closer. "Well, not everything, but it will make life easier."

"Then it is very good news." He took her hand. "Did he write about anything else?"

She wanted to lie. For a day or two more, she wanted to silence all the voices in London. "He writes that a trial date has been set. Were you not informed?"

"A letter came for me too. I did not open mine yet."

"You are smarter than I am about delaying the calls of duty."

"More experienced, that is all."

"When did you think to open it?"

"Perhaps tomorrow. Maybe the next day."

He appeared a little sad. That touched her. "I am sure I have lost my letter, Ives."

"How careless of you."

"Wasn't it? It is nowhere to be seen in my chamber. I doubt I will find it again for a day or so."

He stood and offered his hand. "Two days, then. We will not speak of it until then. Let us go back to the house."

Everyone knew. Padua could tell. Just what they all knew, she was not sure. The conversation at dinner sounded too merry and fast, however. The jokes made everyone laugh too much. Eva acted normal, but the gentlemen forced a gaiety.

Not for Ives's benefit, she realized. For hers. They all knew that the love affair to which they had given safe harbor would end soon. Ives in particular knew it, and he joined his brothers in surrounding her with light-hearted banter and wit. She joined in, so the nostalgia already creeping into her heart would not ruin what time she had left.

She could not control it that night, however. It colored every reaction. Ives made the pleasure long and slow, and sent her crashing over the edge three times before they joined in a poignant union that left her close to tears. He handled her as if he knew her mood, and shared it, and perhaps foresaw the longing to come.

"We will go riding tomorrow," he said when she walked toward the bed in the middle of the night. She had slipped away to the dressing room while he slept, but now he waited, propped on his elbow, for her return. "Eva found something you can wear, didn't she?"

"She did, but I will look foolish anyway, because I do not know how to ride."

"It is easy. You will like it. Think of it as another new experience."

"You do not think I have had enough of those?" She leaned against the bedpost and admired how he looked amidst the sheets with the warm illumination from the lamp etching his torso and arms. Just the sight of him stirred her. It always had, but those stirrings knew their own mind now, and held memories and a purpose, and she could not control them well.

"Not nearly enough." He shook his head like a man overwhelmed by duty. "There is so much to teach you—"

He caught himself, but her mind finished his little joke. *And so little time.*

He cocked his head and studied her standing there. Wicked lights entered his eyes. He threw back the sheet and walked over to her, giving her a good measuring from crown to feet.

"What?" she asked, looking down, wondering what was wrong.

"I am just calculating."

"That is an odd answer."

He stepped closer. So close he trapped her against the

bedpost. He frowned. "No, I don't think so. We were wrong."

"We were?"

"Not you and me *we*."

"Wrong about what?" The feel of him all along her body had her arousal jumping again.

"Whether, with your height, I could take you standing without having to lift you. It was a point of curiosity."

"Curiosity for *we*? Not you and me *we*, but another *we*?"

His expression fell, then he flashed a disarming smile. "The royal we. Me."

She eyed him skeptically. His attention returned to the problem on his mind.

"There is only one way to find out. Are you comfortable there, against that post? The wall might be better, in the event the experiment fails. Yes, I think so." He took her hand and led her over to the wall.

It did not take long for her to be ready. She always experienced the pleasure more intensely when she remained upright. Raw physical sensations puddled low, incited by his penetrating kisses and wicked hands. He slid inside her, high and deep. She thought he would lift her to her toes before he stopped. The fullness made her gasp.

She felt him differently. He pressed new places, inside and out. Exciting ones. He moved once, twice, then paused. "It is cheating, but—" He lifted her left leg by the knee and held it hooked over his hip. He moved again. "Better. Perfect."

She would have agreed, if she could speak, but she could not stop gasping with amazement. He grunted each time he pressed up into her, each sound an affirmation of pleasure. It was the noisiest joining they had ever shared.

He did lift her at the end, so her legs circled him and his final thrusts slammed her against the wall. Carrying her like that, he staggered to the bed, where they collapsed.

CHAPTER 16

I ves left the house through the terrace doors. He wanted to talk to the grooms about the horse Eva would ride. On exiting, he saw Lance standing near the steps, surveying his domain.

"Do you never sleep?" Lance asked without turning around.

Ives stopped walking. "Often and well. Thank you for your concern."

"I suppose it is good someone does. I certainly did not last night." He turned a pursed smile on Ives. "Someone kept slamming around one of the chambers above me, groaning from whatever exertions occupied him."

"How peculiar. Perhaps you were dreaming."

"It sounded like you."

"My chambers are not above yours."

"Miss Belvoir's are, in part. Her bedchamber is above part of my dressing room."

"I doubt she groans like a man, no matter what her exertions."

"You might, however."

"How could it be me? My chambers are across the way. If you are implying that I was in her chambers, that is not possible. There is an edict abroad in the land. Remember?"

Lance raised an eyebrow. Ives smiled.

"I will be riding out after dinner tonight," Lance said. "Do not ask where I am going. Do not presume to lecture me on appropriate behavior. This infernal abstinence is bad enough, but to have to endure it while I listen to you pummel your lover into oblivion is asking too much."

The pummeling had been fine enough that Ives experienced a spot of chagrin. "I do not think I will be noticing what anyone does tonight, Lance. If you sleep so lightly these days, a long ride might do you good."

Ives continued on to the stables and had the chestnut mare brought out. All of the horses were spirited, but the head groom assured him that this one was not skittish or impulsive. "She'll take an easy hand, sir. A lady should like her."

"Bring them around in half an hour. Saddle the mare yourself, so I am sure there are no mishaps."

Upon returning to the house, Ives went up to his chambers. He strode to the writing desk, opened a drawer, and removed a letter.

He looked down on it. It bore the seal of the high chancellor. He lifted a knife and sliced through it.

Only one word of the missive surprised him. As expected, he was being appointed prosecutor for the Crown in the case of Hadrian Belvoir. The Crown did not ask or request such things. That would imply one could decline one's king, or would want to.

The rest of it did not read quite as he had thought it would. The charges, it explained, were counterfeiting and *sedition*. He wondered if any evidence of that had been dug up, or if he was expected to argue with nothing more than innuendo and supposition in his pocket.

He dropped the letter back in the drawer and slammed it shut.

"I still think I am going to fall off." Padua pouted with worry as her horse bore her over the field, slowly. Very slowly.

"You are doing fine. Try not to sit so stiffly. Good posture is important, but adapting to the horse's gait will feel natural, and give you more confidence."

She did not appear convinced. With effort she relaxed ever so slightly.

"If you hate it, we can go back," Ives said, taking pity on her.

"No, no. I do not hate it as such. You want to give me this experience, so I should be accommodating. I am only a little afraid, but it gets better with each step."

"I am forever grateful for how accommodating you

are, even when you are a little afraid. Have I ever told
you that?"

She glanced over, understood his reference, and
blushed. "It is not as if I suffered."

She did not suffer, because she allowed herself to
be passionate. He remembered the list he had written
about the ideal mistress.

Loyal
Good-humored
Intelligent
Uninhibited
Passionate
Accommodating

Padua was all of those things, and surpassed most
women in some of them. She would never agree to be
his mistress, but the list applied to any lover, no matter
what her status. Unfortunately, the most important quality, the one on which there could be no compromise, loyalty, promised to be the biggest problem. Not because
she lacked loyalty, but because she excelled there too.

He paced along, keeping an eye on her and the horse,
noticing how she slowly became accustomed to it. By
the time they crossed the field, she looked to be almost
enjoying herself. He picked up the pace just a little, and
she did not mind.

She took interest in the farms, and waved when they
passed a family working outside their cottage. The man
and woman stopped and stared.

"They appear surprised," she said.

"It has been some years since they saw a woman ride the estate. Probably not since my mother gave it up."

She instinctively looked down at her blue riding habit. Another of Eva's miracles, it had been redone from one of his mother's. The long train of riding habits had allowed a refitting.

"They do not recognize it," he said.

"The woman does, I promise you." She laughed. "Did your mother have dark hair? If so, word might spread that her ghost was seen."

"Her hair was dark, and her eyes, too, and, I suspect, her moods and perhaps her heart. When she passed, I realized how little I knew her."

"That is sad."

It was, he supposed. She had favored Percy, as most mothers would their firstborn. He and Lance had seen an alliance when perhaps it was just a mother being a mother. "I am not only ignorant about her, but about my parents' marriage. Gareth is evidence that it was not happy, but I do not know if she drove my father away, or if he fled, or if the fault was his."

"Perhaps that is why none of you married. All of those ambiguities would not give you much faith in it."

What an odd thing to say. They had not married because . . . He smiled to himself. Because none of them wanted to. Gareth had just married, but then he had the least to lose, and his character had been formed differently. He did not run at the front of the herd. He did not run with the herd at all. It would be like him to decide that, evidence to the contrary aside, marriage would be a good idea if the woman were Eva.

They approached the high hill from a different direction. They were halfway up before Padua realized where they were. "Thank you for bringing me back here, so I can see it again."

He insisted they get down once they reached the top. They stood on the crest. Padua's eyes glittered while she feasted on the vista.

"I brought you here for a reason, Padua."

"I do not think this dress, with all this skirt, is manageable for that."

He laughed and took her hand. "When we were here the last time, I raised a subject that I want to talk about again. I would like us to marry."

Nothing changed in her expression. She continued to look out over the farms. Her half smile did not alter. She remained at peace. Perhaps, just perhaps, a few lights went out in her eyes.

"You want to do the right thing," she said. "That is decent of you."

"On such matters I can be a scoundrel with the best of them. I am not proposing out of obligation. I think we suit each other very well."

She looked at him. A million stars sparkled now, because there were tears in her eyes. "We do, don't we? If this were truly another world—what a scandal you would cause, if you married me. Could you survive it through your birth alone? To marry the daughter of a criminal, a man who might be hanged? I doubt it. I think your brothers doubt it. They know you cannot have me. It is in Gareth's eyes when he looks at me. The apology for what will come."

"I do not care about any of that, damn it."

"You *will* care. To have been in the center, then pushed to the edges—I think it is easier to have lived as I have, on the edges from the start. And when do you think to make this marriage? Before you serve as prosecutor, or after he is gone?"

He pulled her into his arms. "Never. I have decided I will not do it."

She gazed up at him in shock. Her eyes blazed. "But you must."

"The hell I must. I will not be responsible for giving you that pain."

She twisted and squirmed out of his hold. She stepped back, and faced him, straight and tall. "Yet I will know the pain anyway. Your refusing to prosecute spares me nothing, and may make it worse than it has to be."

"It is perverse to suggest that after what we have shared, I go into court against your father, Padua. It is out of the question now. I will remove myself."

"If you don't, who will?" She strode to him and stuck her face up at his. "Some fool who will only think he has won if the accused swings? A man more interested in the coin he earns than in justice? My father may be guilty of playing a minor role in a big crime, but there are those who will make it sound as if he planned it all and grew rich in the process, and worse."

His temper spiked. He walked away from her, so he

might leash it. "After this week, for me to prosecute would be dishonorable. I could never be effective. I must remove myself. Hell, I knew I had to before we even left London."

"You did?" It was more an accusation than a question.

"Of course. A man cannot do to a woman what I did to you at Langley House, then claim impartiality regarding her kinsmen. Did you really think I would have you like this, then pretend I represented the Crown when your father was tried?"

Her expression cracked. Shattered. She bit her lower lip. She hugged herself, and stomped her foot in an effort to contain her emotion. "But you must. You must." She stomped her foot again. Her face twisted in anguish. "I have made such a muddle of it. I am an idiot."

His worst misgivings resurrected from where he had buried them. They spread all through him like a bad chill. He almost choked on the disappointment they bred. "Padua, in my house that first night, you were tempted to try to bribe me. It was in your eyes. Is that what you have been trying to do? Convince me to do other than my best in court?"

She just looked at him, her eyes filming all the more.

"I could not blame you for it," he said. "You are nothing if not brilliant. And loyal."

She shook her head. "Please do not think that. Please do not. I did not open my door to you because of any of this. If I had known doing so would mean you walked away completely, however—your best is honest and just, and others' might not be." She turned away and pressed the palms of her hands against her eyes.

He went up behind her and wrapped his arms around her. Her tears convulsed her, then started to ebb. When she had collected herself, she leaned against him and held his arms against her body.

"Did you read your letter?" she asked.

"Yes."

"But you will refuse. Is that normally done?"

"No."

"You cannot help him at all, then, can you? After refusing to prosecute, to defend would be a slap in the face to whoever wrote that letter."

The high chancellor was the least of it. She did not need to know that, however.

He helped her onto her horse, then mounted his own. They headed back to the house. She remained thoughtful.

"Ives, you spoke of pretending to represent the Crown. Is that who the letter was from? The king's men, or the regent?"

There were moments when Padua's quick mind proved inconvenient. "The prince regent first mentioned it to me, over a month ago."

She stopped her horse, closed her eyes as if absorbing a blow, then opened them and moved on. "You would have been wiser to pursue one of those mistresses, Ives. A new wardrobe and a few jewels would be nothing compared to what I am going to cost you, I fear."

* * *

As with their journey to Merrywood, Ives did not travel inside the carriage with Padua during their return to London. They had shared their parting kiss in the first light of dawn before leaving the magic behind. She did not mind. It would be too sad to sit with him for days, trying to pretend her heart was not breaking.

He did climb in after her when they rolled away from the last coaching inn. "I have told the coachman to bring you to Langley House," he said. "I will leave you after we pass the last tollgate."

"I do not need to go to Langley House again. I should not."

"You will, for tonight at least. Tomorrow I will join you and help you find a place to live. You have the money I found in the books, so letting an apartment should not be a problem."

She almost reminded him that she had promised not to spend that money. She worried that he saw giving her that money as one more compromise in a whole line of them.

After the last tollgate, the carriage stopped. He grabbed the door latch, ready to hop out. He stopped and looked at her, then took her face in his hands and kissed her deeply.

Then he was gone.

She allowed the carriage to bring her to Langley House. She even stayed there that night. The next morning, however, she did not wait for Ives to call on her.

She packed her valise, asked for a hired carriage, and set off.

She had no appointment, but Mr. Notley received her. She sat across from him in his office, as she had before, with his clerk to the side jotting notes.

Mr. Notley smiled, pleased with himself. "I have been very clever regarding this inheritance, if I do say so myself. It took some doing."

"I am grateful."

Notley leaned back in his chair, his fingers forming one of the steeples he created when he thought. "I had to convince the gaoler to trick your father into giving his place of birth. You do not want to know how he did that. It will only distress you. Once I knew the parish in Essex from which he hailed, I sent a clerk down to investigate his family back two generations. We mapped the family tree, then began looking for wills under those names. And, dear lady, we found it."

He leaned forward. "Did you know that your father's name is actually John Hadrian Belvoir? Had we not learned that at the parish, all would have been for naught, since in this will he is called John H. Belvoir. No wonder it took the lawyers forever to track him down."

"Perhaps Papa thought Hadrian sounded more scholarly than plain old John. He can be vain that way."

"John Belvoir inherited a property as you hoped. Right here in London. A house."

"If he owns a house here, why did he let rooms?"

"I assume he lets out the house. He would not need all that space himself."

I could have lived there, too, however. She pushed the spike of resentment aside. "Have you seen this house?"

"I have not. I was not authorized to visit, and assess it. I would have no standing to enter."

"I have seen it," his clerk said.

Notley turned to him. "Have you now?"

"I walked past it. I was curious. It is a handsome house, Miss Belvoir. Larger than most, on a good street."

The clerk's report heartened her. "May I have the address, please."

The clerk wrote it down and brought over the paper. She stuffed it in her reticule.

"Now," Mr. Notley said, "I am afraid I have other news that is not so happy. As I wrote, the trial date has indeed been set. I was able to see the full charges, and a new one has been added."

She dreaded hearing more, but of course she must. "What new one is that?"

Notley's lips folded in on themselves. "Sedition. That means—"

"I know what it means."

"Do you? It is not treason, as such, for example. With the counterfeiting, it could have been that bad. So this is bad news that could have been worse."

"I will remember to think of it in that light. Has he spoken to you now, with such a charge hanging over him?"

Notley shook his head. "I went and stood outside that cell for an hour, and he ignored me the entire time."

"Thank you for trying, and for such diligence regarding the inheritance. I hope that I can call on you if he can be convinced to cooperate."

"Absolutely, Miss Belvoir." They both stood. Notley left the office. The clerk opened his account book and told her what was owed.

"What do you mean, she is gone?" Ives made the demand of the footman who opened the door, after being told Miss Belvoir had departed the premises.

"She left early this morning, sir. Valise in hand."

Ives strode back out of the house and swung onto his horse. Had he not told Padua that he would come by and help her make arrangements? She had no experience with estate agents and contracts. She was only doing this because she wanted to prove she did not need him to take care of her.

She did not want to marry? Fine. She did not want to be his mistress? Accepted. She assumed returning to London made an affair too complicated, too dangerous? Dangerous for him, not her, that is? He would disabuse her of that eventually, but for now, she was homeless and adrift and the least he could do was help her get settled. The least she could do was allow him that.

He headed into the City, to see if she had called on that lawyer. Notley had written he had news, and she would want to hear it.

"Miss Belvoir was here, sir," the clerk said. "She left a good hour ago."

"Where did she go? Do you know?"

The clerk fingered his pen nervously. "Perhaps if you waited until Mr. Notley returned—"

"I do not have the time for that. If you know where she went, tell me and spare us both a long argument that, I assure you, I intend to win."

The clerk heard the threat, or saw it. He grabbed a scrap of paper and jotted. "She most likely went to this house, sir. She was very excited to learn her father owned it. An inheritance, it was."

Ives read the address. Belvoir owned *this house*? He almost did grab the clerk by the neck then. "Mr. Notley allowed her to go here on her own? Is he familiar with this property?"

The clerk glanced left and right, as if seeking an escape route. "He is not. I saw it, however."

"You did not go in, did you?"

"I only walked by, so I could be useful. I reported it was a fine, big house."

"So *you* sent her there?"

The clerk squirmed. "Not sent as such, sir. That was her own decision. If she went at all. She did not say she was going today, or any day, now that I think about it." He smiled weakly.

Oh, she had gone there. Ives did not doubt it. On learning her father was a man of property, she would have to go see the house. Anyone would.

He left the clerk and returned to the street. He aimed his horse back west.

CHAPTER 17

There was nothing else for it. She had to carry the valise with her to the door. She hoped the family that lived here did not think she intended to move in and displace them.

She paused to admire the neatly dressed buff stones that formed the four-storey façade on Silver Street. Impressed, she used the fine brass knocker someone had recently installed. A tall African man in livery opened the door. He looked at her, frowning beneath the edge of his white wig. He boldly eyed her from head to toe.

She examined him too. Liveried servants decked out in blue velvet and pumps seemed excessive for this street. The house was large, that was true, but it was hardly in a fashionable area.

"I am Padua Belvoir, Hadrian Belvoir's daughter. Your employer may know him as John Belvoir. He lets this house. I am hoping the family would not mind if I asked them a few questions. My father is indisposed, you see, and—"

A white glove rose, stopping her. The man stood aside so she could enter. He carried over a salver. She opened her reticule and pretended to search it.

"I am sorry. I left my calling cards at home. How careless of me," she said. "Just tell them it is the land-lord's daughter."

Unimpressed, the servant walked away.

Padua sat on a leather bench in the reception hall. There were several along the walls. She thought it a rather masculine way to decorate an entry.

The servant returned. His white glove beckoned. She followed him.

He took her to a chamber set up like an office, with desk and chairs and bookcases. She guessed it was the butler's pantry. She hoped the servant had not fobbed her off on the staff. She really wanted to speak to the tenants.

She sat in the chair the glove indicated. He left her alone. The house seemed very quiet for midday. Perhaps the family was not in residence.

She waited a good while. Finally the door opened. A woman walked in, wearing a lovely morning dress of gray wool with black embroidery. The color complemented her red hair. Padua judged her to be around fifty years in age. Not the housekeeper, if she wore dresses like that.

"Miss Belvoir, I am Mrs. Lavender. I believe I can help you, if anyone can. Forgive me for the delay. I had not dressed yet."

"I apologize for the intrusion. It is kind of you to see me."

Mrs. Lavender sat in a chair near Padua's. "You told Hector your father is indisposed. He is not ill, I hope."

"No, not ill as such. Just having a spell. I confess I came here partly out of curiosity. I did not know my father owned London property." She looked up at the ceiling. "It is very large."

"We find it comfortable. The rent is reasonable, but fair, if you are concerned someone has taken advantage of Mr. Belvoir. He is, I know, not the sort to inspire confidence in his business sense."

"You have met him, then? I thought perhaps it had been let through an agent."

"We were here when he inherited. We have been here a good long while, you see."

"I suppose any children are grown, then."

Mrs. Lavender just looked at her and smiled.

"Would it be possible to see the house? I know it is asking a lot, but—"

"But it may be yours soon, so you are curious."

"Yes. Very curious."

Mrs. Lavender narrowed her eyes. Her hesitation was obvious.

"Not every chamber," Padua said. "I do not want to interfere with your family's day."

"I will show you every inch if you want. However, this is not a family's home, Miss Belvoir. Not in the normal sense of a family. Young ladies live here."

"Is it a school?"

"Not in the normal sense that word is used, no."

Padua's head turned blank. Mrs. Lavender watched her closely.

"I don't understand."

"Of course you don't. Miss Belvoir, this is a place of business. My place of business. The young ladies provide services for which gentlemen—"

"Oh." Padua felt her face heating. "You mean, this is a—a—"

"Yes."

"My father owns a—a—"

"He only owns the property. The 'a—a—' is mine. He also inherited a minority partnership, of which he had no interest. He receives the rents and his share of the profits, and ignores us."

Padua's head felt as if someone had doused it with cold water. The shock just grew and grew.

"When it went to him as a legacy, we were already here. He did not facilitate the opening by letting it to us. Our lease is a long one. He could not remove us even if he wanted to."

"Of course he could. He need only have asked the magistrate to close the business."

"I assure you the magistrate already knows all about

this house. Everyone does. I opened twenty-five years ago. Mrs. Lavender's is a fixture in London, well respected, and our visitors include gentlemen from the best families. Many a future peer has had his first appointment with Venus here. Their fathers send them."

She was an idiot. An unsophisticated, ignorant, trusting child. No wonder Papa had never told her much about the inheritance. No wonder he did not like having her in London. She might stumble upon the discovery that he was a partner *in a brothel*.

"I would still like to see the property, if you do not mind." Someday it would be hers, and it would not remain what it was now. Perhaps she would have a school here, if the house were as big as it appeared. Maybe she would live here herself.

"If you wish. I cannot show you most of the bedchambers. The young ladies are sleeping."

Of course they were. Padua followed Mrs. Lavender out of the office.

If she had seen the drawing room upon first entering, she might have guessed the business conducted here. It contained a lot of big chairs and several chaise longues. A sidebar held a good number of decanters. A riot of feminine patterns and colors combined to create a flamboyant and exuberant decadence. The library beyond it was more of the same. She wondered if any of the young women ever used the books, or if they had come with the house and had never been moved since then.

By the time she had peeked into all the chambers on

the first two levels, she could tell which were used to entertain guests and which served as true living spaces. The dining room appeared simple and functional, the back morning room contained no fur rugs, and the garden would be fitting for a prosperous merchant family.

Mrs. Lavender led the way to the third storey. "We have ten small chambers up here. One is vacant. A girl got married two weeks ago. That rarely happens. She was very popular, and profits will be down this month until I replace her."

The one vacant chamber was not large. Padua suspected larger ones had been broken up. Other than a bed and washstand, it contained nothing, not even a writing desk.

They went up one more flight of stairs. "This area is forbidden to our guests. I have my chamber up here, and the servants sleep here as well. Lest you think I lure innocents to their doom by first hiring them as servants, I want you to know that I am very strict that no servant ever moves downstairs, even if she wants to. They come and go by these stairs outside, and never set foot in the drawing room after five o'clock in the evening."

"That is commendable."

"I do not expect you to approve, or to understand, Miss Belvoir. I long ago ceased attempting to justify myself to women like you."

"Did you attempt with my father? After all, he could have closed this place down, even if the magistrate turns a blind eye."

"It took your father two years to realize what occurred here. I told him I ran an informal inn for women. We all need to lay our heads on a hired bed sometimes, do we not? If not for an unfortunate episode regarding one of the girls and a boy who sought to protect her from herself, your father might have remained ignorant forever."

Padua could imagine that being true. Even if he saw that drawing room, half his mind would be on some arcane calculation, and he might well have only thought it oddly furnished.

Padua paced down the narrow corridor flanked by servants' chambers. She had overcome her shock, but in its place an ugly humor had taken hold. Her view of herself, of her father, of her world had been so wrong. Ironically so. She thought she was the daughter of scholars. Instead she was the daughter of a whoremonger.

"How much?" she asked. "How much do you send him?"

"The rent is—"

"Not the rent. The rest of it. How much?"

Mrs. Lavender's lids lowered. "His fair share."

Padua looked her straight in the eyes.

"Every quarter he received thirty pounds."

"I will want to see the accounts that show that is his fair share," Padua said, continuing down the hall.

"Excuse me? Your father—"

"My father cannot see to his affairs right now, so I will be doing it. I am far more practical than he. He would never question his fair share, but I am the sort who likes to see proof. There is no insult in the request."

At the far end of the corridor, a door stood open. A few pieces of furniture occupied it.

"There are six servants and seven chambers," Mrs. Lavender explained.

"And these are the stairs you mentioned." Padua opened a door. It gave out to a small wooden terrace, and long flights of wooden stairs leading down to the garden.

Mrs. Lavender's head poked out beside hers. "Fifteen years ago there was a small fire. It frightened me enough that I paid for these myself. As I said, they are useful in allowing the servants to avoid the trade, or the eyes of the gentlemen."

Padua looked at the stairs, then the empty chamber. "Where do the male servants sleep?"

Mrs. Lavender pointed to an outbuilding that ran along the side of the garden. "Hector and the groom sleep there, in chambers above the carriage room and stable."

"It is a big stable."

"It was not always one. Before my time it was used for some kind of business. Smithing or ironworking. I had most of it cleaned out and put my carriage and horses there."

Padua entered the empty chamber. She looked around. "For a short while, your original description of this house will be partly true. As it happens, I need a place to lay my head until I settle myself. Unless you object with good cause, I will use this chamber."

Mrs. Lavender's eyes widened. "You cannot be serious. It will not be appropriate."

"What is inappropriate about it? My father owns part of a brothel. Who am I to have her nose in the air about using such accommodations? I will pay for a new mattress for this bed, if you will arrange for one to be brought. I will use these stairs, and avoid interfering with your trade. And while I am here, I will study the lease and those accounts."

"Your father did not interfere with my business. He went his own way. That was our understanding of how it would be."

"I will not interfere, either, if all is in order."

Mrs. Lavender's mouth flapped, but no more objections emerged. She shook her head in resignation and astonishment. "You are a strange duck. We both know where you got that, don't we?"

Indeed they did. The difference, as Padua saw it, was the strange daughter would not be ripe for fleecing the way the strange father probably had been. If this was the family business, so be it, until that lease ran out.

"If Hector would bring up the valise I left in the reception hall, I will begin to get settled."

Mrs. Lavender left her. Padua opened the window to air out the chamber, then turned her mind to deciding what furniture to keep and what to move out.

I ves grew impatient. The footman, Hector, had put him in Mrs. Lavender's office at least a half hour ago. He checked his pocket watch. No, only ten minutes had passed. Ten frustrating minutes. Hector refused to answer any questions, even the most basic one: Did a very tall Miss Belvoir call at this house this morning? If she had not, every minute he sat here was another minute wasted.

He looked around the office. It was a little cramped, deliberately so. Mrs. Lavender could have arranged the desk differently to make more room. Placed like this in the center of a small chamber, it effectively confined visitors to a slice of floor between it and the door. The forced intimacy and close quarters, the cat sleeping on the hearth and the wool throw waiting in a basket, gave the office a cozy quality.

The door finally opened. Mrs. Lavender walked in. Her mouth fell open in surprise when she saw him. Then she smiled. "Hector said only that a gentleman awaited me. He did not say it was you."

She patted him on the head, like he were a boy, then went to her desk.

"It has been so very long," Mrs. Lavender said. "You are as handsome a devil as ever. Did your family ever come around to your choice of life path? I see your name in the papers sometimes."

"My late brother, never, I am happy to say."

She pursed her lips. "I am sorry for your loss."

"Do not be. We muddled through, splendidly. We recovered from the shock so quickly that some found it heartless."

"He came here, a few months before his passing. I reminded him he was not welcomed. He created a scene.

Hector almost had to throw him out. Thank goodness not. All the friends in the world will not help if a duke speaks against a business, even one like this. I reminded him there were houses better suited to his preferences." Her eyes twinkled. "I told him to ask his brothers if he had forgotten where those houses could be found."

Mrs. Lavender's house specialized in polite, romantic illusions for men who did not seek too much variation in their erotic experiences. As a young man, Ives had visited, like most of his friends. Some of them still did, he expected. Others had graduated to the more exotic tastes that Mrs. Lavender now alluded to.

"Of course, some of my more sophisticated gentlemen return now and then. I find that heartbreaks bring them here, or other disappointments. Is that why you have come? It is early, but I am sure one of the girls—"

"I am here about something else. Not one of your young ladies, but another woman. Did a Miss Belvoir visit today?"

Mrs. Lavender lowered her chin and looked up at him like a vexed mother. "She did. Nothing but trouble that one will be."

"So it is true that her father owns this house."

"It and a quarter of the business was left to him by my late partner. I had come to think no relatives would be found. It was to be all mine in that event."

"A disappointment, I am sure."

"Belvoir kept out of the way, at least. I think it embarrassed him, but not so much that he would sell to me, or refuse the filthy money. Now his daughter is sounding like she will be very much in the way. She has already questioned my accounting. Can you believe it?"

"What gall."

"I'll say so. If I am not careful, she will be trying to change things to her liking. She has that look to her. Noting all the furniture and such, she was, when I showed her about the place."

Ives pictured Padua facing off against the formidable Mrs. Lavender. The latter normally worried about men overstepping the lines, and had Hector available when that happened. He doubted she ever tangled with the likes of Padua.

"Do you know where she went when she left here?"

"Left here? She hasn't left. She is up above right now." She leaned forward, her eyes furious. "She thinks to move in. Up with the servants."

"Move in? *Here?*" Surely Mrs. Lavender had misunderstood.

"*Here.* If she is a friend of yours, I trust you will explain to her how that *will not do.*"

He stood, and shook off his astonishment. "Up with the servants, you say."

"Turn left on the top landing, then the last door on the right at the end."

He strode off and mounted the stairs with firm purpose. No doubt learning the use of this house had shocked Padua and she was not herself. Disillusionment with her father had led her into some peculiar decisions. He would indeed explain to her how it would not do, although by now she had probably realized that all on her own.

The door at the end on the right was closed. He heard her moving around inside. Refusing to treat the chamber as her home, he opened the door and let it swing wide. Padua, in the process of pushing a washstand along the wall, did not hear him.

Eyes narrowed, face taut, she shoved the stand along the boards. Her valise sat on the bed. She had removed her pelisse in order to free her arms for her labor.

"Padua."

His voice made her freeze. She collected herself, her gaze on the washstand. Then she looked at him. A hard smile formed. She stepped into the center of the chamber and gestured widely. "What do you think? It is better than my chamber at Mrs. Ludlow's. With a new mattress and some decent lamps, it will be comfortable and more than adequate."

"You are not going to do this."

"Oh, I am. I am going to live here for free, and make sure that woman pays as she should, and save the money, and in six months I daresay I will have what I need to go abroad. In the meantime this will be my private *studiolo*, where I will read and study and prepare."

"And your father?"

"You mean John Hadrian Belvoir? The partner in a brothel? If by some luck he is acquitted, he can return to his chambers on Wigmore Street. He prefers it there."

She sounded bitter and angry. He could not blame

her. She had lived her life with her father on a pedestal, only to discover his feet were covered in mud.

"His judgment is rather abstracted, Padua. When presented with this property and its lease and the steady income, he probably could not even imagine how to fix it to be less notorious."

"*No.* No more. I am finished making excuses for him. I am done thinking of him as an addled but brilliant scholar, when in fact he is a very, very shrewd whoremonger." The outburst had her eyes flaming. "It will come to me eventually, I assume. When it does, I will decide whether to find a more respectable use for it. Perhaps I will not. Maybe by then I will have grown accustomed to the steady income too. Now, please help me with this washstand."

He lent his strength to it and got it to the spot she wanted.

"A bookcase. I need one over here. The wardrobe will do as is." She opened her valise, and took out a garment to put away.

He went over and stopped her. He placed his hand in the valise, on top of hers. "You will not do this. You will regret it for certain."

"Who will know? I am no one, Ives. It is perfect. I will use a mail drop, not this address, and I will come and go through the garden. Look, there is a fire stairs right out here." She took him to the corridor, and opened a door. "The servants who work here do so with the world in ignorance, and are not tainted. I will not even be visiting the lower floors."

"No. I will not allow it."

She crossed her arms. "It is not for you to allow or not, Ives."

"You are not thinking clearly. You will see that in a day or so, but in the meantime you must not spend one more hour under this roof."

Her eyes narrowed on him. "Do you think I will become corrupted by Mrs. Lavender?"

"No, of course not. You would not— She would not—"

"She would not? You know her that well, to say she would not?"

Damnation.

She grinned.

He did not like being the source of her amusement. He took a deep breath. "When I was younger, much younger—"

"You do not have to explain to *me*. I expect men need to practice a bit before they pursue opera singers."

That was a low blow. He would not engage in this ridiculous argument any longer. "You will come with me now, Padua. We will find you a chamber in a respectable house."

"A family's house, you mean. Or a spinster's. It will still be a chamber up with the servants, I suspect. I prefer this one. I would not like the women in those other houses watching me, judging me. It would be like being at Mrs. Ludlow's again."

She turned and pulled a dress out of her valise, to emphasize her decision. "If you are too scandalized by my address, our friendship can end. Or, if you prefer it not, we can meet sometimes in the park." She looked over her shoulder at him. "Of course, you can come up those stairs out there, as surely as I can go down them, if you like."

He had been ready to drag her out, but that invitation took the wind out of his resolve. He hardened at once, like the slave to pleasure he had become. The possibilities lured him. She was correct, he could come up those stairs, unseen. The woman of the house would hardly object if she knew, considering the trade down below. Should anyone else become aware, they lived under a roof where discretion ruled. Only putting Padua in her own home would be better, and she had rejected that even before he offered it.

She had found the perfect solution, should they want to continue the affair. He certainly did, even if it had become complicated and even dangerous.

Temptation worked its wiles on him. His body would tolerate only one choice. He wavered badly.

She turned and waited, lips parted, ready to take him into her arms right now. One step, that was all. One smile—

"Absolutely not, Padua. You may choose to live above a brothel, but I will not be joining you here." He turned away. "Please come out on these stairs, where the air is fresh. I have something to ask you. To tell you."

His body gave him hell as he walked out that door. He waited on the little wooden terrace, wondering if she would follow. Eventually she did.

"Besides news of this property, did Notley speak of anything else?" he asked.

"If you mean the charge of sedition, yes." She speared him with a direct glare. "You knew at Merrywood, didn't you?"

"I did. It was in the letter I received."

He waited for her to upbraid him for not sharing that. Instead she sighed heavily. "A few days ago, I would have insisted that was so wrong as to be comical," she said. "Now I do not have confidence that I know him at all."

"They may not have much, or anything useful. I will try to find out."

"It does not take much to spin a good story."

They were back to her concerns that the prosecutor would be more aggressive than honest. Ives wished he could reassure her, but he could not.

She moved to him, and stretched up to kiss him. "Not only a criminal, but a whoremonger and perhaps a man involved in a seditious plot. You became entangled with the daughter of a man sure to make the newspapers happy."

"You are not him."

"No one will remember that once this becomes the talk of the town. I had a moment of weakness inside, when I tried to tempt you. A desperate, hopeful moment. I think perhaps you should leave us to our own devices, and look for a mistress to entertain you in the future."

He found it hard to believe she had said that. "No."

"I love how you say that. No. It is as if you assume the world will conform to your preferences. Your birth and position give you that confidence. If you want to preserve the privileges both bestow, you will agree I am correct."

"Only this is not my preference. I do not want this."

She laid her hand against his face. Her eyes sparkled up into his. "I *do* want it. We both knew how it would be." She kissed him again, then went into the house.

He stood there a moment. Then he walked down the stairs. Only at the bottom did he accept what had just happened.

Padua Belvoir had thrown him over, totally and completely.

Padua returned to the bedchamber. She stood in the middle, hands on her hips, enumerating the things she would do to make a home here. Yes, a bookcase, good sized, right over there. A decent set of bedclothes, too, so it did not remind her of Mrs. Ludlow's too much. She would tell Hector to bring someone in to check the fireplace. She did not want the room full of soot the first time—

She ran to the door to the stairs and looked out. Ives was just leaving by the garden portal. Her heart knew relief that he had heard her words, and it was over. It also began breaking.

She hurried back to the chamber and closed the door before her effort to hold in the tears failed. As soon as the latch clicked, the flood started. The pain inside built until she thought it would suffocate her. She gasped for air as she wept, doubled over. Her strength left her and she slid down until she sat on the floor, sobbing into her hands, trying to smother the sound.

CHAPTER 18

I ves firmly believed that when a lover said it was over,
it was over. Not for him the humiliation of cajoling
and begging. Not only would that be undignified but it
would also be hopeless. His experience had been that
women know their own minds very clearly on the
question of whom they wanted to be naked with.

Rarely had he been thrown over, but it had happened.
He knew what to do. First, a night of drinking with
friends—male friends—to balance out too much time
spent in feminine company. Second, renewed energy to
matters of the mind—his cases, reading, and intellectual pursuits. Third, the very prescription Padua had
given him—find a mistress.

The steps did not have to be taken in order, or even
one at a time. And so it was that two nights later, he

found himself deep in his cups at Damian's gaming hall, commiserating with Belleterre about the complications women brought to one's life.

Belleterre had his own problems, far more colorful than Ives's. A well-known courtesan had pursued him last season, finally running him to ground at the very end of the festivities. She had then discarded discretion and all sense, and fallen in love. All summer long high drama built, until even Belleterre's wife became aware of the affair. Not a woman to suffer whores gladly, she had four days ago confronted him and issued her terms. The mistress, or her. He had dutifully broken with his paramour, who now went around town announcing she would kill herself due to a broken heart.

"She has broken all the rules," Belleterre complained. "Miranda has never minded before, when it was kept quiet. This might as well have been a theater show listed in the papers. Now should anything happen to Charlene, it is my fault. Don't tell me I won't be blamed. I am sure to be, and all I did was take a bite out of an apple that fell onto my head."

"It will pass. She won't kill herself. You aren't *that* fascinating, and you sure as hell are not irreplaceable. None of us are."

"Hell of a thing anyway. It is all backward." Belleterre gulped more of the whiskey they shared.

"I can tell you about backward, but—" He pantomimed at locking his lips.

"Have you been busy? A secret affair? Who is she? Do I know her?"

Ives shook his head and locked his lips again. "The important thing is we must get back on the horses again. And ride."

Belleterre cackled into his glass. Ives realized that had sounded more bawdy than he intended, but laughed too.

"You should call on Mrs. Dantoine. My situation with Charlene need not stop you. Mrs. Dantoine was most interested in you, as I said. She is sweet. If it did not mean sailing too close to the rocks already battering my ship, I would set my course there myself."

Ives idly wondered if Mrs. Dantoine would fit any of the qualities on that list he had made. Not that the list existed anymore. He had burned it last night when it fell out of the book he was moving. Why have such a list if the woman who fit every adjective did not want you?

"What ho, are you going to drink all of that yourself? I could use a few fingers."

The voice hailing them came from Strickland. He dangled a fat, heavy gambling purse from his hand. Ives gestured for him to sit beside him. He pointed at the purse.

"Winning again?"

Strickland patted the purse and smiled like a contented cat. He helped himself to some whiskey. "Good to see you are back in town. Word was you had left for parts unknown."

"Were you out of town?" Belleterre asked. "No wonder you did not know about my sorry plight."

"I went down to Merrywood. My brother Gareth returned from the Continent."

"Your half brother, you mean," Belleterre said with a smirk.

Belleterre could be an ass when he drank. Ives had forgotten how much of one.

"It is good you are back, now that things are coming to a head with that case," Strickland said.

Ives caught his eye and glanced to Belleterre. Strickland took the hint.

"I have to go piss," Belleterre said, unaware of their silent messages.

As soon as he left them, Ives put his head to Strickland's. "Sedition now? I don't believe it."

Strickland sipped whiskey and smacked his lips. "Not what you believe that matters, is it? What the jury believes is all anyone cares about."

"Do they have anything at all to convince a jury about that?"

"Enough for a good barrister to get the job done. More than enough for you to do it. Belvoir was told there would be hell to pay if he did not cooperate. Them that said it, meant it."

"One more reason for me to decline to prosecute," Ives muttered.

Strickland stared at him. "You cannot be thinking of it. I heard you were firmly committed." He bent forward and whispered, "That word came from way on high. Do you understand? *He* has every confidence you will do your duty, it is said."

"I have a conflict."

"A conflict? Well, get rid of it."

He had gotten rid of it. Or rather, it had gotten rid of him. Still, he remained a far cry from committed. It did a man's soul no good to do his duty if he had lost faith in it.

Belleterre staggered toward them. "Let us go find some women," he declared.

"The way I heard it, the woman you married has your cock under lock and key these days," Strickland said.

Belleterre looked at Ives, pained. "See? The whole town knows. If Strickland quips at my expense, imagine what is being said by those with some wit?"

Ives sent Strickland a sidelong glance. Strickland's own glance met his. They burst out laughing. "Trust us," Ives choked out. "You do not want to know what those with wit are saying."

Dispirited, Belleterre downed more whiskey.

Padua entered the gaoler's office. He eyed her from head to toe.

"It has been some time, Miss Belvoir."

"It has."

"No food? No books?"

She shook her head. "It will be a very brief visit."

"Make it so. He has been designated dangerous, I'll have you know. We are supposed to keep a closer watch on him."

She left the office and strode through the prison. Dangerous. What nonsense. Were the authorities blind?

Then again, what did she know? Perhaps Papa was a criminal mastermind.

She found him sleeping in his corner. The other inmates of his cell had changed over time. She did not recognize most of them. She gestured to one, and then at her father. The big fellow went over, and gave her father's hip a good kick.

He startled awake, cowered, frowned, then saw her. He closed his eyes again.

"I know about the house," she called. "The one on Silver Street."

His eyes opened again. Wide. He scrambled to his feet and shuffled over to the bars. "Padua, I—"

"Do not say a word. You have had precious little to say to me in ten years, so do not start talking now. Just listen. I found the house. I have been there. You have no pride left to protect with me. I should turn my back on you, as you have done with me so often. I will not, however. I promised Mama, and I am your daughter. I only want to hear one word from you. Will you now, finally, make some attempt to defend yourself?"

"You have been there?" His face flushed.

"I am living there."

His eyes widened. "No. You cannot have—"

"Oh, Papa, for heaven's sake. I have not begun working there. I am not one of Mrs. Lavender's young ladies. I am up with the servants. I have to live somewhere, don't I? If you were not too proud to own such a place, who am I to be too proud to take sanctuary under its roof?"

"It is different. It is—"

"One word, Papa. Yes or no. Will you finally fight

this? If not, I will leave you alone, as you have so often insisted."

He looked down. Emotion twisted his face. "I am sorry you know."

"Yes or no, Papa?"

He weighed his answer for a long time. Exasperated, she turned to leave.

"Yes," he said. "Yes."

"Sir." Vickers spoke lowly. "Sir, you have a visitor."

Ives opened his eyes. Low flames in the fireplace greeted him. He had dozed off while reading a long, boring brief regarding a contested inheritance. It was the kind of family argument that made lawyers rich and the family in question much, much poorer.

"Send him away. Tell him to return tomorrow afternoon."

"It is a woman, sir."

Ives held out his hand.

"She has no card, sir. It is the same woman as before. The very tall one."

Padua? Here?

He stood. "I will see her."

"I put her in the office, sir."

He wanted to tell Vickers to go and get her. Instead, he strode to the office.

She sat where she had been that first night. She appeared less distraught than that time. Less vulnerable. He paused at the door and admired her bright eyes and self-contained poise. Damnation, but it was good to see her. Too good.

She noticed him and he walked forward. "Padua."

"I am sorry to come at this hour. Again."

"You are welcome at any hour. Come to the library."

"No. I would prefer we talk here. I have come to speak with the famed barrister, you see. Not my former lover."

Her last words sliced at his heart. With difficulty, he became the barrister she sought. He sat in a chair facing her.

"I know you will not prosecute, and I know you cannot defend without great cost to yourself," she said. "However, I hope you will speak to him. To my father. You know everything—about the house and that income. Mr. Notley does not as yet. If you question him, you may learn things Mr. Notley never will. And, I trust you, as I never will trust another."

Another what? Man? Lawyer? He did not ask.

"Do you have reason to think he will talk to me, Padua? Or anyone?"

"I saw him today. I told him I know about the house. He was ashamed. I think he did not want me or anyone to know about it. That was why he would not speak, I think."

"Did he say as much? Will he cooperate now?"

"Yes. He told me he would. Will you do it? I know I have no right to ask it, but—"

"You have every right to ask it. What we shared does give us rights, Padua. Both of us. We are not made out of stone. Of course I will do it, if you ask it of me."

She flushed. "Thank you. Do I need to do anything? Will the gaoler permit it?"

The gaoler would permit it because he still believed Ives would prosecute. The letter begging off lay on his writing table upstairs, waiting for the morning post. He had labored over it for hours, trying to find words that would not imply indifference to duty, or to the royal favor he had enjoyed. A second letter, directly to the prince regent, tried even harder.

Neither would be well received. They could wait another day to be posted.

"He always receives me, Padua. He will allow me to speak with your father. I will go tomorrow."

"Thank you. I feel better now, knowing it will be you. Do not let him slither out of full answers. Make him tell you everything, Ives, even if it is the worst news."

"Even a snake cannot slither out of answering me, and your father is nowhere near that sly."

She stood and he followed. She smiled weakly and made a clumsy gesture with her hand that almost looked like a wave good-bye.

"You can stay, you know," he said. "No one saw you enter. No one will see you leave."

She appeared torn. He urged her silently to follow her hunger if not her heart. One step toward him. Just one, and he would—

"I have spent three days crying, Ives. Mourning. I do not want to cry all over again." She took that step then. And another, until she could kiss him. He fought the impulse to grab her, and hold her close, and caress her the way that would overcome her worries and fears, for a few hours at least.

He accepted her kiss of thanks, and branded his mind with the softness of her lips. Then she was gone, gliding to the door, and away.

"If you like, you can use this chamber here," Mr. Brown said. "I'll have him brought here for you."

Ives knew the chamber well. There were men who went in there for conversations, and who came out battered.

Belvoir had faced no physical coercion. Those who use such tactics know their men, and Belvoir was not a promising candidate. Belvoir had the look of a fanatic to him, a man who would die before betraying a principle. Such men did not talk on the rack. They died on it.

Ives waited in the small, windowless chamber while guards went for Belvoir. Unlike some barristers, he did not plan elaborate strategies and stage directions when he performed. A few facts and a lot of instinct stood him in good stead. He would wait to see if Belvoir needed to be lured or browbeaten to be fully forthcoming.

Tall and lanky, thinner by far than several weeks ago, Hadrian Belvoir shuffled in, his hands and legs manacled. Ives told the guard to wait outside the door, which he then closed.

"Guard said you are my prosecutor," Belvoir said after sitting in the one chair.

"All you need to know is that your daughter asked

me to come. She thinks you will tell me the truth that you might avoid telling her."

"Why would I do that?"

"Because I am a man, and no relative or friend. The charges against you are severe. The odds are even that you will hang if convicted. It is time to add your side to this story."

He hung his head, breathing hard. Ives realized some malady of the lungs afflicted him. Newgate was taking its toll.

"It all is because of that damned legacy," he said, shaking his head. "I should have refused it, or sold that woman the whole damned thing. Got greedy, didn't I? A steady living was something I had never had for long. I figured I could just take the money, and pretend the property weren't mine."

"How does that involve you in counterfeiting?"

"These men came to me. Strangers. They knew about that house. They said either I stored that trunk for them, or they would let the world know. I'd be branded a whore-monger. All who knew me would know of it." He looked away. "My daughter would know. This was a year ago, maybe fifteen months now. Had to do it, didn't I?"

"No, you did not have to do it. Your interest in mathematics has led you to forget your readings in moral philosophy. Do not expect me to approve the bargain you made."

Belvoir's head went down again.

"Did you open that trunk? Did you know what was in it?"

"After they took the first one away and brought the second, I opened it. I had never seen so much money in my life. I knew then I was deep into something that was probably illegal. I figured the money was no good. It smelled when it first came. Like the ink on it still had an odor. It was all fresh, crisp. Either they were robbing the Bank of England, or they were printing that up themselves."

Belvoir was a smart man. Too bad. If he could claim ignorance, if a jury would believe he might be too dim-witted to understand what he had in that trunk—

"I chewed it over a lot after that," Belvoir said. "They knew about that house. No one else did. Even the deed uses my whole Christian name. No one has called me John in thirty years. So I wondered if the counterfeiting was not tied to that house too. How else did they find me?"

"Do you think Mrs. Lavender is a counterfeiter?"

He shook his head. "I'd be surprised. She is old-fashioned, and honest in her way. I assume she cheats me on the accounts, but not too much. That is the sort she is. Even her trade there. It is so proper a brothel it is a wonder she gets any business. It is wrong, but not too wrong."

Ives bit back a smile. For a man in perpetual distraction, Belvoir could show remarkable insight when he paid attention to something or someone.

"There are the servants, though. Hector and the groom and a couple of others. I wondered if one of them might be up to no good, and pulled me into the web."

"You said they came to you. Who were they? Describe them."

"Two men. One tall, one short. There was nothing special about them. I'd never seen them before, nor later. Even when one trunk left and another arrived, they did not carry them. Regular transport movers did that work, and I don't think they even knew what they carried."

"Do you remember the name of the transport company?"

He closed his eyes, then shook his head. "Brown wagon it was. Painted. I don't recall a name on it."

"Do you have anything else to add? Anything at all, that might shed more light on this?"

Belvoir shook his head.

"Then I have a few other questions for you. Answer honestly. If you do not, no one can help you. Do you have any associations with radicals or revolutionaries? Even old friendships that might be misunderstood?"

"I have no interest in politics. Never have. I also have no old friends. I'm not a man who needs them much. I like being alone." He paused, then added, "I have books, of course. Pamphlets and such. I read many things. Reading isn't the same as doing, or even agreeing. Everyone knows that."

Not everyone. Ives pictured the prosecutor reading from one of the more lurid revolutionary tracts, waving it around, describing it being found by the accused's bedside.

"One more question. You are not a man much engaged with the world. You say you have no old friends, and you have no living that would be threatened by scandal. Why, then, have you refused to speak until now? Why agree to the blackmail you describe? It is hard to believe you cared if the whole world knew."

"It wasn't the whole world I cared about. Just one small part of it. My daughter. I did not want to taint her with the story, and I never wanted her to know." He covered his eyes with his hand. "But she does now. She must despise me."

"She is surprised, and disappointed, but she does not despise you. She is glad, I think, to learn there was a reason you refused her help." He gave the man his handkerchief. "Regarding your daughter, I have a few more questions now, if you will indulge me."

P adua listened to Ives's description of the meeting with her father. He had asked to meet in Hyde Park, and they strolled along the Serpentine while he reported her father's explanation.

"I guessed as much," she said. "As soon as I realized what went on in that house, I knew that was why he would not speak. Eventually it would come out, to my humiliation."

"It is not the thinking of a man who is indifferent to you," Ives said.

"Perhaps not." She was not sure what to think of Papa now. Her old image had been destroyed, and a new one had not yet formed.

"This is England. I cannot believe owning some radical tracts can be used to prove sedition," she said.

"It is all in how it is presented at the trial."

"Could you use it well enough?"

"Yes."

That was not the answer she wanted to hear. "Would you?"

"If I were convinced a man plotted assassinations, I might."

Could you do the opposite, and present it so everyone decided it meant nothing at all? She did not ask. She did not have to. Of course he could. She already regretted having compromised him to where he would not prosecute. She would curse herself before this was over, she feared.

He had told her all there was to tell. Walking with him, seeing him, made her sad and wistful. Her heart wanted to stay, no matter how painful it might be. She knew, however, that was not wise.

"I must go."

He pulled out his pocket watch. "Not yet. We are meeting someone soon."

"You arranged a rendezvous for me?"

"I am the rendezvous. They are the friends." He looked above the heads surrounding them. "Ah, there they are." He guided her down the path.

Up ahead, Eva and Gareth waved.

"What brings you to town?" Padua asked when they all continued on the path.

"We are meeting with estate agents, looking for a house to let," Eva said.

"Also, Lance had become poor company." Gareth looked apologetic. "He will be following us, I think. We are sorry, Ives, but I could not listen to his moaning about dying of boredom in the country another day. I promise to play nursemaid if he turns up."

"I expect we will both be needed. If he issues another challenge, however, you can be his second this time. I am all talked out where he is concerned."

The two brothers pulled ahead as they chatted on. Eva fell into step with Padua. "Where are you staying? I will call on you."

"It is a simple room in a house. I would love to receive you, but I do not even have a sitting room."

Eva's little smile matched the sly way she looked ahead at Ives's back. "I can't imagine Ives is happy about that."

"He is not happy about much where I am concerned."

Concern replaced Eva's mirth. "Did you break with him?"

"I had to. London is not Merrywood. We both knew such a liaison would only bring scandal to him. Surely Gareth told you about that, and how Ives has already paid a cost for befriending me even if the affair is over."

"He only told me that Ives's refusal to serve against your father would not be well received at court. He is doing the right thing, however. If he made a different choice, it would be despicable."

On the face of it, yes. Eva would not think any better of Ives if he did make a different choice, in order to do less than his best for his lover's sake. Whether cruel for his own benefit, or dishonorable for hers, Ives could not win. It had been heartless of her to force that dilemma on him.

"I do not like picturing you in some tiny chamber in a stranger's house," Eva said. "Once we have settled into our new home, you must stay with us."

"I could not intrude. You are still almost newlyweds. Please do not try to cajole me, Eva. You have a kind heart, but I am contented where I am. And please do not let Ives know that you offered. He does not approve of the arrangements I made for myself."

Eva cocked her head. "Did he offer to make a better arrangement for you?"

Eva had bluntly asked if Ives asked her to be his mistress. Padua never thought she would speak so frankly with a woman, but Eva had found Ives in her bed. That had created a special intimacy between them. An instant friendship.

"He did not offer directly. He intended to help me find a home, however."

"And when a suitable one proved too expensive, he probably intended to help you afford it." Eva narrowed her eyes on Ives. "He has formed some bad habits over the years. It may be cruel of me, but I am glad you did not accept that help, Padua. His dealings with women have been too efficient for my liking. It will do him good not to get his way for once."

"We neither of us have gotten our way, Eva."

Eva's expression fell into one of concern. She stopped walking, and her hand on Padua's arm stopped Padua too.

"Padua, did you fall in love with him? It is not the same thing as desire and passion. I trust you know that."

Had she? She did not have enough experience to know how it was different from passion. Perhaps passion did not have the ability to break one's heart. Maybe only love made it so difficult to be near Ives today, and so hard to pretend she did not ache for his touch, his smile, and the sound of his voice.

Up ahead, the brothers had also stopped and chatted. Padua looked at Ives, so handsome in his face and form, a smile softening a mouth so easily stern. She wanted him to hold her again. She wanted to let him have his way, whatever that way might be.

"Eva, I am going to leave you now. Please make my apologies to Gareth and Ives. Say I promised to meet a friend."

"But—what are you—"

"Please, Eva. I am in grave danger of making a fool of myself. I must go."

Eva leaned in to give her a kiss on her cheek. "Call on me. Promise you will."

She only nodded, because emotion choked her words. She turned and walked away quickly.

CHAPTER 19

For two days Padua thought about the things her father had said to Ives. He claimed he had been coerced to store that bad money in his chambers. The men who did it knew about the brothel. He logically guessed they had something to do with the brothel, or else they would not have known of his connections to it.

The obvious suspect was Mrs. Lavender. Eva had proof the woman was at least mildly dishonest. Upon examining the accounts, she discovered a small but repeated irregularity in the way her father's share had been calculated. Of more interest was the lease. Mrs. Lavender had omitted one significant term when describing it. The lease renewed every five years, unless one party chose otherwise.

Presumably the rent could be renegotiated then.

Shrewd of Mrs. Lavender to give the landlord part of the business. It was not in his interest to demand a rent that would kill the golden goose.

If those men still made their counterfeit notes, would they not want to find a new way to store them? If they used the house in other ways, or were in league with Mrs. Lavender, would they not want the other partner in their net, too, once again? Perhaps the men involved in this scheme had written to her, to inform her of her father's incarceration. If so, that sounded as if they indeed hoped she would take his place.

The next day Padua went downstairs at the dinner hour, and entered the dining room. All the women ate together, along with Hector and the groom. They all looked at her. Silence fell.

"I thought I should introduce myself. My name is Padua Belvoir. My father is John Hadrian Belvoir. He is Mrs. Lavender's partner."

Faint buzzing suggested all the young women did not know there was a partner.

"My father is indisposed, so I must stand in for him here. I will be executing his responsibilities and obligations."

All eyes turned to Mrs. Lavender. Her eyes pierced Padua.

"My father is easily distractible, and did not involve himself in this business. I am cut of different cloth. I have ideas for improving everyone's lot here. I do not mean to interfere, but my father has been foolish to neglect such an important part of his income." She sat in an empty chair, and looked expectantly at one of the serving girls. The girl hurriedly brought her a plate and fork. Two of the soiled doves passed her the tureens of stew and rice.

Conversation resumed. The woman sitting next to Padua, a plump, pretty young woman with sandy hair, spoke to her. "I do not think Mrs. Lavender appreciates your interest in the house."

"She has borne the burden on her own for so long, and she can imagine no other way. However, in a few weeks she will be glad I am here to help her. She must grow tired of taking care of everything."

"Do you think to greet the guests too? I doubt she will give that up."

The very idea terrified Padua. "I see no reason to ask her to, then. However, what happens if she takes ill? Does Hector do it instead?"

The woman laughed, drawing Mrs. Lavender's attention. "Goodness no. She has a friend who joins us when she needs some money. That is who takes her place if she cannot take the helm. It does not happen too often, I am glad to say. I do not care for Emily."

Padua looked down the table. "Is Emily here now?"

"Not today. She has her own trade, with longtime patrons. A carriage trade, to hear her tell it. The Honorable this and Lord that. She comes here maybe one night a week. You will notice her. She is older than most of us. There's some men who have a fondness for older women. Some even try to convince Mrs. Lavender to take a turn again, but I think it has been twenty years since she did."

Little cakes passed along the table. Padua helped herself to one. At least Mrs. Lavender fed her doves decent food. Far better than what had been sent up to Padua's chamber the prior evenings.

"Are we to call you Miss Belvoir?" her tablemate asked. "Mrs. Lavender permits no informality with her own person."

"Then it might be best if you did address me that way."

"I am Susan. Most of us don't have last names here. Not real ones, anyway."

Being of inquiring mind, Padua had a lot of questions she wanted to ask Susan, most of them rude and personal.

Susan ate the last of her cake and licked her fingers. "You've never done this work yourself, have you?"

"No, I haven't."

"Mmm. I didn't think so. We can tell. You ain't one of those reformer ladies, are you? We don't need that sort here."

"I would not presume to try to reform you." Actually, it had crossed her mind.

"Then welcome." She grinned, and pushed back her chair.

Mrs. Lavender walked over to Padua. "A nice little speech, Miss Belvoir. I will brook no interference, however."

"In just under six months, the lease on this house renews. Or not. I will not interfere. But I will be keeping an eye on my father's interests."

Mrs. Lavender barely contained her anger. "Gentlemen will be arriving soon. I suggest you make yourself scarce, unless you want them in my office, bargaining for *you.*"

Padua would not have minded being a fly on the wall of the office, observing how those bargains were struck. As an idea, a brothel repelled her. Now that she was in one, however, she found it interesting.

She climbed the stairs to the deserted top floor, and repaired to her chamber. She wondered if announcing her presence would bear any fruit. If her father's problems had begun here, and if he had become unavailable, would someone now approach her? She hoped so. She could think of no better way to help him now than to point the authorities to the source of those bad notes.

"So I stopped my horse and had it out with him," Lance said. He lounged on a chair to the side, watching Ives and Gareth fence. "I said, *Listen here, Radley. Why are you showing up like a love-struck boy whenever I go riding?* He did not care for the boy part, but I swear I feel as if he has improper designs on me sometimes."

Gareth smirked, but did not lose his concentration.

"I wish he had declared his passion then and there," Ives said. "That would have stunned the wit right out of you."

"Such a man would never admit those inclinations if he had them. He is never seen without a hat. He always talks as if he is addressing a bishop. I don't think he has any passion at all, and hates me because I know how to have fun."

"How like you to assume you are admired for your excesses," Ives said. "But do go on. What did Radley say to your challenge?"

"He said, and designs on my person would have surprised me less, he said that he hoped to gain my confidence and friendship, because he wanted to introduce his female relatives to me."

That impressed Gareth enough that he stepped back and lowered his foil. "For what purpose does he pursue this introduction?"

Lance shrugged. "So I will receive them, I suppose. So they can drop my name at the county assemblies. So he can tell people he has a connection."

"So you might marry one of them?" Gareth added.

Lance looked up, surprised, then began laughing. "He is a fool, but not an idiot, Gareth," he choked out. "A ride or two with me is one thing, but that—even Radley is not so stupid as to aim that high."

Ives waited for Lance to stop guffawing.

"Did he say anything else?" Ives asked.

Lance sobered up, and thought. "He implied he would call off the hounds if I accommodated him on this small favor."

"Implied?"

"He could not say it outright, could he? That would be asking for a bribe. Radley does not want me off the hook only to find himself on one."

"What did he say?" Gareth asked.

Lance waved his hand in a circle. "Something about friends and neighbors and the good of the county and, wait, something else. What was that now?" He frowned while he searched for it in his somewhat foxed head.

Ives's patience thinned by the moment. "You grab him," he muttered to Gareth. "I'll duck his head in a bucket of water to clear his thinking."

Gareth chuckled. "Do not blame him that you are out of temper. He has been behaving fairly decently since he came up yesterday. He is only half-foxed, and you have to admit that Lance happy is far preferable to Lance miserable, since he insists on infecting everyone with his humor good or bad."

"I'll blame him if I want. I did not plan on spending days on end with him as my shadow, nor I as his."

"Ah, I have it." Lance stuck a finger into the air. "I remember his exact words."

"Are you going to share them?" Ives asked. "Or am I supposed to shake them out of you?"

Lance's expression fell. He looked at Gareth. "He is talking like a vicar again."

"Vicars do not thrash people," Ives said.

"I trust you will remember that, *Vicar*," Lance shot back.

"Ives has important matters on his mind," Gareth said.

Lance's eyebrows rose a fraction. "That woman? Of course it is. She is still a ticklish subject, I see."

Ives prayed for forbearance. "Could you please turn

your half-addled mind back to the exact words that Radley said to you, to imply he would call off the hounds?"

"Ah. Yes. He said, and I think you will agree his meaning was unmistakable—I certainly comprehended him immediately—"

"What. Did. He. Say?" Ives said.

"He said, *County neighbors should look out for each other, and friends even more so. I always honor my debts when I am beholden to a man, especially if I have the means to resolve his greatest concern.*"

"It certainly sounds like an overture to me," Gareth said.

"I am more interested in what means he thinks he has," Ives said. "Radley cannot end that investigation on his own. He is not the only authority involved."

"What do I care how he will do it?" Lance said. "I allow an introduction to these women, I nod to them at an assembly, I receive them and Radley when they come to call once or twice, and *it is over.*"

"I don't like it," Ives said. "Don't agree to anything until I have a chance to speak with him. If it is as simple as that, he will not mind some frank negotiations on the matter."

Lance threw up his hands. "He isn't one of your mistresses, Ives. A little subtlety is in order at times."

"What would you know about subtlety? Just do not agree to anything."

One of the servants at the fencing studio approached them. "Milords, there is a man outside. He asked to speak with you, sir." He addressed the last to Ives.

"What man?"

"A big one. Black. He did not give his name."

Rather suddenly, his brothers lost interest in Radley. Lance eyed him. "Didn't Mrs. Lavender have a big black man at her door? An ex-slave from the islands. What was his name? Achilles or something."

Ignoring him, Ives walked to the door and stepped outside. Hector waited there. "Mrs. Lavender said you are to come. Very angry, she is."

"Tell her I will come tomorrow."

He shook his head. "She said you are to come at once."

"Fine, go and tell her I will be there soon."

He strode back to his brothers, unfastening his padded vest as he went. "I must do something."

"Are we going to Mrs. Lavender's?" Lance asked.

"You are not."

"I think I am. I have not thought about Mrs. Lavender in a long time. Years. I always liked her. She reminded me of a mother."

"Not our mother, I hope."

"Of course not our mother. A real mother. Warm and concerned. Don't you agree, Gareth?"

"I never visited her."

"No? I thought everyone did, at first."

"Take him to his club," Ives said to Gareth. "He will have to be Aylesbury there. That should make him manageable."

"I am not a member of his club," Gareth reminded. Damn. He kept forgetting. "Then take him home."

"I'd rather go to Mrs. Lavender's," Lance said.

Ives glared at him. "Don't you dare show up there. I mean it, Lance. You have all of London to distract you. Do not go to that house."

He threw off his vest and turned to go.

"You heard him," he heard Lance say to Gareth. "We have all of London, with the vicar's blessing."

Ives did not know what he expected to find at Mrs. Lavender's. Nothing good, that was certain. He imagined the various ways Padua might have caused enough trouble to cause Mrs. Lavender to send Hector to find him.

Hector let him into the house. The night was far enough along that Mrs. Lavender had taken her position in the office. He had to wait while some business occurred behind its closed door. Eventually it opened, and a young man who looked all of eighteen came out. Mrs. Lavender escorted him away, to make the introduction to the woman she had just sold him.

She returned, gave Ives a stern frown, and entered her office. He followed, closed the door, and sat in the patron's chair much as he had when he was as green as its last occupant.

"Miss Belvoir is not keeping to herself, as I was led to think she would."

"Why don't you tell me what she has done to distress you."

She treated him to a long description of Padua joining the household for dinner, making a speech, and threatening Mrs. Lavender with the loss of her lease. "She intends to look after her father's interests, she says. She intends to watch the accounts most closely, she says. She intends to involve herself in the running of things, she says."

"I will talk to her."

"I'll not be tolerating such cheek. She thinks she can threaten me about the lease? Well, I have a few aces in my pocket, too, if need be."

He took his leave and walked to the stairs. Above one level he heard laughter coming from the drawing room. He kept climbing, past the chambers, up to the servant quarters.

Padua opened her door a crack when he rapped. She peered out, startled.

"Let me in, Padua."

"I don't think I should."

"Open it, or I will kick it in."

"I don't like your tone."

"What you hear is as restrained as I am likely to be, and I grow less restrained by the moment. Open the door. Now."

She did, but gave him a pinched, low-lidded look he suspected she used on students who challenged her authority.

He paced around the little nest she had made for herself. "You said you intended to use this chamber as a free bed. You said you would go and come by those stairs outside, and no one would be the wiser."

"That is true, I did say that."

"Mrs. Lavender says you dined with the prostitutes."

"We call them the young ladies."

"*We?*"

She backed up a step. "Mrs. Lavender. And, um, Hector. And . . . me."

"Have you decided to enter the trade now? Should I offer you coin, when you refused less insulting forms of support?"

"That is uncalled for. I am not one of the young ladies, nor will I be one."

"How reassuring. You will, however, be a madam, like Mrs. Lavender."

"If she told you that, she exaggerated."

He sat on the bed, and pulled her in front of him. He looked up. "Tell me how she exaggerated. What are you up to? Are you so disillusioned with him that you want to rub your own ruin in his nose?"

"I am not doing this to spite him. I am doing this to save him." She laid her hand on his face and leaned down so her gaze filled his own. "Do you believe me so stupid as to risk everything for no worthy reason?"

Her touch both soothed and seared. He reacted like he had been starved for years, not mere days.

"I have a plan, Ives. I think it will work." She spoke seriously. Earnestly. He barely heard her.

He pulled her onto his lap and raked his fingers into her hair. "Later." He kissed her. "Tell me later."

She accepted a consuming kiss, and returned one just as fiercely. She tried to turn her head. "What are we— We should not—"

He went to work on her dress's fasteners, impatient
to see her, hold her. "We are blameless. Eros is present
in this house. Have you not sensed his spell, even up
here?" He kissed her neck and sucked on her pulse.
She groaned, and nodded. "Then do not tell me we
must not, Padua. The wonder is I do not take you every
way I have known or imagined."

He pulled her garments off impatiently. Clumsily.
She knelt beside him on the bed and took his face in
her hands. She kissed him a long time and forced some
calm on him. Not much, but enough that he allowed
her to slide his coats off, and unbutton his shirt, and
tantalize him by undressing him.

"What do you imagine? You said the wonder would
be if you did not take me every way you have imagined. What wicked things do you dream of doing?" She
pushed his shirt open and gently rubbed her breasts
against his skin.

"They would shock you."

"I have not been too shocked so far." She worked at
unbuttoning his trousers. "Are they the things you needed
to negotiate with your mistresses?"

"Some of them."

"Not minor variations, then, if such women might
not be amenable."

"Nothing dangerous, however. Nothing cruel."

She scooted off his lap, and helped him to shed his
lower garments. Then she straddled him, her long
white legs dangling on either side of his lap, the dark

hair of her mound revealing flashes of dark pink flesh. "Perhaps I will not be shocked. At least not too much."

She lured him to a path he had avoided. He might have forgone it forever. With Padua such things became unnecessary indulgences. Now that she spoke of it, however . . .

He put his hand to her, and used his fingers to explore the most sensitive spots she had. She draped her arms on his shoulders and accepted the pleasure. A dreamy expression softened her face.

"The first thing is that you do as I say," he explained, leaning forward to lick the dark, hard tips of her breasts.

"You command me, you mean."

"Yes."

"No seductions."

"No."

"Negotiations?"

"You can say no."

Her hips swayed to his hand's arousing touches. "It sounds— It should not be exciting, but I find the notion is. A little frightening, but—" She looked into his eyes.

"The second thing is, you will answer my questions."

"We will be chatting?"

"You will be telling me things I want to hear."

"Anything else?"

"You will address me as my lord."

That amused her at first, but he watched understanding

dawn in her eyes. "That has nothing to do with your title, does it?"

He shook his head.

She pressed her forehead to his and looked down. She took his cock in her hands. "What does my lord want? This?" She trailed her fingertips up the shaft, then wrapped them around it.

"That is the least of it. But first things first." He lifted her forward, so her knees rested on the mattress. He raised her until his mouth could reach her breasts. He wanted her so wild that she denied him nothing. He aroused her without mercy until she swayed and clawed at his shoulders.

He inserted two fingers in her passage, then three. She bore down on them hard, panting in short, desperate breaths.

He controlled her carefully, giving her just enough to leave her on the edge. She sought more with her hips and objected with frustrated whimpers.

"What is it you want, Padua?"

"I want— I need— Can't we—"

"You must wait for that. Does this help?" He withdrew his fingers, and caressed around the outside of her lower lips. A low, guttural scream trembled out of her. Her response had him gritting his teeth to control the urge to throw her down and relieve them both.

"Or do you want this?" He stroked forward to the nub and rubbed.

She buried her cries in his shoulder while the pleasure sent her crashing higher. He let her have her release, but not totally. He removed his hand at the point where she had calmed and known the best of it but remained aroused.

He set her on her feet, and stood with her. He released some of his own hunger in an embrace too tight and a kiss too savage, but anticipation had his blood scorching his mind.

"I want you to kneel now," he said.

She gave him a glance of curiosity, then lowered herself. He gazed down on her long dark hair, and full breasts and pale arms and shoulders.

"How do you feel, Padua?"

"Small." She looked up. "Vulnerable. If my lord were a different man, I would not like it. If I did not know you so well too. As it is, the fear is not real fear, because—"

"Because it excites you?"

She nodded.

On her own, she took his cock in her hands. He watched, thoughts deserting him, while she stroked him.

"Do you know what I want now?"

"I am not sure."

He told her.

Her fingertips circled the tip of his cock. He all but heard her mind working. "My lord said I could say no if I want."

"That is true." Her lord might die if she did.

She contemplated the demand for an excruciating minute. He thought his body would split open.

Tentatively, she stuck out her tongue and tested. She

thought some more. "You do this for me, and it is wonderful. If you would know something similar—it is only fair to try." She looked up. "You will tell me what to do?"

He told her. She kissed, then she licked, then she used her mouth fully. Keen bolts of feral pleasure prodded him to spectacular erotic heights. She did not retreat, not even at the end.

He lifted her up and dropped on the bed with her in his arms. For a long count he lost himself in a dark mist of an encompassing pleasure that spun out of his climax.

Later, he did not know if it was one minute or twenty, Padua moved. She raised up on her elbows. "Are we done, my lord?"

He opened his eyes and looked at her. "Hardly."

Padua had always known that her submission aroused Ives. She had not called it that, but it had been there, from that first night when he held her hands together during the first kisses. She had sensed it in the ways he handled her. Even in his possessive caresses.

She supposed all men liked it. They were not far from the animals in such things. Nor, she was learning, were women.

She lay on the bed, waiting for Ives to finish preparations for the next wicked game. He had stacked two pillows and told her to lie facedown with them under her hips. She now spread naked on the bed.

The waiting aroused her terribly. Again the vulnerability. Again the fear that was not fear because it excited. Her arms angled out toward the bed corners, to which they were loosely bound. Behind her Ives did the same with one of her feet.

He moved to the other foot. Her legs spread now, like her arms. Her bottom rose high, exposed. Waiting.

She could not believe what it did to her. She had never been in such a state without being touched before.

"How do you feel, Padua?"

He stood behind her, next to the bed near her leg. Even with her face turned on the mattress, she could not see him.

"I am comfortable enough."

A small slap smacked her bottom. "That is not what I meant and you know it."

That smack had not hurt. It had been too gentle for that. But it had— She blocked her mind against the fantasy that he might do it again. She would not like that, she was sure, but the thought of it, the waiting—

"I am surprised, my lord. I do not feel the way I expected. I am already half-mad."

A caress fluttered up her leg in a feathery touch he had first used in Langley House. "Do you like how you feel?"

"It is intense. I grow impatient, however."

The mattress depressed as his weight joined hers. She looked over her shoulder. He knelt high between her legs. Low, deep throbs began torturing her. She set her head down again. He caressed her bottom and she throbbed more. "And you? How do you feel?"

He warmed her back as he came over her. Braced on his arms, he dipped his head low so he spoke right into her ear. "I feel in possession, when I know I really am not. I feel as if you are mine, and I will make sure you never leave, when I know that is not true. I can want you without reservation, as I have never wanted another woman before, and make you admit your own passion, and pretend I am indeed your lord." His lips brushed her cheek. "And I like that I can make you ache with desire, and totally surrender to the pleasure I give you."

He moved back. "Tell me what you want, Padua." He caressed her bottom firmly, taunting her.

"You," she whispered. "Everything."

He entered her slowly. She caught her breath. She closed her eyes so she might feel it all as intensely as possible. He filled her. Completed her.

He took her then. Restrained as she was, she could only accept whatever he gave, both the tenderness and the fury.

"What are you doing out here?" Padua turned to the door. Ives stood there. He had thrown on trousers and shirt.

She hitched the blanket in which she cocooned her own nakedness. She held her finger to her lips, then pointed to the long carriage house. "Look low. Near the ground, halfway along. There is a deep shadow there. I think it is a small window."

He peered through the night. "There may be a cellar underneath."

"I think there is. I have spent a long time looking at that building over the last few days." She opened the door and returned to her chamber. She climbed onto the bed and drew up her legs. He lay beside her, resting on his elbow.

"I told you I had a plan. I let everyone know I was taking my father's place, because I think whoever coerced him to take that trunk is connected to this house. If so, perhaps they will now approach me as they did him. Then I will know who else is involved, and can use that information to help him. They sought to catch a whale, you said. Well, I intend to find the whale, or someone who knows where he swims."

She expected praise for her cleverness. Instead his gaze pierced her. "If you are correct, you have put yourself in harm's way, Padua."

"I do not think anyone will hurt me here."

"You do not know they will not. Men facing a noose will do desperate things."

"I will be very careful."

His severity did not dim one bit on her reassurance. He sat up on the edge of the bed. "You will move out tomorrow. I will bring you to Langley House."

"I cannot leave. I have things I need to do tomorrow."

His head snapped around. "What things?"

"A walk in the garden, for example."

He captured her face in his hand. "A walk very close to that carriage house, is my guess."

"I only want to see if there is a cellar like it appeared tonight."

"I should have smacked your bottom much harder, and more often. I still may. I forbid you to go within fifteen feet of that building."

She rose on her knees and wrapped her arms around him from the back. She nuzzled his neck. She thought it charming, and very male, that he did not understand that even if he were her lord, which he was not, she would not always obey him.

"Do not try to work your wiles on me, woman. You are not to—" She nibbled his ear. "Stop that, I am serious. You are not to leave this—" She ran her hands down his chest. "I will not tolerate—" She slid her hands lower yet.

He caught them, turned around, and threw her down. "I will do it," he said. "Tomorrow night, I will see if there is a cellar and what it might contain. Nothing more than rusting carriage parts, is my guess. I will check if you want. You do not go near it or show the slightest interest, however. Do you understand?"

She nodded, and tried to look meek.

He pushed her over, unswaddled her from the blanket, lay down beside her, and unfurled the blanket over them both. "As for the rest of your plan, I will be here every night. If you are correct, you will not face or meet such men alone if I am alive to prevent it. Since you set things in motion on your own—" He gave her one more glare. "There is no choice but to await developments."

"Every night?"

"Until it is clear you are wrong, or until it is proven you are right."

"You plan to sleep here?"

"I'm not going to sit awake in a chair, Padua."

"It is a fairly small bed."

He turned, and pulled her close. "We will manage. You do not take up much space."

It would be like Merrywood again, his lying with her. Her sleeping with his presence around her and in her soul. She might not regret the passion, but this—

Her heart swelled with poignant emotion as the intimacy descended, claiming her. But she trembled too. She would endure the worst of the heartache again, raw like a fresh cut.

"Does anyone come here in the morning?" he asked in a drowsy voice. "One of the servants?"

"I must go and get one. Mrs. Lavender will do nothing to aid my comfort."

He settled himself deeper on the pillow, and rested an arm over her. "That is because she suspected you were troublesome baggage at first sight." He yawned. "As did I, God help me."

CHAPTER 20

I ves arrived at Langley House the next evening. He found Gareth in the library as planned. He poured himself some brandy and stood by the window, watching twilight begin its fade to black.

"Where are the others?"

"Eva is in her chambers, reading. Lance is in his study, pretending to attend to estate affairs," Gareth said. "The solicitor sent a stack of documents around late in the afternoon, with a message they required his immediate attention."

"Convenient."

"Damned convenient. Good of him to help out."

"He does not want Lance in more trouble any more than we do."

He opened the window and stuck his head out. He

could see the moon low in the sky. There were few clouds to interfere with what light it would give.

Gareth stood. "Shall we go?"

Ives nodded. They walked side by side to the reception hall.

"Ives. I did not know you were here." Lance's voice sounded from the stairs.

"Keep walking," Ives muttered under his breath. He shot a quick glance back at Lance, who stood on one of the stairs with a stack of papers in his arms. "I just stopped by to get Gareth." He aimed for the door.

"Where are you going?"

Gareth turned and shrugged. "Out and about. No place of interest. No place that is any fun. I am married now, so it is bound to be a boring few hours all around."

"Not as boring as mine." He frowned at the documents. "I think we need a new solicitor."

Ives hung back while Gareth engaged.

"It is quite a lot of paper," Gareth said.

"I was going to spread it out in the library and see if it makes more sense that way."

"Such are the duties of the title, eh?" Gareth gave Lance's shoulder a firm clasp. "We will let you get to it, then."

"Hell. It can wait. Even being bored by you is better than this." He gestured for a footman, and deposited the stack into his arms. He brushed off his coat sleeves. "So, where to first?"

Ives inserted himself. "You cannot come."

"Why not?"

"It would not be appropriate," Gareth said. "If we are caught, it is one thing. If you are, it is a huge scandal and the talk of the town."

"Caught doing what?"

Ives wanted to throttle Gareth. "None of your business. Which is why you cannot come."

"Is it his business?" Lance jerked his thumb at Gareth. "I didn't think so. It is *your* business."

"Correct. So I get to make all the decisions, such as the one that says you are not joining us."

"Yes, I am. An adventure is afoot, I can tell."

"A very small one," Gareth soothed. "So small it is almost as boring as those documents."

Lance frowned peevishly. Then his expression cleared. "It has to do with that Belvoir case, doesn't it?"

Ives often regretted forgetting that Lance, for all his self-absorption and distraction, had a mind as sharp as a sword when he chose to use it. That he so chose at the most inconvenient moments was a source of unending annoyance.

"I am right. You are investigating something, and I'll wager it is not for the Crown's interests. You will only make a mess of it without me, whatever it is." He snapped his fingers at a footman. "My horse."

Gareth sighed, defeated. Ives wondered if they could lose Lance between this house and the one they would visit.

"Do not follow your own nose in this," he said to Lance. "If you insist on coming, at least do not get in the way or cause more trouble than we need."

"I am insulted and wounded. I do not cause trouble." He strode to the door, paused, and turned to them. "Say, do we need our pistols?"

"It is not that kind of adventure."

"If you say so. Pity."

L ance stood in the alley, gazing up at the house.

"Are you coming?" Ives whispered.

Lance joined him. "The house appeared familiar to me. Have I been here before?"

"I am sure you have never stood in this spot before."

They crowded Gareth, who bent over the lock on the carriage house, working a pick.

"Where did you learn to do that?" Lance asked.

"Here and there. It mostly requires concentration, and silence."

"You will have to teach me. It might be a handy skill to have. Don't you agree, Ives? We will have Gareth give us lessons on lock picking some rainy day."

"Concentration and *silence*," Gareth repeated tightly.

Lance folded his arms and waited.

Thus far bringing him had not created any particular problems. By arriving by the mews behind the house, and entering along the alley on which the carriage house stretched, Lance had not even realized just where they were. They would be done here and he would be back in Langley House with him none the wiser.

The lock clicked. Gareth straightened, removed it,

and swung open one half of the carriage house door. They all slipped in.

Windows allowed moonlight at least. The bulk of a carriage filled most of the space. "A groom has his chamber above," Ives whispered. "He may be there, so move quietly."

"Move where? And why?" Lance asked.

"We are looking for evidence of a cellar, and access to it," Gareth said.

They walked the perimeter of the room, then went through the door to the stables. The horses had been noisy and nervous, and became more so on their arrival. Lance walked to the stalls and calmed them. Ives paced the plank floor, evidence that this building once had had a different purpose.

Suddenly his boots made different sounds. Hollow ones. He crouched and felt the floor. His hand found a ring. He gestured for his brothers, and pulled.

A hinged door in the floor opened. Darkness gaped below. "Wait here," he said.

He lowered himself through the hole. There were no steps, so he dropped down. There was a cellar after all, one so low ceilinged he had to bend his shoulders to move about. A small window high on one wall must have been what Padua saw last night. The vaguest light leaked in, but it was enough to show the lamp on a table nearby.

He went over, found the flint, and lit the candle in the lamp. The cellar took on form. Shapes and shadows stretched into view.

"What is down there?" Lance's loud whisper poured through the hole.

"Stay there. It is not large enough for all of us."

Silence. Then a few scrapes, huffs, and boots landing on the cellar's dirt floor.

"I said to wait."

Lance ignored him. He looked around the cellar, then advanced on a corner. "What is this here? Some kind of machinery."

"It used to be an ironmonger's or some such factory."

"This is iron, that is certain. Bring that lamp here."

Ives carried over the lamp. The machinery's parts jumped out of the dark. He looked at it and knew at once what it was. "Shit."

Lance played with the wheel and poked at the roller. "Is it a press? It is rather small."

"It is a rather small cellar."

"You make a good point."

"How heavy is it?"

Lance set his arms under it and tried to lift it. "Heavy, but not immovable."

Of course not. Men had to carry it in. Which meant men could carry it out. Ives set down the lamp. "Let us see if we can hoist it up to Gareth."

"You are going to steal it?"

"I am. Since you insisted on coming, so are you."

Lance did not argue. "I hope you know what you are doing."

Together they lifted the press and carried it to the hole in the floor. Straining, they pushed it up through the opening. Gareth helped from his end, until the press rested on the stable floor.

"There is a door to the garden, near the carriage," Ives said. "Can the two of you take this out that way, and hide it? Just tuck it under some shrubbery for now."

Gareth gave him a direct but curious look. Then he extended his arm for Lance to use to get out.

Up above, Ives heard them shuffling along the floor toward the carriage room. He returned to the lamp. He carried it back to where he had been, near the window.

It cast its glow over the wall, and the two objects he had seen there when he first lit it. A good-sized wooden box sat on a large trunk. He set down the lamp and threw the box's top back.

It contained thin metal plates, stacked one atop the other. He ran his fingertips over one, and felt fine ridges and depressions. He lifted it and held it to the light. The ghostly image of a banknote showed.

He lifted the whole box and set it on the table with the lamp. Then he opened the trunk. Its contents surprised him less. Paper filled it. Half was blank. The other half consisted of sheets with six banknotes, each sheet about the size of the bed on that press that had just been carted away.

Padua had not only been correct, she had been completely correct, more totally than she guessed. The counterfeiters were not only connected to this house. They had worked here, right in this cellar.

He gazed at the irrefutable evidence of that. Evidence that, if Hadrian Belvoir's ownership of this property became known, would send him to the gallows for sure. It would be assumed he was not the dupe of a whale, but the whale himself.

And Padua . . . He shook his head. He did not have to speculate how it would look. She had announced she was taking her father's place. She lived in the house right now.

He cursed under his breath. Cursed long and hard. This was all evidence in a serious crime. He was supposed to give it to the authorities. To ignore this, to turn a blind eye—that was not who he was. It violated all that he believed and would leave him without honor or integrity, even if it never came to light. And if it did . . .

He closed the trunk. He blew out the candle. Steeling his strength, he lifted the box with the plates and carried it over to the hole. He lifted it over his head and slid it onto the floorboards, then jumped, grabbed the sides of the opening, and leveraged his weight up.

Gasping for breath, he rose and carried the box to the next chamber, and out the door.

"What have you there?" Lance's whisper carried through the silent night as he and Gareth approached on the path.

"Do not ask."

"Let me help you." Gareth moved to take one side.

"No. Go and wait for me near the door. I will join you in a minute."

They moved away. He lugged his burden to the back of the garden, and dropped it with relief on the ground.

He looked for a place to stash it near the portal. A bench backed by low, thick boxwood seemed the best place. Lifting the box again, he carried it there, and shoved it under the bench, then back until the boxwood swallowed it.

Spent from the effort, he stretched his arms, then found his way back into the garden and along the wall. Up ahead, near the door into the carriage house, he saw Gareth and Lance. And someone else.

"But you know me, Hector," Lance was saying. "I am a duke now. A peer. You really should not threaten one of us. It isn't done."

"It really isn't," Gareth said.

"I know you be a thief, not a duke," Hector said.

Ives walked up and joined them. He saw the problem. Hector had not merely confronted his brothers. Hector had brought a very, very big knife with him, that he brandished in the moonlight.

"I told you we should bring pistols," Lance muttered when he noticed Ives by his side.

"You come with me now," Hector said. "I bring you to Mrs. Lavender. You rob her, so she can decide what to do."

He gestured for them to go in front of him. They walked to the house.

"Did he see you leaving with the press?" Ives asked.

"I don't think so," Gareth said. "He appeared to have arrived just as we did."

When they got near the house, Ives looked up the long fire stairs. At the top, on the little terrace beneath the eaves, he saw a figure move. He hoped Padua had enough sense to stay up there.

Into the house they marched. Into the dining room. Hector went to the doorway, and called a servant girl. He spoke lowly, then took position, arms crossed and monstrosity of a knife at the ready.

The door opened and Mrs. Lavender hurried in, fussing. "I do not know what could be so important that you pulled me out of my—" She froze, and took in the three guests.

The knife pointed at them. "I found them in the garden, up to no good. Near the carriage house. I think they were going to steal the horses."

She peered at the three of them. In particular she narrowed her eyes on Lance. He opened his arms and smiled.

"Mrs. Lavender, it is such a joy to see you again. It has been too long. Surely you have not forgotten me?"

Her eyes widened. "Oh! *Ohhh.*" She collected herself and executed an impressive curtsy. "Your Grace, we are honored."

Poor Hector looked confused. Mrs. Lavender glared over at him. "This gentleman is an old friend of ours from years back. Surely you remember Lord Lancelot. Only he is a duke now. You have threatened a duke, Hector. A *duke.*"

Hector lowered the knife, and his head. Mrs. Lavender shooed him away. He left, much subdued.

She returned her attention to her guests. "Gentlemen, why were you in my garden?"

An awkward moment. Silence quaking.

Lance stepped forward, all smiles. "I thought to revisit the site of my fondest hours of my misspent youth. I could hardly walk in the front door, however."

"Oh, goodness no, of course not. We are honored, Your Grace. The young ladies will be overwhelmed." She peered at Gareth. "I do not recognize you."

"I have never been here before."

"He is my brother Gareth," Ives said. "He is the youngest."

"How unfair that the duke did not see to your initiation too."

"Gareth took care of that himself long before my father would have thought of it," Lance explained.

"Well, he must finally enjoy the refinements of our entertainments."

"I must decline, generous though the offer is," Gareth said. "I am only with Ives, who needed to show Lance where the garden entrance could be found."

"You will find that little has changed, Your Grace, except the faces. If you would wait just a minute, I want to prepare my young ladies, so they greet you properly." She sailed out of the dining room.

"I told you that you would make a mess of it if I were not with you," Lance said. "Hector would have chopped you to pieces by now if not for me."

"And now you will fall on your sword to spare us yet again," Ives said. "How good of you."

"That is what brothers are for."

The door opened, and Mrs. Lavender beckoned. "Your Grace, all is ready."

Lance squared his shoulders. "Gentlemen, enjoy your evening, and raise a toast to my sacrifice when you are in your cups."

"Your selflessness moves us both," Ives said.

"It should." He sighed. "The things I do for the family."

Ives shed Gareth once they left the house. He then circled back to the garden portal and climbed the fire stairs.

Padua waited for him in her chamber.

"I saw," she said. "Did you get in before Hector found you?"

"We did, and I found the cellar. It contained nothing of interest." He hated lying to her, but he had not completely reconciled his mind to what he had just done. Nor what he would do tomorrow night, when he returned with a carriage and moved the box and the press from this property entirely.

Hiding evidence was contrary to his sworn duty. It compromised his honor without recourse. No one would care that he did it to protect Padua.

He had acted on impulse. It could still be undone. One note to the Home Office or the magistrate would set all to rights.

With the choice weighing on his soul, he joined

Padua in bed. He let her know through the kiss he gave her that there would be no passion tonight. He lay in the dark with her in his arms, assessing the fine mess this had become, considering his limited options and their unacceptable consequences.

"After your father's trial, what will you do?" He knew she did not sleep yet, but the question sounded stark in the way it broke the silence.

"If I inherit—" She broke off. She would only inherit for one reason. "If I do, I think I will sell this house. Not to Mrs. Lavender. She can go elsewhere if she is determined to continue. I would like to see it become a school. I would accept much less if someone wanted it for that."

"It could be your school."

Her hair, so like fine silk, moved against his cheek when she shook her head. "I will take the money and go to Padua, and study. If by some mercy I do not inherit, I will make him give me the money you found in the books and go anyway, and find employment as a tutor while there."

"I may not allow that."

She kissed him, and he felt her smile. "You know you cannot stop me. I will have to go. I will be notorious here."

He was risking his good name, his reputation, and everything that mattered to protect a woman determined to leave him. He was either an ass, or . . . His embrace closed on her tighter as he acknowledged the truth behind what he did. Behind the desire and even the pleasure now. Behind the tightness in his chest.

"If I cannot stop you, perhaps I will follow you."

"To drag me back? It sounds romantic, but I do not think I would like it."

"Not to drag you back. To join you."

Her head turned. "Why would you do that? Your life is here."

Tell her. She has a right to know. "So I can have my fill of you." *Coward.*

She nestled down. "I would be happy if you visited me for a while."

He pressed a kiss to her crown. "It might be a long while, Padua. A few months at least."

She nodded subtly, then yawned.

He held her until she fell asleep. *A few months. Perhaps a few years. Maybe forever.*

CHAPTER 21

Two mornings later, Ives let himself out the door and began to descend the fire stairs of the house. A movement caught his eye and he halted in his tracks. Down below a woman strolled in the garden. He watched her a good while. Then, when she aimed toward the back portal, he retraced his steps to Padua's chamber.

She looked up from where she prepared to wash.

"There is someone in the garden. A woman."

"They often take the air after they rise. She will not be there long."

"I find it hard to believe this woman is one of Mrs. Lavender's young ladies. She is too old, for one thing."

"That must be Emily. I am told she is older, and works here on an itinerant basis. She lives elsewhere. Mrs.

Lavender had complained of feeling poorly yesterday, so Emily took her place in the office. She does that too."

Ives went back to the door. He did not step outside again, but he watched Emily as best he could through its opening. When she turned toward the house again, the suspicion that had been nudging him was confirmed. He recognized her.

"Has she met you? Does she know you are here?" he asked Padua, upon returning to her chamber again. He sat on a chair to watch her finish her ablutions. It charmed him, this simple, common task. She appeared domestic and fresh in the dawn's light, with her night-dress down around her waist and her lithe back flexing softly while she washed her breasts and arms.

"We have not met. I heard two of the servants complaining about her last night, however."

"I recognize her."

Padua looked over her shoulder. She grinned. "Is your past haunting you?"

"Not the way you mean. If you saw her, you might recognize her too. She has rooms right below your father's on Wigmore Street."

"She is that blond woman who likes to sit at the window?"

He nodded. "Her name is Emily Trenholm. I prosecuted her husband."

"I expect she does not like you much."

"I thought her living below your father an odd coincidence. That she also has a connection here is one too many."

Padua slipped her arms back into her undressing gown. "Do you think Mrs. Lavender is involved after all? I hope not. I rather like her."

"We will not know until all is revealed. However, assume she is for now. Do not let her know we are suspicious."

"I have been waiting, expecting some kind of overture from her or someone else, and nothing has happened."

Ives went over, kissed her. "It is time to fix that."

"How?"

"By setting a trap."

Padua tucked her mother's blue wrap around her shoulders more snugly, and cast her gaze over Berkeley Square. On this overcast, chilled morning, most of the people dotting the paths and grass were governesses with small children.

"Padua." The voice behind her made her jump. She turned to see Jennie walking toward her, arms open.

They embraced, then Jennie stood back and gave her a good look. "That is a new pelisse. It suits you."

It was one of the garments Eva had redone for her. "I wore it just for you, so you would know I am not starving."

"I feared you were, or that I would never see you again. What were you thinking, writing that you were leaving town for an indeterminate period, then never writing again? I have worried the whole time."

They locked arms and strolled along the path. "I have made some new friends, and learned some things about my family too. It has been an amazing few weeks, Jennie."

Jennie's blue eyes glanced at the pelisse again. "Did one of your friends buy you that? I promise I will not scold."

"Yes, but not a man, if that is your insinuation. A very nice lady gave it to me. An artist." She told Jennie about Eva and Gareth, and their recent trip abroad.

"Such circles you have moved in, Padua. How did such doors open to you?"

"It is all due to my father." It was the truth. "There is much I cannot confide yet, but eventually perhaps I can explain everything. I wanted to see you mostly to know you are doing well, Jennie. Please tell me that you are."

"Little has changed, except I no longer have you to complain with. The woman hired to replace you knows little more than the girls. She has them doing the most basic problems. Mrs. Ludlow does not know, or does not care."

"London could use a proper school for girls," Padua said. "One that taught them the way boys are taught. Girls are just as smart. Why should they have to tolerate teachers like this one you describe?"

"Because the one who could do it better got herself thrown out?" Jennie's eyes glistened with humor.

Padua laughed. "Someday I hope to have a school, Jennie. Would you teach there if I did? Would you be the Mrs. Ludlow?"

Jennie laughed, too, then realized Padua no longer did. "You are serious?"

"It is something I think I may be able to convince my father to support someday."

"You do?" Jennie gave her an odd look, then averted her eyes.

Ten paces on, the little frown on Jennie's brow had not smoothed.

"What is it?" Padua asked. "You are subdued all of a sudden."

"You speak of your father as if there has been a rapprochement between you. If there has been, I am truly happy for you. But—"

"But?"

Jennie took a deep breath. "I saw a newspaper that had a small notice about a man with your name. Belvoir. He is to be tried for serious crimes. I wondered if he was your relative, and asked Mrs. Ludlow. She insisted he was not. But—" She looked embarrassed, and hopeful.

Padua watched poor Jennie try to believe the best, the way dear Mrs. Ludlow had encouraged. If she were told that Hadrian Belvoir was not relation at all, Jennie would probably believe it.

"The notice was about my father. A mistake has been made."

"Of course it has. I am sure it has."

"I know he will be acquitted."

"I know he will be, too, if you have cause to think that. Truly."

Did she imagine that Jennie moved away? Not a step

was taken, but a shifting of weight had Jennie more distant. Her eyes looked worried, and her reassuring smile polite and forced. She fussed with her reticule and straightened her gloves.

"I really must hurry back. I must take my class after lunch."

"Jennie—"

Jennie stopped walking. "I wish I were as brave as you, Padua. Brave enough to stand up to the world. Brave enough to be different. To think differently. I am not."

"You do not have to be."

"Don't I? Your father— It is the kind of trial that all the papers report. Every word. He will be infamous, once it starts."

"And I will be too. That is what you are saying, isn't it?" Jennie could ill afford to have the taint spread to her too. She could not risk this friendship any longer. Padua felt the cut deeply, but she could not blame her friend.

Jennie's eyes teared. "I really must go." She walked off, her expression stricken. "I am sorry, Padua. So sorry."

"Are you ready?" Ives asked.

They sat in his carriage, two streets from her father's chambers on Wigmore Street. They had ridden past the building, to ensure a blond head sat near the window on the first floor.

"I am ready, but you must do the shouting. I do not think my voice will carry enough."

"I will make sure she hears." Every day this continued, his situation became more untenable. He was in far deeper than he ever thought possible, and he wanted it finished.

Padua stepped out of the carriage. Posture rigid, she walked toward Wigmore Street.

Ives's mind followed her to the building's door, and up the stairs. Only then did he set off on the same path.

He approached the building, and spied Mrs. Trenholm at her window. She peered out, then pulled back, out of sight. He mounted the stairs like a man on the trail of an elusive quarry. He found Padua at the bookcase in her father's apartment, running her finger along the spines. She paused and pulled out a small, thin schoolbook. A blue one this time. She held it upside down and shook.

"What are you doing?" he asked.

"Checking to see if you missed any money. As long as I am here, I thought I might as well see what other of my books were here."

Finding that money had been the first step on the path that had brought him to where he was today. He did not regret any of it, but abandoning one's honor would leave any man in a dark humor.

He pointed to the floor. Performance time.

"Miss Belvoir, it is time you and I had a right understanding."

"Regarding what, sir?"

He raised his voice. "I think that you have the evidence that is sought regarding your father. I am sure of it. If you do not tell me what you have found, it will go badly for you."

"I am sure I do not know what you mean."

"The plates, Miss Belvoir. The equipment," he boomed. "He told you where to find it. A man was put in the cell with him, to watch you both. He reported a conversation, full of whispers and instructions, through that grating. Your father has made you an accomplice, and if you do not reveal all, you will end up on the gallows beside him."

"You are all bluster, sir. You know nothing."

"Then there is something to know!"

Padua waited a five count. "If there were—and I am not saying there is—would I be able to bargain for my father's freedom if I revealed it?"

"His freedom? I should hope not. Some mercy, perhaps. For him and for you. You know where it is, don't you? The equipment used to print the notes. The place where the bad money is stored, while it gets passed bit by bit into the economy. Tell me now."

"If I knew these things, I would expect a lot of mercy before handing the information over. I would need to have more than your word as guarantee too."

"My word is the best you will get."

"I am sure you believe it is all anyone would need. I do not agree. We have nothing more to say to each other. Please leave now. You were not invited in, but I will indeed invite you out."

Ives came over to her. "You did splendidly," he whispered.

"I actually grew angry with you. Your tone was very high-handed. I did not care for it at all."

"Let us hope the woman below heard every word."

"What if we are wrong? What if she has nothing to do with any of it?"

"Then we will find another way to discover who does." He gave her a kiss. "I must go. You have just thrown me out, remember?"

He used heavy steps on the stairs, and frowned hard as he left the building. He strode away, then waited for Padua at the carriage.

She took some time to arrive. He grew annoyed, then worried. Finally she walked around the corner.

"What were you doing?" he demanded.

"I finished looking in the schoolbooks. You missed twenty pounds." She shook her reticule. "That was careless of you."

"This was not the time."

"It was an excellent time. Between your leaving and my leaving, someone else left." She climbed into the carriage. "I think you were correct about her."

He settled onto the other seat. "Let us hope so. Take your supper in your chamber this evening. I will join you early, in case we have had success."

They held vigil that night.

Padua ate her supper, then they played cards. When that bored them, they read. The hours passed slowly. No one came to her chamber door. No messages arrived.

Padua considered that her chamber was big enough for one, but not two. Unless the two were in bed, that was. They could not occupy themselves that way, however.

She took pleasure just being with Ives. She hoped he felt the same about her. This was, she realized, the longest they had been in each other's company like this, not even talking, sharing silent companionship. It created a domestic intimacy that she enjoyed. She tucked it away as a memory for later in her life, when she needed some cozy warmth.

After midnight, Ives grew restless. She could tell he doubted matters would develop as quickly as he had assumed. The chamber became even smaller then. Ives at peace took up less space than Ives agitated and impatient. He did not actually do anything different, but his spirit churned and roiled.

They had begun to give up that it would be this night, when a scratch sounded on her door. Both of them snapped alert. Ives moved silently to the wall behind her door, then nodded.

They had rehearsed what she would do and say, assuming the demands were those they anticipated. She opened the door a crack and looked out.

A man stood there. A stranger. The door to the stairs remained ajar. He had entered the way she did, and Mrs. Lavender would be none the wiser.

He had known where to find her. He had learned that from someone in this house.

"You are Belvoir's daughter." He spoke lowly, with a thick Cornish accent.

"Who are you?"

"Never you mind. You've something that's ours, or know where it is. I'll be needing that information now."

"I don't know what you are talking about." She made to close the door.

His boot, heavy and big, stopped her. He thrust it into the opening on the floor. He bent closer. "You don't want to be causing trouble. A bit of iron and copper won't help your father. If you turn it over, you will only ensure he hangs."

"If I turn it over to you, what will I get instead?"

His eyes narrowed. "What do you mean?"

"You think I have something you want. If I give it to you, I expect something in return."

"You are blackmailing us?" He appeared incredulous.

"I am negotiating. Here are my terms. I want two thousand pounds. The real kind, not the kind printed up at night. It is a good bargain for you. Rebuilding your trade will cost much more."

He scratched his chin. "I'll be needing to talk this over with the others. I will come back tomorrow or the next day or so."

The tiniest tap on her elbow made Padua ease back enough to see Ives out of the corner of her eye. He shook his head.

She thought fast. "If you must do that, you are not

the one making decisions. Tell him, whoever he is, that I will only bargain with him so we can make quick work of this."

"That is not how he likes to do things."

"It is the only way he will get what I have. If he does not agree by week's end, I will hand it all to the local magistrate, and take my chances."

He shook his head. He gave her a stare full of disdain. "Just like that, you sell your father. What kind of daughter are you?"

She felt her face warming, but she held her hard pose and expression. "The kind who would rather have two thousand in good notes than even thirty thousand of the amateurish forgeries you print up. I want this settled by week's end, or I will become a dutiful daughter again."

She closed the door in his face, and held her breath. Neither she nor Ives moved a hair for a long time. Then, on his nod, she opened the door again and peered out. The man had left.

"Do you think he will return tomorrow night?" she asked.

"Two nights hence, or three is more likely. It sounded like the man we want is not in London. He will have to journey here."

"At least it is not Mrs. Lavender."

"She may still know of it. She may use the bad money in that office of hers." One of his eyebrows went up. "I just realized I may know how to find out if she does." He turned her around and began unfastening her dress.

She waited until he was done. "It does not appear I will need protection tonight. Or until two nights hence, at least, you said."

He turned her to face him. He looked down, his hands still on her shoulders. "I have grown accustomed to it, but I will leave if you want."

She did not want that. It had taken all her strength to say what she had. She had grown accustomed to having him beside her too. Too much so, she feared. It had become normal. Expected. She wondered if she could even sleep now without his arm slung over her the way it was all night.

"If you don't mind that narrow bed and cold water for the first washing, I am glad if you stay."

Later, while she thought he slept but she stayed awake storing memories, he spoke into the peaceful space. "I want you to stay at Langley House tomorrow night."

"You are not sure I will be safe here?"

"It is not that. I truly think nothing will happen for at least two days."

"Then . . . ?"

"It would be nice to use a good bed for one night."

She had to laugh. "What? You do not find this one comfortable? You are not sleeping well?"

"It isn't the sleeping so much that is limited."

"I would have said you managed the other more than well enough, *my lord*."

"I did, didn't I?" He sounded pleased with himself. "A resourceful mind can always find a way. However, a night of comfort is still called for. For your sake, I mean. We will join the others for a good dinner, and you will remain there as a guest."

"I would not mind being spoiled for a night."

"Good. We will feed you delicacies, and put you to bed beneath lovely drapes, surrounded by soft pillows. And I will spend the night spoiling you without mercy." He turned on his side, then tucked her back against his body. She nestled close, and felt the evidence that he would not sleep soon.

Kisses on her back ensured she would not either. That possessive arm moved until its hand could fondle her breasts, then caressed lower to raise her nightdress. Experienced, efficient touches aroused her quickly. When she was dizzy with pleasure, he bent one of her knees up in front of her body and pressed into her.

She smiled at the welcomed fullness. "How . . . resourceful."

"More than you know. Here, I will show you." He demonstrated how he could reach her breasts and elsewhere easily, and how the front of her body remained available to him.

"How wonderful," she managed to say despite her short, shallow breaths. "It was naughty of you to save one of the best for last."

"Not quite the last, Padua."

Much later, when they were again entwined and he truly slept, she wondered if he had spoken of the way they joined, or when they would part.

CHAPTER 22

"I think a turn outside is in order," Gareth said. "That was quite a feast and I suddenly feel portly."

"Eva said Ives here requested half of it," Lance said.

"I had a taste for a few old favorites. It was kind of Eva to tell the cook to indulge me," Ives said. "Regrettably, I overindulged myself as a result. I will join you, Gareth. We can waddle down the street like two old uncles."

"I will enjoy my port, then retire," Lance said. "The ladies have already gone above, so I will entertain myself."

Outside in the crisp, damp air, Ives and Gareth strolled in the mist. The houses at the far end of the block appeared ghostly, with only diffused light coming from a few windows and their dark shapes bleeding into the fog.

"Eva is delighted that you convinced Miss Belvoir to visit," Gareth said.

"Your wife has been very kind to her. Not all women would be, after—"

"After finding you in her bed?"

"Yes. And after learning about her father."

They paced on, around the corner.

"How compromised are you, Ives?" Gareth asked.

"Thoroughly."

"Does it go beyond losing the Crown's favor?"

"Far beyond it."

"What Lance and I carried out of that carriage house was not in itself incriminating. You never mentioned what was in the box you hauled away, however."

"No, I did not. And do not ask."

"You are risking a lot for this woman. Lance thinks you have lost your mind."

"In a manner of speaking, I suppose I have. Not the way he means, and not the way he would ever understand. You would, I think."

Gareth gave him a long look, then stopped him with a hand on his arm. "I am the last one to lecture. I have no right, and—"

"You have every right, if any man does. As much as Lance. You will probably make more sense than he does too."

Gareth laughed lowly, then turned serious. "I have always been outside. I know the prospects from that vantage point. You have never been there. Do you think to keep this affair going once that trial starts? Even being the son and brother of Aylesbury will not help you much if you do. The scandal will be unbelievable. Your dealings with her, for her, will be poked and prodded and dissected until leaving your house will be something you dread."

Gareth was correct. A year ago he might have braved it out. Secure in his honor, he could have withstood anything. He no longer owned that safe haven, however. He might never again.

"Is there a way out of this?" Gareth asked.

"She thinks so. She tried to throw me over. She will again."

"Then, perhaps, for a while—"

"She does not know about that box, you see. I made a choice that night that I cannot, and will not, undo. A love affair with the daughter of a criminal has become the least of it."

Mood subdued, Gareth continued their walk.

They had almost circled the block when Ives resumed the conversation. "I have spent most of the night debating whether to ask something of you."

"I hope you know you can ask for anything."

"Do not be so quick. It draws you into it, and more than I like. I have scoured my mind for an alternative, however, and there is none. I need to trust the man involved completely. Other than you and Lance, there are no such men."

"I hope you do not want me to commit highway robbery."

"Not quite. I need you to stand guard at that building the next few nights. With a pistol this time."

Gareth was not so foolhardy as to ignore the implications. "Just me? Will Lance—"

"Aylesbury should not be further involved. He would not be at all if he had not inserted himself the other night."

"He inserted himself quite a lot that night, didn't he? Especially after we left him, I think."

Ives smiled at the bawdy entendre. "He did speak of the ultimate sacrifice."

"He did not return the next morning until ten o'clock. Mrs. Lavender has how many young ladies? Ten? Twelve? You don't suppose he enjoyed them all, do you?"

"I have tried not to wonder. Now I will picture him staggering from chamber to chamber until he drops from exhaustion."

They laughed, and Ives was grateful at Gareth's ability to lighten even the darkest night.

"I will clean my pistol," Gareth said as they entered the house. "Just tell me where, when, and what. I will be there. Now, I am going to retire."

"I think I will have a smoke before I leave."

Gareth grinned. He came over and cocked his head closely. "The servant stairs are more convenient to her chamber. Also more discreet."

Ives entered the library, prepared to dally for the length of one cigar before seeking the servant stairs. He did not find the chamber empty the way he expected. Lance still sat in a comfortable chair near the fire, his port on a table near his arm.

"I thought you were retiring," Ives said, taking a cigar from the box and preparing it.

"I have been thinking."

"You cannot do that in your apartment?"

"I chose to do it here. Do you mind?"

He did. He would have to wait Lance out now. A very big, very comfortable bed waited, with a very lovely, very willing woman in it. He did not want to humor Lance when he could be with Padua instead.

Lance gestured lazily to a nearby chair, inviting him over. Ives poured himself some port and carried it and the cigar to the fireplace. He settled in. This might take hours.

"Miss Belvoir looked lovely tonight," Lance said.

"I thought so."

"Eva was happy to have another woman here."

"We probably bore her."

Lance fingered his glass, then looked over. "Did you know Miss Belvoir has been living in a chamber at the top of Mrs. Lavender's house?"

Ives almost choked on cigar smoke. He cleared his throat. "Who told you that?"

"Susan. She is the young lady who entertained me there. She had all kinds of revelations."

"You were chatting? You were supposed to be fucking."

"We chatted between fucking. Have you never done that? Do you just lie there, silent, while you recover?"

"I am mostly astonished to learn you spent all that time with one of them. I assumed that you intended to spread the ducal favor far and wide."

"It was my plan, but when Susan let me know she was not averse to ignoring many of Mrs. Lavender's fussy rules, I thought I would do best staying the course, as it were."

Ives trusted Lance would now lose himself in waxing nostalgic about his visit to his youthful haunt. Alas, it was not to be.

"She said that Miss Belvoir introduced herself to all of them. Sat to a meal with them. Said her father was a partner, and she was now too. I am not a fastidious man, Ives. It is not for me to lecture—"

"I'll say."

"However, is it a good idea to bring her here when Eva is in residence? For someone who never let his women near the family, your blindness to basic propriety with this madam is troubling."

"She is not a madam."

"So Susan had it wrong?"

Ives puffed away.

Lance waited, all curiosity.

"It is very complicated," Ives said.

"Take your time. I have all night."

"I don't."

Lance glanced to the ceiling. "Ah. Of course. The dinner was only the prelude. The symphony has yet to play. Well off with you then, to lead the tempo with your baton. You can explain it all tomorrow."

"I have nothing to explain to you."

"But you do. Our breaking into that building, for example. We stole something. You stole something else. All of it is important, I am sure. All if it has to do with Miss Belvoir. I think another adventure is going to occur as well, because it all smelled of a job unfinished. Do not even try to leave me out of the denouement, when it comes. I will make your life hell if you do."

Ives stubbed out his cigar. Lance *could* make his life hell. He managed to do that without trying. If he put his effort to it—

"Out of curiosity, how did you pay Mrs. Lavender, Lance?"

"With a twenty-pound note."

"She gave you notes back, then?"

Lance laughed. "Many. There isn't a whore in London worth more than two or three."

"Do you have any of those notes on you now?"

Lance thought about it, then rummaged in his pockets. He deposited several crumpled banknotes on the table beside him. "I expect those are them. They were on my dressing table. I must have thrown them there when I came back."

Ives picked up the notes. He smoothed them, then carried them to the lamp.

"I trust they are good," Lance said.

Ives set them back on the table.

"Good, and not printed on that little press we found in the cellar, that is," Lance added.

"They all look to be genuine."

Lance peered at them. "You are sure? Some of these fellows are experts with the burin."

"I am sure." He walked to the door. "I am leaving now."

Lance just smiled at him.

"If you cannot sleep, Lance, you might spend the time doing something more worthwhile than wondering about my inexplicable lack of propriety. You might, for example, clean your pistols."

Padua heard the door to the dressing room open. She heard boot steps, then saw the tall shadow at the dressing room's threshold. It disappeared, and muffled sounds came out of the other chamber.

Her body grew sensitive to the sensation of the sheet's fabric against her bare skin. Her breasts swelled and firmed as anticipation teased her.

Ives reappeared and walked to the bed. He was naked. He stood beside her. He drew off the sheet and looked at her.

She looked at him too. The small lamp's light washed him in a golden glow that defined his form in highlights and deep shadows. His eyes appeared as deeply green as a dense forest's foliage. His face, always so handsome, held the hard angles that reflected his desire.

She wondered what game he would choose to play, or if there would be a new one. It surprised her when he joined her, and wrapped her in a commonplace embrace. His gaze moved over her face slowly while his fingers twisted lazily in a strand of her hair.

"There is nothing ordinary about you, Padua. Not even your beauty."

It was not said like an easy flattery, but instead thoughtfully while he subjected her to that gaze. She believed he really meant it, even though no one before Ives had ever called her beautiful.

He rose up on his arm, so he could watch his fingertips trace along her body. She had expected hard, even violent passion, so this meandering caress charmed her. Then she realized what he was doing. He was making memories, much as she had done several times now. He was storing this night in his head where he might visit again.

It touched her deeply that he sought to do that. He had not liked it when she broke things off. Perhaps there had been more to it than wounded pride, the way she had assumed.

He kissed her slowly, deeply, wonderfully. Her heart stretched and filled until it ached. His caresses began guiding her out of the everyday world, toward the rare existence that she experienced when he controlled her pleasure. He knew her very well now, knew her body and how to make the pleasure sweet, then maddening, then so powerful it shattered her hold on herself.

He used all his skill, as if he wanted her to remember too. The intimacy deepened along with the pleasure, the two so intertwined that they became one. It awed her, moved her, so that her heart held on to both desperately, just as she held on to him. *Yes*, her mind chanted, accepting everything she experienced, even the sweet ache that colored the beauty with sadness.

He came over when the first tremors of her release tantalized her. He bent her knees, then lifted her legs over his shoulders. Braced on his arms, he looked down between their bodies and watched how he entered her. He closed his eyes at the sensation. "*Yes*." His own affirmation echoed hers.

She watched what it did to him. She never had before. She watched how the pleasure both hardened his expression and transformed it. She watched how his gaze both ravished her and adored her. She saw how he sought signs of what she wanted, and made sure he answered her need.

Yes, she breathed as he moved in her. *Yes*, aloud now, when he thrust harder. She laid her palms on his chest above her, and his heartbeat pulsed into her body. *Yes*, she cried as wildness set in and her mind narrowed until it knew only him. Then she even lost hold of him, and the pleasure tightened and broke and screamed.

He waited for her on the other side, his heart pounding beneath her palm, his breathing ragged. He moved her legs down and lowered onto her with a never-ending kiss on her neck.

She filled her embrace with him, and her head with

his scent and sounds, and her soul with his care. *Have you fallen in love with him, Padua? It is not the same as desire or passion.* Yes, not the same, but not so different. Not separate. *Have you fallen in love with him?* Yes.

CHAPTER 23

For two nights Ives and Padua waited. Two nights Gareth held vigil in the alley. For two nights nothing happened. On the third day, Ives made a decision on a matter he had been debating. He rode to the Home Office, and called on Strickland.

"Do you want to catch a whale?"

Strickland's eyes lit. "Hell, yes. Nothing would advance my career faster. Do you have one in your sights?"

"I do. Bringing you into it comes with conditions, however."

Strickland grimaced. "A lot of lawyer talk is coming, isn't it?"

"Some. I will be relying on your friendship more than any formal terms, however. That, and your word as a gentleman."

"You had better let me hear those conditions. I am suddenly uneasy."

"I have reason to think that Belvoir's accomplices will be making themselves known tonight. You are welcome to join me when they do."

Strickland eyed him. "And the condition?"

"If I am wrong, you never speak of what you see or hear."

Strickland thought that over. "That is a damnable condition."

Ives shrugged. "Have it your way. Do not say I did not offer." He turned to the door.

"Now *wait*. Give a man a minute to think things over." He did. "How bad might things be if you are wrong?"

"No worse for you than for me."

"I don't find that reassuring, for some reason."

"Your choice is simple, as is mine. We can let a man stand trial for crimes that far surpass his guilt, or we can attempt to bring the real culprits to justice. Remember justice? It is why we do what we do. This is England, and the word used to mean something here."

Strickland flushed. "Do not preach at me. I'll not sit for it when I know in my gut you are up to something that you shouldn't do."

"You are right. I should not preach. I will instead appeal to your baser desires to further your career."

Strickland's face reddened more. "What must I do?"

"Go to Langley House at eight o'clock this evening. My brother Gareth will be there. He will tell you what to do."

* * *

They waited again, but it was different this time. Padua sensed something in the air, a pending excitement. Ives remained more alert, listening to every sound that came through the walls.

"Mrs. Lavender took ill after dinner," Padua reported. "She seemed fine, the servants said, then later complained of a malady of the stomach."

Ives looked over from where he sat, looking at nothing, thinking. Waiting. "Was Emily Trenholm at that dinner?"

"Perhaps so. It was said Mrs. Lavender was relieved Emily would be able to stand in at the office."

Ives stood and went to the door. He looked out, then closed it. "I think it will happen differently from what we expected. I do not think the man we seek will come to this door."

"Then how?" She had accommodated her nerves to the idea Ives would be right near her when that man arrived.

"If Emily has taken Mrs. Lavender's place, I think he will walk in the front door, like a patron." He raked his hair with his fingers. "I will return in two minutes. If anyone comes here, do not leave the chamber. Put them off if they try to call you away."

He slipped out, leaving her to worry. This was far worse than waiting the last time. Her stomach churned. She experienced a wave of relief when Ives returned. He took a look at her and crouched near her chair so he could see her face.

"You do not have to do this. We can find another way."

"What other way is there? I must do it. If I do not, I will have nothing to use to bargain for my father."

"I do not like to think of you afraid."

"A little fear will not harm me. Deep in my heart, I am not as fearful as I may appear either. I know you will not be far away. I know they are not so stupid as to harm me."

He grasped her hand. He stood and bent down to give her a kiss, but froze when a scratch on the door interrupted.

Ives stepped out of sight, pressing to the wall. Shaking, Padua opened the door a crack.

A servant girl stood there. "Emily asks that you come down, miss. To the office. She is having trouble with a patron over payment. With Mrs. Lavender gone, she wants your help and advice."

Padua almost said to tell Emily to have Hector throw the patron out, before she realized this was the other way Ives had expected.

"Tell her I will be down very soon. I need to make myself presentable."

The servant girl walked away. Padua closed the door.

"Agree to nothing right away," Ives said. "Even if he wants to give you two thousand, bargain for more to keep him talking."

"But what do I say if he wants to know where the equipment is? I have claimed to know, but I don't."

He appeared torn. "Say it is in that cellar."

"Is it?"

"It was. There is still some paper and bad money there."

"Now you tell me?"

"If you did not know, you would not have to lie. Questions might have come from others besides the man you will meet tonight. Scold me later if you want."

She would definitely do that.

She closed her eyes, to compose herself. She did not need to do anything to her person. She already was presentable. She had dressed tonight to look like a prosperous business owner, not an impoverished schoolteacher.

Ives tapped her shoulder. Before he opened the door, he gave her a kiss.

She battled excitement and fear as she walked down the stairs. She wanted to sound poised and in command, and sought that voice inside herself. She would think of them as students, she decided. Students who had not learned their lesson for today.

Hector stood guard by the door. Before going to the office, she approached him. "Is Mrs. Lavender faring better?"

He turned black, worried eyes on her. "Not worse, at least. I thought the food, maybe—no one else is sick."

"Send for a physician, Hector. Tell him that her food may have been tainted or poisoned."

The whites of his eyes showed more at the last word. Hector angry was a sight to behold. "Who?"

"I do not know. Send for the physician, then keep your ears open."

* * *

Padua entered the office without asking permission. Emily was not Mrs. Lavender, after all.

She found Emily in a tête-a-tête with a man. Not especially tall, he wore riding clothes and his face was unshaved. Close-set round eyes peered at her from his narrow face. He gave the impression of having ridden a good distance recently.

Emily snapped her mouth shut upon Padua's intrusion. She appeared older and harder up close. Sitting in her window, one might think her attractive. Now deep lines by her mouth marked her character. A sharp chin gave her a belligerent appearance.

"Is this the gentleman who is objecting to the fees?" Padua asked.

"Not objecting as such," Emily said. "He wants to use a bank draft."

Padua remained standing, and noted how the man did not stand, too, as a polite man would. "We do not take bank drafts, sir. In all the years here, Mrs. Lavender never has. There can be no exceptions."

The man just looked at her. Judging. Assessing.

"If your business is concluded, sir—" Padua began.

"Not yet concluded, Miss Belvoir. You've something I want, and it is not one of those whores you sell."

"I cannot imagine what that might be."

"Of course you can. You sent for me. I am not pleased about that, so let us settle matters quickly."

Padua looked pointedly at Emily.

"She can stay," he said. "Although she has been nigh useless to me recently."

"I found your men a place to store it all, didn't I?" Emily snapped.

"Aye, the chamber of an idiot who left it in plain sight for anyone to see. You were supposed to keep an eye on it too. You just watched as they carted it away."

"What was I to do? Object? Say it was mine, and the magistrate couldn't have it?"

"You could have taken the next trunk when it came, instead of telling my boys that the constables had visited. You scared them off to hell knows where, without them leaving so much as word of where they had the press. That has cost me plenty."

Emily jabbed her thumb toward Padua. "I got Mrs. Lavender to talking about that partner of hers and I learned about this one here, didn't I? So you could write and let her know her father was in prison, so's he might tell her what he knew."

Padua interrupted. "My father is not an idiot."

The man looked at her, astonished. Then he burst out laughing. "Defending him, are you? Now that is pretty coming from a daughter willing to sell him out for two thousand."

"I am glad that we are turning the conversation in the correct direction. Did you bring it with you?"

He leaned forward. His eyes narrowed. "I'll see you dead before I hand you two thousand."

* * *

Ives almost burst in the door on hearing the threat. Strickland's firm grasp on his arm stopped him.

Out in the anteroom to the office, Lance spoke. "They are closed today, gentlemen. An illness. See yourselves out, will you? Hector is occupied."

"Why is Aylesbury here?" Strickland whispered.

"He insisted. Who am I to refuse a duke?"

"He has a pistol on him, I hope you know."

"Does he? I'll be damned."

Ives and Strickland bent their ears to the door again.

"You will do no such thing," Padua said. "It is not in your interest to harm me. I have your equipment. I have your plates and your paper, and a large amount of printed notes. If you get it all back, you can continue on. Two thousand is a small price for the fortune you will make."

"I don't pay for what is already mine. All I needed to know was you were here, and wanting to bargain, for me to figure out where it all was. I should have guessed. Or this fool of a woman should have known. They were working right here, under your nose, and you did not realize it, Emily. Is your brain going soft?"

"I'm not here often. I'm never in the garden at night, being as how I am busy. No one is, considering the trade here."

"Two thousand," Padua repeated. "For that I return your belongings, and I will not object if you continue using that cellar. Except for the unfortunate development with my father, the plan your men used worked very well."

"Not his men," Emily mumbled. "He made them bring him in, then took over. Didn't you?"

"Be silent, you old whore."

"Threatened to bring the government down on them if they didn't agree."

Ives stiffened. Ever since he began listening, something had struck him as oddly out of place about the conversation. He suddenly knew what it was.

He glared at Strickland. "That is Crippin in there. I swear, if you or anyone else is trying to trap Miss Belvoir I will—"

Strickland waved his hands. "He is not working for us in this. He isn't!"

"That is what you said when I caught him outside Langley House."

"He wasn't then either. I kept telling you that."

"Here is how it will be, Miss Belvoir," Crippin was saying. "Right now I've my men looking into that carriage house. I think we will find everything there, just as the others left it. There is no way a woman, even an Amazon like you, could carry a press out of there, or a box of plates, or a large amount of paper. I won't be needing your permission to continue use of the cellar either. I'll be telling them that matter that you tried to sell me more notes that you found on your father's property. The authorities trust what I tell them, you see. My information should put you in the dock beside that old fool."

"Have you heard enough, Strickland?" Ives asked. Strickland nodded.

"I certainly have," Lance said.

Ives pivoted. Lance stood at his shoulder. He pulled a pistol out from under his coat. "I'll carry this visibly, so we don't waste time with fisticuffs and such." He looked down pointedly at Ives's clenched hand.

"Let's do it, then." Lance pressed down the latch, threw open the door, and marched in with the pistol pointed upward, held high near his head.

CHAPTER 24

The house swarmed with constables. A few other men, not officially there, huddled in the office. Crippin and Emily Trenholm waited in the dining room under the watchful eye of Lance and Hector. The young ladies had all retired.

"Look what I found," Strickland announced. He led a small parade in from the garden. Bringing up the rear, Gareth kept a pistol trained on the two men they escorted.

"Put them to the dining room, with the others," Ives said.

Strickland stuck his head into the office. He closed the door, and came over to Ives. He whistled a little tune of astonishment. "Did you send for Sidmouth?"

"Lance did. As a courtesy, he said. Peer to peer."

"I wish I could have read the message he sent."

"As I recall, he wrote something about the immediate danger of both Sidmouth's reputation and that of the Home Office being engulfed in excrement. He gave him one hour to arrive, or he would feel obligated to next write to the prime minister, and the prince regent, lest a scandal that would shake the government erupt."

Strickland chuckled. "Sidmouth looks stricken. One of his own agents takes over a counterfeiting ring—you must admit, that is rich. I think I will go join him and my colleagues from the Home Office, and enjoy the show." Strickland walked to the door of the office. He dropped his smirk before entering and replaced it with a pensive frown.

Lance and Gareth came out of the dining room. "Hector is in there. No one is going anywhere. He has his knife," Lance said. He looked at the office door. Loud voices penetrated. "He came?"

"Oh, yes," Ives said.

"I should go help them. They are bound to miss the obvious solution unless I point it out."

"They are not stupid, Lance. They will see it."

"The problem is no one will want to voice it. It will sound too much like what it is. A compromise of honor to avoid humiliation and scandal."

"Perhaps a little scandal would do them good. Rein them in. Crippin was inevitable. Eventually men given leave to disobey the law will do it without permission."

"Neither they, you, Miss Belvoir, or the realm can afford that. Lest Strickland be thinking such nonsense, too, I had better be Aylesbury."

He strolled to the office door, opened it, and made his ducal presence known. "Gentlemen," he said as the door closed behind him. "This is a fine mess, isn't it?"

"Where is Miss Belvoir?" Gareth asked.

"She went above, to see Mrs. Lavender. She is worried that an innocent was harmed by our scheme."

"Bold of them, to have that Trenholm woman make her sick. It is good you realized he would not go up those exterior stairs after all."

Ives counted it as a close call. Had he not fathomed Crippin's plan, Strickland and Lance would have been deep in the garden when the servant came for Padua, and not waiting at the top of the stairs. He had needed Strickland to hear what transpired. He needed a witness other than Padua and himself.

"Here she comes," Gareth said, looking to the stairs. Padua was walking down. "Take her out to the garden. I will inform them that you are there, if anyone looks for either of you."

"Tell Strickland to find me before he leaves."

Ives guided Padua into the garden. No one remained in it now. She had watched a good deal of confusion out there earlier, as constables poked into shrubbery and dragged a big box out of the carriage house.

They sat on a stone bench up against some boxwood. Ives removed his frock coat and set it around her shoulders.

"Did they find everything?" she asked.

"It was all still here. I thought to remove it, but decided it would be easier to remove you. Alas, you proved almost unmovable." He embraced her with one arm. "Is Mrs. Lavender out of harm's way?"

"The physician thinks so. It might have been tragic. Poisons are not to be used carelessly. Emily could have easily put enough in the food to kill her, not incapacitate her."

"You know about such things, do you?"

"It is just chemistry."

She laid her head against his shoulder. She had calmed, but it would be some time before she knew real peace. "What will happen now?"

"There are men inside the house who want nothing more than to have all of this disappear. They will do anything to keep the truth about Crippin quiet."

"Can they do that?"

"If they want it. The constables will be sworn to secrecy. Hector and Mrs. Lavender and the ladies will be threatened. Crippin will be offered the noose or exile. Emily Trenholm will receive a similar choice. Should Hadrian Belvoir even go to trial, which would surprise me, since if he does it will all come out, he will be adjudged a victim of his own befuddled confusion."

"My father is neither befuddled nor confused."

"No, he is not. However, he will be free, Padua. It is not an outcome to be quibbled over."

She hung on his words with hope. Would it all end this way? Could it? "What if those men do not do any of this? What if they decide to send everyone to prison or the gallows?"

"Then that is bad news for Crippin and Mrs. Trenholm."

"And my father?"

"He will fare the best. I am told he has an excellent prosecutor who will ensure justice is done."

"You think too highly of your colleagues, I fear. You cannot be sure that this man will arrange it so justice is done."

"I can be very sure, since I am the prosecutor."

She sat up and turned to him. "I thought you withdrew."

"It appears I neglected to post the letters."

"When did you decide this?"

"After I spoke with him. I saw he was the worst kind of defendant for a prosecutor. He is incapable of dissembling. He exudes honesty and a childlike innocence. Also he shows just enough befuddlement to appear incapable of knowingly committing a crime. A jury would love him. If he spoke for himself, my histrionics would have at best even odds of gaining the conviction. As it is, my position as prosecutor is influencing events right now. Strickland is telling them I can never be convinced to leave out half the story."

She took his hand and kissed it. "Thank you. Another might have been so convinced." It could not have been easy for him to decide this. His sense of honor must have rebelled. He probably still wondered if she planned it so he might indeed do less than his best.

He pulled her back into his arms. "He told me something else that day, Padua. I think you should know what he said about you."

"He talked about me?"

"After I heard his story, I asked him why he would rather die than let you know about that house. After all, he had shown little interest in you for years."

Her throat tightened. The disappointments had been many, and still pained her. "What did he say?"

"He wept, darling. He explained it was not lack of love that made him keep his distance. It was because seeing you broke his heart. You look just like her, he said. You look just like your mother. He has never stopped mourning her, or loving her."

She held in her tears, but they burned her eyes and throat. Ives must have felt them in her, because he pressed a comforting kiss to her head.

Footsteps heralded another person in the garden. The moonlight reflected off fair hair.

"Over here, Strickland," Ives said.

The man who had burst into the office with Ives and Aylesbury joined them. "It is done. Your brother proved eloquent in describing the repercussions if it became known a government agent had become a rogue. Sidmouth looked ashen when Aylesbury finished talking.

They are taking Crippin and the Trenholm woman to a place of confinement, until arrangements are made for them to go away."

"And Belvoir?"

"There were a few curses about the bad luck of having a stickler like you on the case. It will take some doing to find a story the magistrate will swallow, but they will fix it."

"Thank you for your help."

"I enjoyed every minute." He took his leave and walked away.

The garden fell silent. And the house. "I think they are gone," Padua said.

"Then we can be too." Ives stood and offered his hand. "You will not stay here tonight, or any night again, Padua. You will come with me now."

He took her to his house on Lincoln's Inn Fields. His man Vickers only blinked once at her arrival before announcing he would bring some refreshments.

"I think we have shocked him," Padua said.

"We have certainly surprised him. I do not bring women here."

"You should not have brought me either."

"I have some things to say to you, and they are not appropriate to an inn or a carriage or that house. Come to the library."

She loved the library. Everything about it spoke of comfort and informality. Good chairs, a plump divan, a big table, and a handsome fireplace filled a good-sized chamber lined with books. One wall held law books, but the others showed a wide assortment of tomes in leather bindings.

She toured it all, taking in the appointments. She realized Ives watched her. "It is perfect," she said. "Just the right size. Luxurious, but not overwhelming like the one in Langley House."

He took her hand and led her to the divan. He sat and pulled her down on his lap. "I am glad you like it. I will show you the rest of the house tomorrow, to see if it suits you as well."

"What matters is that it suits you."

He quirked a half smile. His gaze drifted lower. "I'll be damned. I had not realized this before."

"Realized what?"

"Due to your height, when you sit like this, your breasts are most conveniently placed." He kissed one, to show what he meant. "A bit of unfastening and unlacing and I can drive you mad from the comfort of my favorite chair." His hand toyed with buttons on her pelisse to show what he meant.

"Mr. Vickers—"

"Damn. I will have to wait until after he brings the refreshments. Until then . . ." He kissed her breast again, and caressed the other.

She looked down on his fine hand moving on her body. A most contented arousal purred. Perhaps one more time—she kept saying that, didn't she?

"Padua, we must speak of serious matters now."

"Perhaps you should stop doing that, then. Soon I will be incapable of thinking at all."

"I will leave you with some ability. Enough. But I am inclined to keep at it, to make you pliable to my will."

"Are you going to propose another game?"

"It is no game, I promise you." He looked up in her eyes. "I broached the idea of marriage once before. You did not want to hear a proposal then. It was tainted by obligation. I would like you to agree to hear one now. I think I have a right to that."

She thought he had a right to much more. "I will listen."

"We suit each other, Padua. Not only in bed. In all ways. I enjoy your company, your mind, your laugh. I am never bored when I am with you, and I am often vexed when I am not." He kissed her breast once more. "You have stolen my heart, Padua. I do not want you for a mistress. That is not good enough. Or a lover alone. That is not permanent enough. I want us to marry, so I can love you forever."

She filled with light and happiness. She lay her hand against his face and kissed him. "That was a perfect proposal, Ives. Far better than I ever expected to hear. Not one word about the notoriety that will still attach to the name Belvoir even if my father goes free. Not even an allusion to all of the trouble I have caused you."

"None of that matters, if you say yes."

"I am not sure that I should."

His expression fell. "If you do not feel the same, I understand. However, with time perhaps—"

"Oh, no. Oh, dear. Do not think that I do not feel the same. I have loved you for so long. I cannot contain my love sometimes and I want to shout or weep from it. It is only that—my father has owned a brothel, and been in Newgate for a month on suspicion of the worst crimes. You may be able to spare him future suffering, but the past is already written in indelible ink."

"It will take more than a few ink spots to dissuade me, darling. Or to affect my position. And if I am wrong, that is my choice, I think. Having you is worth it to me, as so much else already has been."

Love spilled out of her heart. She did not think it possible to be so happy. "If I say yes, is that all there is to it? We are engaged?"

"The rest is just formality."

"Then yes." She kissed him. "Yes!"

A discreet cough interrupted. She looked around, but could not see its source.

"Yes, Vickers," Ives said.

"The refreshments are in the dining room, sir." The voice came from just outside the door.

"We will find them. You should retire now."

"Very good, sir."

Padua giggled into Ives's ear. "Do you think he was listening?"

"Undoubtedly." He set her on her feet. "Let us see what he prepared." He walked over to a writing desk, and made a stack of some paper and two inkwells and pens.

"What is that for?"

"The formalities."

Vickers had prepared a little supper of ham, cooked eggs, bread, and cheese. A pot of coffee and another of tea waited as well. Ives divided up the paper while they ate. He set one inkwell near her, and kept one for himself.

After their meal he tapped her paper. "The solicitors will handle most of the settlement, but we should have our own. One that considers things other than property and pin money."

She stared at her blank paper. "What do you expect me to do?"

"Write down your expectations. Anything at all, that you want in this marriage. Except the right to take lovers. I will not agree to that."

"I would never demand that."

"No, of course not. You are nothing if not loyal." He looked at her most seriously. "It is one of your finest qualities, and one reason I love you so much."

His flattery touched her. It was rare, to see something of yourself through another's eyes. "And you, Ives. Will you take lovers? Will you still have those opera singers?"

He took her hand in his and held it firmly. He looked right in her eyes. "I cannot blame you for asking, even if I am wounded that you do. No, I will not, Padua. I love you. I hope you come to know how much, and how deeply. You are my only lover now, forever. I promise you that."

It was one expectation she had not dared to have.

She learned then and there that her love could still grow, despite the way it seemed to fill her, because it took on a new depth and confidence while they held hands in that pact.

She lifted her pen and checked its tip. "Do all lawyers do this when they get engaged?"

"I doubt any do, but they should." He dipped his own pen. "I grew up in a house that knew little happiness, Padua. I think that unfulfilled expectations caused a lot of that grief. Indulge me, please." He gestured to her paper.

She tried. Her mind remained as blank as the page. Ives did not understand. She had never had *any* expectations. She could hardly construct them out of thin air. She managed to jot a few things, but halfheartedly.

Ives, on the other hand, wrote and wrote. She glanced over at the list that just kept growing. Finally he set the pen back in its well.

He slid her page over and read it. "This is all?"

She shrugged.

"*A new wardrobe of at least four dresses.* Padua, four dresses do not a new wardrobe make. I am a man, and even I know that." He grabbed the pen and crossed out the number of dresses. "A new wardrobe, period. Now, as to this one here, of course we will make sure your father is never destitute. What do you take me for? However, you will see on my list the requirement that he sell that house and his share of the partnership to Mrs. Lavender. I will make sure she pays fairly for it."

"I accept that term. I would have noted it myself, except it seemed more a formality for my father."

"The rest of this is easy to accept. Too easy." He set down the paper. "There is nothing here about going to the Continent. Studying at a university. Have you given up that dream?"

"I thought I had to, if I married."

"Darling, the first item on my list is that you do not go without me. Of course you will still do it. Next spring would be a good time for us to embark, don't you think?"

She jumped up and threw her arms around him. They shared a long kiss that had her wondering if dining tables were ever used the way those in morning rooms might be.

Unable to stop smiling, she sat down again and plucked his list out of his hand. She began reading. After a few practicalities, the list took a turn in a different direction. The sort that was never included in marriage settlements, but perhaps should be.

She kept reading. "You will have those negotiations in the end, won't you?"

He just watched her.

She got past the amorous variations she knew about. Matters became a bit obscure after that. She pondered the meaning of one reference. When clarity struck, she cast him a dubious glance. He responded with a charming smile and wicked eyes.

After working through it all, she picked up the pen.

She struck out three items. She handed it to him. "Can you live with that?"

He did not look at what she had rejected before folding the paper. "I can live with anything, as long as I am living with you, and as long as you love me."

He stood, and pulled out her chair. He lifted her in his arms. "Come with me now, my rare and beautiful lover. I will show you the most important chamber in the house."

She embraced his neck, and he swept her away.

September 1799

Lydia stared at the cascade of raw silk and muslin falling over Sarah's arms. She barely perceived the colors of the cloths. Her only alert sense had become one of touch, specifically of the texture of the letter crumpled in her tight fingers.

"Which will it be, milady?" Sarah thrust the muslin forward. "The earl always liked this blue one. Since he will be there, it would be a good choice."

The blue dress in question looked like something a girl would wear during her first season. Since Lydia was almost twenty-four years in age, it did not suit her. Her brother, the Earl of Southwaite, did favor it, but then her brother still saw her as a girl and would continue to do so until she married. The likelihood of that ever happening decreased with every year that passed.

Thank goodness.

She blinked away her distraction and smoothed out the crumpled letter on her lap.

Her fist had smeared the ink, but she could still read the words. Once more they sent a chill up her spine. This time, however, instead of heralding shock, the chill collided with the white heat of indignation when it reached her head.

It is in your interest to meet me at Mrs. Burton's this evening to discuss some shocking information regarding you that has come to my attention. I am sure that if we put our heads together, we can find a way to spare you great scandal.

Your servant,
Algernon Trilby

The scoundrel had sent her an overture to blackmail. What nonsense. Would that she had something in her past interesting enough to provoke such as this! The stupid man had probably made a mistake.

She pictured bland Mr. Trilby accidentally addressing this to her, and mistakenly sending an invitation to one of his boring magic demonstrations to the real quarry of his extortion. If not for her interest in sleight-of-hand tricks, she would have never come to know him well enough to attract his attention.

Sarah shook both dresses, causing their fabrics and embellishments to make faint music. The maid's crescent eyebrows almost reached her dark hairline due to her exasperated impatience.

"Neither," Lydia said, waving away both dresses. She stood and walked out of the dressing room. In her bedchamber she settled into the chair at her writing desk. She quickly penned a note while she called for Sarah.

"Bring this down and have it delivered to Cassandra by one of the footmen. Then prepare my green evening dress."

"The green silk? Lady Ambury said it would be an informal dinner, you told me."

"I am not going to her dinner. I am begging off."

"This is rather sudden."

"Sudden, but necessary. I must go to Mrs. Burton's tonight."

Sarah's mouth twitched with an expression of disapproval. Lydia tolerated such familiarity because she and Sarah had played together as children at Crownhill, her family's county seat, where Sarah's father still served as a groom.

"Speak your mind," Lydia said while she walked back to the dressing room. "I cannot bear it when you do so with your face instead of words."

Sarah strolled in behind her and set the two dresses down. "Surely you can miss an evening at the gaming tables to be with family and close friends. I believe Lady Ambury and Lady Southwaite have been planning this dinner with some care."

Lydia pawed through her jewelry box. "That means they invited some man for me to meet. All the more reason to go to Mrs. Burton's instead. Cassandra will add her aunt to balance the table, or Emma will bring one of ours instead. My absence will cause no serious awkwardness."

Sarah opened a wardrobe and took out the green silk. "They only want you to *meet* him, if you are correct about their plan. A mere introduction is hardly an imposition. As for Mrs. Burton's—how much fun can you have now that your brother requested that promise from you?"

"Southwaite requested nothing. He demanded it." That conversation with her brother had been recent enough that she still smarted from the insult.

"He only wants what is best for you," Sarah muttered.

Of course he did. Everyone did. Southwaite and his wife Emma, Cassandra, and her two aunts all wanted what was best for her to their collective mind. Even Sarah did.

"He knew it was just a matter of time until your luck turned," Sarah went on.

Except it hadn't yet. That frustrated her brother. Her uncanny ability to always come out ahead at the tables seemed immoral to those who believe one reaps what one sows. Her small fame as a result of her luck smelled scandalous to them.

So Southwaite, after waiting in vain for her to get her comeuppance with a big loss, had interfered to ensure such a loss never did happen. If she ever risked more than fifty pounds in one night, he would cut off her allowance and make sure every gaming hall in town learned of it.

"Perhaps he was also concerned that the excitement had captured you too much." Sarah kept her gaze on the green dress while she examined it for damage. "That is known to happen to some people. It gets to where they can't stay away, much as a drunk can't put down the gin." She reached for her sewing basket. "They pass up other entertainments, even evenings with family and friends, to return to those halls. Even if they use their winnings in the best ways, the thrill can be too alluring in itself."

Lydia glanced in the looking glass at Sarah's concentration on her needle and thread. They had played in the mud together as girls, and remained more friends than they were lady and maid. Lydia had defied both of her aunts to insist that Sarah remain at her side, even though it meant two years of supervision and training by a more experienced servant.

Lydia, however, did not much like this indirect warning from Sarah. Too many people felt free to warn her, direct her, scold her, manage her. She was a grown woman, for heaven's sake.

"Do you fear I am such a person, Sarah? Drunk on the excitement? Unable to stay away? Doing it for the thrill instead of a means to an end?"

"No, milady. I would never—" Her face reddened.

Of course she would. She just *had*. "Rest assured, I am not changing my plans tonight in order to gamble."

"Yes, milady."

"The truth is—and promise you will tell no one—I am going to Mrs. Burton's in order to meet a man."

She glanced again in the looking glass and noted with satisfaction how Sarah's eyes bulged with shock and curiosity.

"Please bring that letter down now, then help me prepare quickly."

Clayton Galbraith, the Duke of Penthurst, believed that a man, no matter how elevated his station, could not claim good character if he did not show patience and politeness to the older relatives of his family. He therefore sought equanimity while he attended on his aunt Rosalyn while she gambled at Mrs. Burton's gaming salon.

She had requested he escort her. He waited for her to reveal her reason. Thus far it appeared she merely sought his company so she could share a month's worth of gossip.

She did not need to drag him here for that. She lived in his house, as she had all his life. She had never married because, as she liked to explain, for the daughter of a duke to marry often led to a loss of status and precedence. He suspected the real reason was that marriage would remove her from the ducal residence, and infringe on her ability to meddle in the lives of its inhabitants. Since he was the only other person living there now, that meant him.

Her fashionable evening dress, the color of an iced lake, complemented her white skin, gray hair, dark eyes, and regal bearing. She lost her money at a very leisurely pace between her *sotto voce* confidences. The whole table's gaming slowed as well, to accommodate her. One by one the others excused themselves until he and she sat alone. Which, he suspected, had been her intention.

He slid the dealer a guinea by way of apology while his aunt squinted at the new hand she had just received. As age thinned her face and sharpened her features, he and she looked more and more alike. He had not realized the similarities until one day, when seventeen, he had visited her while she was sick and seen her without paint or smiles or distracting wig. The same chestnut eyes and winged, straight eyebrows, surely, and perhaps even the same wide mouth, although her feminine version of the features appeared less severe.

"It is too bad about Kendale," she murmured while she studied the cards. "He waited too long, of course. The older a man gets, the more likely some young flirt will turn his head."

Penthurst debated whether to defend his friend Viscount Kendale, or pick up the challenge just thrown at his feet. Damnation, if his aunt had plotted this evening in order to broach the tiresome topic of his lack of a wife, he would make her be blunt and not smooth the path for her. "He appears very happy, and very much in love. Would you wish less for him?"

"Kendale in love? Whoever thought to see the day." She *tsked* her exasperation, then called for a card. "She is not suitable. Everyone knows it, including him. He should have married correctly. If he is very much in love, he did not have to deny himself."

"He is too honest for that. And you should hold now. You are likely to break twenty-one if you take another card."

"Honest? Is that what it is called when a peer indulges in romantic notions better suited to a schoolgirl? I hope that you have much more sense than that kind of honesty."

"Rest assured, I am so ruthlessly practical with my women that no one will ever pity me as you do Kendale."

She called for another card despite his advice. It put her over. "Yes. Well, at least he *did* marry, didn't he?" A note of aggrieved censure sounded. "She is very lovely, I have to admit. And, despite her birth, she has some style."

He refused to humor her. He turned his attention to the ballroom that served as a gaming hall in this Mayfair home. Mrs. Burton ran the most polite place in London aside from gentlemen's clubs in which to gamble away fortunes, and perhaps the only establishment that ladies could visit alone without raising eyebrows. There had been some official moves against other gam-

ing salons run by well-bred women in their homes, but
Mrs. Burton's aristocratic clientele afforded her a special dispensation.

"Speaking of lovely girls," his aunt said while the
dealer slid away her money. "Did I mention that Lady
Barrowton's niece is coming up to town? Her beauty
is said to be celebrated."

"Said to be? Has no one seen for certain?" Only a
corner of his mind heeded the conversation, since the
rest already knew what it would hear. Most of his
attention had riveted on the entrance to the ballroom.
A dark-haired, soulful-eyed woman had just arrived.
Lydia Alfreton.

That was odd. He was certain Southwaite had mentioned that his sister would be at that little dinner party
being held tonight at Ambury's house. Yet here she
was, ready to press her considerable luck at the tables
instead.

The green dress she wore flattered her dark hair and
very pale skin. She appeared happy. She only looked
like that when she gambled, unfortunately. If one met
her during the day, her eyes stared right through you,
opaque and unseeing, and her face remained expres-
sionless.

"Of course some have seen her niece. Otherwise
she could not be celebrated. However, she has never
been to town before. She is coming for her final fin-
ishing prior to coming out."

"A child then. All children are lovely. Sweet too.
And boring."

"Hardly a child. A fresh, innocent girl. I would like to introduce you."

"I am not interested, but thank you."

The proximity of the dealer suddenly discomforted her. She dismissed him in an imperious tone that had him backing away at once, leaving a good deal of money unattended. She turned her whole body. She angled her gray head so her next words would not be missed. "You must marry eventually, and this girl sounds perfect."

"I told you long ago that I would not be managed in this. If you think I will be more amenable because you raise the matter in a public place instead of at the house, you are mistaken. And, surely by now you know that I will have no inclination to marry a fresh, innocent girl when the day comes that I marry at all."

She heaved a sigh of forbearance. "I have never understood your preference for older women."

"Haven't you?"

She flushed and looked away to avoid acknowledging the question. Something distracted her. Her brow furrowed. "I suppose I should bow to your preferences, since your instincts proved so wise regarding that one there. Her poor mother must be turning over in her grave."

He did not have to look to know she spoke of Lydia Alfreton. He did anyway, in time to see Mrs. Burton greet Lady Lydia and escort her to the hazard table.

"I had no instincts regarding her. I had an understandable annoyance at you and Lady Southwaite deciding whom I would marry before the girl was one day old. Such prearranged pacts are antiquated, lack any legality, and are not to be tolerated." Upon inheriting at age fifteen, disavowing their ridiculous arrangement had been among the first things he did. No one but his aunt spoke of it anymore. He doubted anyone else even remembered it.

"Celeste was my dearest friend, and so sweet and good. Whoever expected her daughter to—well, to turn out like that." Her hand gestured at Lydia, who had just won a throw. People had gathered around to watch her. Perhaps her reputation for winning drew them. Maybe her vivacious excitement did. Eyes afire with lights that normally the world never saw in her, she raised her gaze and her arms upward while she laughed after each win, as if thanking Providence for once more favoring her wagers.

His aunt clucked her tongue. "During the day she is a sphinx, and unknowable. Here at night she is like a bacchante drunk on wine. She is going to ruin Southwaite if he does not rein her in. Everyone says so. She will ruin herself, and him, and that whole family."

"She wins. If she keeps at it, she is more likely to double the family fortune than ruin it." That was the problem. Southwaite was sure that if she would lose even once, big, that would end it.

"I am not talking about the gambling."

That got his attention. "You cannot be talking about men."

"Can I not?"

"She has no interest in them. Gambling, yes. Horses,

yes. Art and literature, yes. But if there are rumors about that other kind of ruin, they are not accurate."

"You heard this from Southwaite, no doubt. As if he would know!" Her eyes narrowed on the other side of the chamber. "She has befriended a number of men while she games, and is hardly demure in her conversations with them, I am told. Her aunt Amelia is most distressed about it." She shook her head. "My dear, dear Celeste. Perhaps it is just as well she did not live to see it."

He swallowed the inclination to repeat that the gossip was inaccurate by a mile. In the end, what did he know? Southwaite certainly worried about his sister. If more than her gambling had become a problem for the family, Penthurst did not expect to be informed.

As if to underline his aunt's whispers, a man approached the hazard table. He squeezed himself through the crowd so as to stand by Lydia's elbow. Penthurst angled his head to have a better look at the fellow's face. He could not prevent a laugh from escaping once he recognized the man. Algernon Trilby? Trilby and Lady Lydia? He did not think *that* likely.

"What is so amusing?" his aunt demanded.

"I am chewing over what you just told me, and could not suppress my reaction."

"Laugh all you want. The *on dit* is rarely wrong on such things." She beckoned the dealer and returned to her cards.

Their conversation turned once more to his introduction to the sweet, innocent niece of Lady Barrowton. He sidestepped any commitments to meet her. While they carefully placed their feet in their dance of interference and resistance, he found himself looking on occasion to where Lydia seemed to be winning nicely with the dice.

She appeared to know Trilby. She spoke to him several times. Whatever she said had the man flushing. Finally Trilby peeled away and went to watch the faro play. Lady Lydia appeared to know how to shed unwelcome attention with grace but finality.

He almost pointed that out to his aunt, so she might spare his friend's sister unnecessary gossip. Just as he was about to speak, however, Lydia herself left the table. No longer bright-eyed, but wearing the aloof, blank expression that caused his aunt to call her a sphinx, she walked directly to the terrace doors and slipped outside.

Twenty steps behind, Algernon Trilby followed.

"You must excuse me. I think I will retreat for a short spell, then you can take me home." His aunt held out her hand so he might help her to stand.

"I will come and find you in a few minutes," he said.

"Not too few. The best gossip will be in the retiring room."

"I will wait until you have your fill."

She sallied forth. She left thirty pounds on the table, as if returning them to her reticule were too much a bother. For a woman supported her whole life by dukes, it probably was. He gestured for cards.

With his aunt's removal, others came to use the table. Spirited play ensued. During the fourth round, he looked around the chamber and realized that neither Lydia nor Trilby had yet returned.

There had been no indication that Lydia had planned an assignation, but with each passing minute more people would assume that to be the case. He pictured Trilby out there now, annoying her at best and importuning her at worst.

He threw in his cards, stood, and walked toward the doors. If she were his sister, he would expect Southwaite to keep one eye on her, after all.

From *New York Times* bestselling author

MADELINE HUNTER

HIS WICKED REPUTATION

Gareth Fitzallen is celebrated for four things: his handsome face, his notable charm, his aristocratic connections, and an ability to give the kind of pleasure that has women begging for more. Normally he bestows his talents on experienced, worldly women. But when he heads to Langdon's End to restore a property he inherited—and to investigate a massive art theft—he lays plans to seduce a most unlikely lady...

"Excellent."
—*Publishers Weekly* (Starred Review)

"Hunter seamlessly marries seductive wit
with smoldering sensuality in her latest impeccably
written Regency romance."
—*Booklist*

madelinehunter.com
facebook.com/MadelineHunter
penguin.com

M1695T0715

From *New York Times* bestselling author
MADELINE HUNTER

The Accidental Duchess

When Lady Lydia Alfreton is blackmailed over the shocking contents of a manuscript she wrote, she must go to the most desperate of measures to raise the money to buy back the ill-considered prose: agreeing to an old wager posed by the arrogant, dangerous Duke of Penthurst, a man determined to tame her rebellious ways...

madelinehunter.com
facebook.com/MadelineHunter
facebook.com/LoveAlwaysBooks
penguin.com